GERONIMO HOTSHOT

A Ben Blackshaw Novel

by

Robert Blake Whitehill

TELEMACHUS PRESS

This book is a work of fiction. Names, characters, places and incidents are either the product of the author's imagination or are used fictitiously. Any resemblance to actual persons, living or dead, or to actual events or locales is entirely coincidental.

GERONIMO HOTSHOT

Cover Designed by Buffalo Gouge
Additional Cover Design by Carol Castelluccio at Studio042
With Photographs by Michael C. Wootton

Cover art:
Copyright © Calaveras Media
Photography Copyright © Calaveras Media

Published by Telemachus Press, LLC
www.telemachuspress.com
and
Calaveras Media. LLC
www.calaverasmedia.com

Visit the author website:
http://www.robertblakewhitehill.com

ISBN: 978-1-942899-44-0 (eBook)
ISBN: 978-1-942899-45-7 (Paperback)

Version 2015.08.18

10 9 8 7 6 5 4 3 2 1

PRAISE FOR GERONIMO HOTSHOT

Without a doubt the most disturbing chapter of the Ben Blackshaw journey to date, Geronimo Hotshot pulls you into the darkest realm of humanity and leaves you clamoring desperately towards the light.
Cyrus Webb, host of Conversations LIVE/Editor-In-Chief of Conversations Magazine, www.cyruswebbpresents.com

I loved Geronimo Hotshot! It is the perfect addition to The Ben Blackshaw Series. I was drawn into the story from the first page and could not put it down. Just like the previous books, Geronimo Hotshot is packed with superb action, political intrigue, and an addicting story. I highly recommend this read. It is the best thriller I've read this year!
Bri Wignall, Editor at *Natural Bri—Pursuits of Life*, www.naturalbri.com

Geronimo Hotshot is an intriguing, enthralling, and intense topical storyline. Robert Blake Whitehill will seduce your mind into a world of retribution and revenge. One thing is for sure: Ben Blackshaw is not your stereotypical hero—more of an antihero—but a man who will command your respect and interest. Prepare to be pulled into a dark and destructive storyline.
Sandy Schairer, Editor in Chief, www.TheReadingCafe.com

Ben Blackshaw returns with a dark fury! In his best instalment yet, Robert Blake Whitehill has yet again delved deep into the psyche of his hard-bitten reluctant hero, Ben Blackshaw. On his own and running from his own life, Blackshaw goes looking for a fight and finds more than even he might be able to handle. Fast moving and engrossing from the first page, Geronimo Hotshot pulls the reader along at gunpoint through Blackshaw's quest for personal redemption, justice, and some very well-deserved violence.
Adam Stephan Gubar, Screenwriter, *Summer Bridge, Section 8,* www.adamstephangubar.com

Geronimo Hotshot is one of those rare works that makes you look at life from a different, more alive perspective. The constant turmoil, combined with the electric dialogue had me wondering at times if the story's fire would consume me before I had a chance to see how Blackshaw was going to escape this uniquely twisting conflict.
Quentin Brent, Author of *The Reason*, www.QuentinBrent.com

Robert Blake Whitehill takes Ben Blackshaw and the series to a new, darker level with Geronimo Hotshot. Whitehill's individual voice kept me on the edge of my seat the whole read as he wove a new friendship between Ben Blackshaw and Native American wildfire fighter Delshay Goyathlay. Nothing is predictable and everything is believable during this intense and fast moving ride. Geronimo Hotshot is both a stellar example of the genre and unique by merit of Whitehill's distinctive style.
Gail Priest, Author, Annie Crow Knoll: Sunrise, www.gailpriest.com

Robert Blake Whitehill has delivered again in his new Ben Blackshaw thriller, Geronimo Hotshot, a story as gripping as today's headlines, crossing the country from the Chesapeake to the desert of Arizona, with themes of illegal immigration, white supremacy, motorcycle gangs, and a giant wildfire sparked by a lightning storm. The lawmen and women are the heroes, but Whitehill paints vivid villains and wild watermen as Blackshaw goes outside the law to make sure the good guys win. I cried at the end.
Bruce Ashkenas, Author, *Playing with the Bund: A Novel of Nazis in New York*, www.bruceashkenas-author.net

Geronimo Hotshot is a masterful blend of sadistic villainous characters interwoven with non-stop action, wit and intrigue. Author, Robert Blake Whitehill, overloads the senses with thrilling ambushes of disturbing suspense and enigmatic genius in this complex revelation of twisted psyches politicking lethal agendas.
Simone Salmon, Author, *Camille and the Bears of Beisa*, Drafnel, www.drafnel.blogspot.com

In Ben Blackshaw, Whitehill has created a genuinely intriguing character who deviates from the typical molds we've become used to seeing. Complex. Hurt. Tough. Haunted by his past. All of these qualities make Blackshaw as real as the book you're holding. Whitehill's ability to create a very real world inside a fictional book is what's so compelling: He is an author who's breathing new life into the thriller genre, a true heavyweight contender for the literary crown. I promise you: This will not be the last time you hear of Robert Blake Whitehill!

Anthony Karakai, Author, The Black Lion, http://anthonykarakai.com

With a host of grudgingly admiring old allies, and ineffably evil new villains, Robert Blake Whitehill's hero, Ben Blackshaw, has his greatest adventure yet in Geronimo Hotshot as he travels cross-country to avenge a horrible death, and stumbles upon a plot that threatens thousands—told with the now-legendary Whitehill verve and page-turning urgency.

Steve Sussmann

For Mom

FOR THE REAL Geronimo Interagency Hotshot Crew (IHC) in admiration of their fearless, selfless dedication and service.

http://forestry.scat-nsn.gov/publicweb/geronimo.html

FOR ALL THE wildland firefighters of the United States Forestry Service, especially the nineteen City of Prescott firefighters of the Granite Mountain Hotshots who succumbed in the Yarnell Hill Fire, 30 June 2013.

https://www.azfoundation.org/About/NewsEvents/View Article/tabid/96/ArticleId/9/Give-Online-to-Help-Those-Affected-by-the-Yarnell-Hill-Fire.aspx

FOR LAURENCE LINDEMAIER, friend and classmate, who walks toward the warm places so the rest of us don't have to. I am proud to know you.

Thank you all.
RBW

CONTENTS

Special Acknowledgements

Geronimo Hotshot would not have come about without the crucial insights and support of Cecily Sharp-Whitehill, www.alliance4discovery.com, Mary Whitehill, www.womanhattan.com, Karl Guthrie, www.theguthrielawfirm.com, Telemachus Press, www.telemachuspress.com, Rusty Shelton, www.sheltoninteractive.com, cover artist Buffalo Gouge, www.facebook.com/AcrylicGD, cover designer Carol Castelluccio, www.studio042.com, the dynamic trio of Stephanie Bell, Tamra Teig, and Michael Lipoma of HatLine Productions, www.HatLineProductions.com, Adam Gubar, www.adamstephangubar.com, and my cousin Walter Whitehill. Thank you all from the bottom of my heart.

RBW
Independence Day 2015
Chestertown, Maryland

GERONIMO HOTSHOT

PART I
STRANGE FRUIT

CHAPTER 1

THE BOY'S LYNCHING was inconceivable to Ben Blackshaw. On this quiet morning, the waterman stood all alone outside the fishing ark contemplating myriad memories woven around its rough, boxy lines. The cramped house-on-a-barge had belonged to his family for generations. His grandfather had towed it every year to temporary shoreline encampments with other arks, other fishermen, in the upper waters of the Chesapeake Bay for the shad season. What grand times!

The planks of the ark's walls had shrunk with the alcohol stove's warmth, but between his father's efforts and his own, tar paper covered most of the gaps, and blocked the chilly winds that could whip up on a Chesapeake island even in late spring. Yes, there was also death lurking in Blackshaw's heart, but it was the brutal last rites for the boy he had once been, certainly not for a stranger's helpless child. Blackshaw had yet to discover the actual bloodletting.

Arranged around Blackshaw on the ground lay his pack, a few provisions, and his shotgun. Three plastic bottles that held alcohol for the stove still sat on the stern of the ark.

His father, Richard Willem Blackshaw, had recently bunked in the old ark here on Lethe Island while convalescing from some illness, likely from an infected bullet wound. Ben glanced at the trunk of the enormous willow tree that draped the clearing, and for the first time noticed how carefully his father had chosen places from which to knife out small sections of its bark which he had chewed, or used to brew a fever-breaking tea. The tree would

4 ROBERT BLAKE WHITEHILL

survive his father's sickness. Unless Blackshaw took action, it would not survive his own deeper malaise.

This ark far from Smith Island was the last place he had recently spoken to each one of his parents, though not in the same visit. His father might turn up again, and might not, as was his wont.

On the other hand, Ben sensed that his mother, Ida-Beth, was gone for good after her recent visit. Each of his parents had tried to explain away their absences from his life for the last fifteen, nearly sixteen years. Their reasons sounded lofty, compelling, and self-serving by turns.

His father had been ruined for any regular existence by his time in Vietnam. If Richard Blackshaw had ever sought treatment to help him settle and find peace, Ben did not know. His father's distemper had a name these days: post-traumatic stress disorder. From Blackshaw's own harrowing experience as a veteran come home from the savageries of state, he could understand the urges, the lurching attempts to flee this wolf that constantly nipped at his heels, urges that drove Richard Blackshaw back into battles the world over as a mercenary; they were now too much a part of him to tame with prescriptions, or with heartfelt talk, or supportive, empathetic camaraderie. The Chesapeake waters around Smith Island had formed a palisade that held many families in and together through hard times. Blackshaw's father had been drafted away for war, and would never feel at home again, no matter on what continent he lay down his head. His long convalescence sheltering here in this ark on Lethe was not enough to bend his thoughts toward coming in, coming home, and staying put on Smith Island. Though Richard Blackshaw seemed to circulate closer to his home waters over the last few months, Ben read nothing into that. Might've been age. Might've been simple curiosity.

Blackshaw put aside thoughts of his father. The tide was high now. It was time. He unmoored, levered, and shoved the fishing ark into the water until it turned heavy, lazy circles in eddies of the gut. He did not bother to check its bilge to see that it was sound and keeping out the brackish bay. It did not need to float for long. Waist deep in the water, he pushed the heavy ark down the gut to a place where it widened at a bend, and hauled it ashore. In a few hours, the tide would have ebbed, and stranded the ark again. At least now, it no longer lay directly beneath the swaying expansive willow that had shielded the barge from aerial observation while his father healed as much as he ever would.

In her visit just a few weeks back, Blackshaw's mother had revealed much less about her own disappearance from Smith Island, and from his life, so long ago. She reluctantly explained, as if it were the price of sitting with him, that she had willingly, happily tried the roles of wife and mother for a good while. Soon, though, she was not living the traditional life mapped out for her. She was marking time, dreaming of places that lay over the horizon where new versions of herself might be free to roam. She bided mostly in her imagination until Richard Blackshaw's old troubles from the war, and his need to run for his life, had provided her own moment to escape this alien existence on Smith Island; it was a life to which she was no longer suited. But she would not run with her husband. Nor would she seek a new path wide enough for a son to walk beside her. Instead, she left behind a void surrounded by a carefully assembled minimum of evidence proving that she had died. For Blackshaw, thinking her dead was better. It had kept his expectations of her low.

Wanderlust, she told Blackshaw, had taken her to other continents for a little while after her departure, but she had returned to the States and settled in, of all places, Baltimore, mere miles from where her son still lived on Smith Island. She had never reached out to him in that time, though she had purchased, and in her own way cherished, his sketch of a Merganser duck that she had bought at a waterfowl art festival.

Like her departure before, this visit on Lethe Island from Ida-Beth was more, much more, to satisfy her own curiosity about her only child than it was to beg his forgiveness and seek a place in his life. She'd shared a single evening's halting, stilted conversation with her son in the ark. The next morning, true to form, the old woman was gone. At least his father had ably plied his trade in death when Ben most needed it before throwing a rucksack over his shoulder and taking his leave.

Blackshaw emptied the alcohol bottles inside the shanty, and outside on its decks, walls and roof. Standing clear on the shore, he struck a single match and tossed it aboard.

He heard the *wump* as the alcohol flashed, but for a moment the flame was so clear it was almost invisible—a mirage's heat-ripples rising into the air. Then it turned blue and climbed the dry boards of the shanty walls. The tarpaper, made mostly of felt that was impregnated with asphalt, burned yellow and smoked gray-black.

Blackshaw walked back upstream through the reeds to his gear. As he entered the clearing where the ark had lain, he looked back only once to be sure the smoke and embers were drifting away from the willow tree.

"A lot of history fueling that fire."

Blackshaw looked up from a final check of his pack to see Knocker Ellis leaning against the willow's trunk, and holstered the Bersa Thunder 380 automatic that had appeared by reflex in his hand.

The black man by the tree, likely in his seventh decade, but wiry and tough in the way of a much younger man, appraised his friend with care.

"Are you being psychological?" asked Blackshaw.

"Am I? Maybe a righteous burning is better than tacking that shanty onto somebody's house as a side room full of old newspapers."

"Some folks come here for the quiet," Blackshaw observed.

"You haven't answered that sat-phone in over a week, Ben."

A torsion of dread and hope crossed Blackshaw's face. To ease his friend's distress, Ellis reported, "There's no change."

Blackshaw's face resumed its impassive mask to hide his deeper sorrow. His wife, LuAnna, had been terribly wounded in a firefight with human traffickers at Dove Point a month ago, and though she breathed on her own now, she had yet to regain consciousness.

Ellis said, "The docs have left. We got 'em on call in case of trouble. And we got good nurses round the clock backing up the Council ladies at your saltbox, but some have said she'd do better in a nursing home."

"No!" erupted Blackshaw. "She's home now, right where she is."

"But you're not. So how do you know anything, moping around here setting fires?"

Blackshaw's anger, never far below the surface these days, rose under the insinuation of neglect. "I was just leaving."

"But you aren't coming back to Smith Island."

Blackshaw said nothing.

Ellis went on, "There's some who put a lot of store by talking to folks in a coma. They wake up, and some who slept for days and weeks remember every kind word said to them while they were dreaming."

Blackshaw flared like the shanty. "You see me doing that? What would I say? Tell her I'm sorry? Tell her she should have listened to me, and stayed clear of that whole shit-show?"

"No," said Ellis, "I don't see you accusing somebody who can't talk back. And you know she'd have something to say about it. It was her call to mix in the way she did."

Blackshaw could not argue this point. LuAnna listened to him better than many women besotted with their husbands but, in the end, she always followed her own leadings. This was the quality Blackshaw loved most about her, at least up until that last near-fatal moment.

Ellis suggested, "Hell, you could read her the phone book, or the newspaper, or some bad poetry, or talk about the weather."

Blackshaw confessed, "I can't face her like that."

"Even though you promised to," said Ellis. "But I get it. Man, you can't even say her name."

"You're overstepping."

"Our friendship? My race? Pray, Ben, how'd I offend the King of Pain? Did I break in on the perfection of your self-pity? Drop too much truth on you all at once?"

"Ellis, hear me when I say you need to leave. Now."

"*Fuck you* I need to leave! You need to quit this place and come home before you take stupid to a whole new level."

A part of Blackshaw knew his friend was right. This did not change his compulsion to take a different course. He shouldered his pack. He picked up the shotgun and tossed it to Ellis.

"You want to talk, Ellis? Then tell her I love her."

"Tell her your own self." Ellis turned and walked out of the clearing toward the gut where his skiff was tied up.

Blackshaw took a last look around the clearing. Downstream, he watched the starboard wall of the shanty crackle and collapse in a plume of smoke and flying sparks. Then he strode toward a different stream where his old deadrise, *Miss Dotsy*, lay.

CHAPTER 2

TIMON PARDUE SHOT his next-to-last horse. He came close to feeling regret about it. That meant his trigger finger hesitated for several picoseconds before the hammer of his Henry rifle fell on the chambered cartridge, and Buckeye dropped dead. The pinto was lame, useless for riding, packing supplies, or anything but steaks, but Pardue still felt that fleeting twinge. It was more than the former sheriff of Cochise County, Arizona felt for any human being. At least Buckeye had kept up his end of the deal, and that was saying something.

Pardue butchered Buckeye under the placid gaze of his last horse, Popper. After a rinse in the little stream snaking through the bottom of the arroyo near his camp, he breathed life into the embers of his fire and got ready for a night exactly like the last sixty or so nights (he had determined that losing count on purpose would help him forget) since he had thrown down his badge in frustration, and walked out of his Bisbee office. After eight years of service, he had been brought down in a recall vote by the liberals in Bisbee, and those Latinos in Douglas, the legal ones supposedly, though he was convinced there had been improprieties at many of the polling places. The kids at Fort Huachuca had been prevented from voting to keep him in office, confined to base by some kind of ill-timed terrorist scare which Pardue would have looked into if he still gave a shit. Which he swore to himself he did not.

He had been stomping around the foothills of the Chiricahua Mountains ever since that awful night, with Buckeye, Popper, and a mule named Asshole that Pardue had shot and eaten first, more to be rid of the animal's foul temper than because it could not, or would not, carry his gear. He suspected the mule of Democrat leanings, or maybe it just looked too much like the political symbol for Pardue's liking. In posthumous revenge, the old animal had tasted terrible, even with liberal or, better put, copious applications of dried chilies from the pack. Pardue had been sick for nearly a week after only two servings of mule meat.

Too hard on illegals, that's what they said about him. *Profiling.* Timon Pardue saw himself, and the loyal members of his department, as the last line of defense of the United States from an invasion of criminals rolling north from Sonora in Mexico. Increased border patrol activity in San Diego and El Paso had not been matched, or at least, had not been as successful, in Cochise County, even though Customs and Border Protection was now the largest single employer in the town of Naco. Pardue believed that the CBP was organized more for the satisfaction of Congress in Washington, and not for effectiveness on the actual border.

So, as sheriff, Timon Pardue had assigned all his officers to a rigorous taskforce of stopping any and all suspicious persons, with particular attention paid to the documentation and immigration status of the subjects in question. The problem of illegals was old. The accusations of profiling were newer. The entire matter got rejuvenated in the media when the newly appointed Presiding Judge of the Superior Court of Cochise County was detained on a routine stop, and spent a long weekend in the Bisbee lockup before anyone realized who she was, other than angry and Hispanic.

The Right Honorable Judge Eleonora Vasquez had been held because the arresting deputy believed she was a prostitute, despite the fact that she was picked up at night near a lonely country road devoid of prospective clients. She swore to the officer that her telescope, which she used for her hobby of amateur astronomy, was just over the next rise. Her jacket, which held her identification, was next to the telescope. She had stepped away from the instrument to relieve herself. It was in that compromising position that the deputy, who had been alerted to the presence of a prowler by the rancher who owned the property, discovered her.

Like her telescope and the coat holding her identification, her Lexus LX was not in plain sight at the time of her arrest. Despite the judge's outraged insistence, the arresting deputy had declined the hassle of stumbling around the countryside in the dark to find these items on what was no doubt a wild goose chase. Vasquez's claims to be a judge, and not a prostitute, were finally corroborated when her Lexus was towed into the county impound the following Monday morning, and the registration was examined by a lot attendant who sometimes watched the news on Telemundo.

To Pardue's consternation, Judge Vasquez had many good friends at the local Hispanic television affiliate. She was also a close friend of the Chief Justice of the Arizona Supreme Court who had appointed her. Her story caught like a wildfire in mainstream media outlets, even on Fox news, which sacrificed Sheriff Pardue, vilifying him in a bid to appear just a little less like a mouthpiece of the Koch Brothers and Rupert Murdoch. Pardue was pilloried. That was eight months ago. The resulting recall election had gone badly for him. Oh, they would miss Timon Pardue. He had no idea how much.

CHAPTER 3

BLACKSHAW HAD NO idea where he was headed. He had a good idea where he did not want to be. For the first time in his life, the Chesapeake Bay felt like a cesspool. He could not understand his own revulsion, this new low regard for his beautiful home. Perhaps the reason was simpler than he wanted it to be. Everything he knew, everyone he loved, and everywhere that felt comforting and life-giving was fouled with his own remorse.

He pointed *Miss Dotsy* south and west. The sky was clear. The waves rolled gently underneath the stern with a gentle rocking motion impelling him onward into the unknown. Then Blackshaw realized what had happened. At some point in the last twenty-four hours, he had deployed himself without orders from any higher authority. He was looking for trouble.

The Windy Point Marina in Calvert County, Maryland was jumping, though it was mid-week. It was the busy time of year. The dockmaster had one free seasonal slip left, and Blackshaw took it. In an office just off the chandlery, which was a high-flying name for the Windy Point bait shop, Blackshaw peeled bills off a wad in front of the manager until *Miss Dotsy's* dockage for summer and fall were covered. He peeled off additional cash with standing instructions to haul and winterize *Miss Dotsy* if he had not checked in by November. And he left an envelope. If he were not back by this time next spring, the envelope contained a name and a phone number dashed off on a sheet of paper. The person appointed therein would be authorized to collect *Miss Dotsy* after settling any outstanding or unexpected bills. Other than the Navy's Standardized Will Intake Form, this was as close as Blackshaw had come to planning for his own demise, with the exception of a few bad minutes looking down the business end of a loaded shotgun.

With *Miss Dotsy* taken care of, Blackshaw used the manager's phone to call a cab. He threw his pack over his shoulder again, walked to the marina entrance, and waited, all the while trying his damnedest not to compare himself to his father.

CHAPTER 4

BUCKEYE TASTED OKAY in Timon Pardue's estimation, but he still felt that chili-rubbed horse meat steaks would never equal the offerings of Sammy's Hot Dog Company on State Highway 92. His canteen of Jack Daniel's helped wash it down. In exile, even self-imposed exile, there were comforts to be had, and certain standards to maintain.

He had stocked up well on provisions before taking to the wilderness, and so hadn't needed to resupply. The lack of human contact, even as minimal as a fellow might get during a liquor store purchase, was taking a toll. Pardue talked to his dwindling animals and thought nothing of it. Given enough Jack Daniel's, he would also haul up his trousers and rant at the stars, convinced that he struck fear into the unseen legion of undocumented intruders from the south. Before he passed out, he mumbled a few words for the ungrateful citizens of Cochise County, a prayer that boils and other indignities be visited upon them.

Well along in his evening trajectory with the booze, it took Pardue a few seconds to realize this new voice was not his own, and to limber his Glock.

Aiming at nothing in particular, he slurred out a surly, "Who's there? Show yourself!"

The reply, muffled by intervening rocks that the speaker had wisely interposed between himself and an armed, inebriated Pardue, was immediate. "It's me, Timon! Sam Wimble! Please don't shoot! Put up the gun, alright?"

"Show me your hands!" growled Pardue. "Step into the light nice and slow where I can see you."

It was close to Pardue's bedtime. He had let the cooking fire burn low. Wimble's paunch, and the dusty points of his cowboy boots, were the first things Pardue saw. The rest of his old friend followed soon after.

"You by yourself?" asked Pardue.

"Just Lobo and me," Wimble's bloodhound loped after him into the circle of firelight. "I swear you read too much Louis L'Amour."

Pardue holstered his gun. "No such thing as too much L'Amour. Sit down. Want a drink?"

"Don't mind if I do," said Wimble. "What's that smell?"

As Pardue tipped whiskey into an enamel tin cup. "Guess it's Buckeye. Might not've got all the hair off his meat before I cooked him."

Wimble was a moment taking this in, and used the time to sip from the cup. Pardue was grateful for company, but Wimble, or Deputy Wimble, the arresting officer, and first casualty in the Judge Vasquez fiasco, would not have been his first choice of visitors. Likely not in the top 100, for that matter. Still, another human being was something, and they had worked together, and both been martyred in the cause of political correctness.

"You found me," said Pardue after a while. "Going to sit there all night, or you got something to say?"

With the effort Wimble had obviously put forth to locate him, Pardue was expecting at least an apology for the moronic cluster that had cost him his job. That's not what he got.

"There's some folks looking for you, Timon."

This came as a surprise. Pardue was short on friends. He was nine years divorced, and his wife had remarried so quickly and so happily that it utterly galled him. He and his two children never spoke. He had been a strict, sometimes cruel father, and in this day and age, discipline was not appreciated, what with kids redefining what *family* was, as if blood ties counted for nothing. Pardue blamed namby-pamby television shrinks and overstocked Self-Help shelves at the bookstores for the dissolution of his little clan.

Pardue said, "That's none of my business, and you best not let on where I am. Not to anybody. I move camp every couple nights, so's you know."

"You're a regular outlaw. So you'll either be here tomorrow night, or a day's ride from here?" Wimble was a real smart-ass; unfortunately, just not very smart. And he was holding out his cup to Pardue.

"Sam, what do you want?" Pardue was already weighing the decreasing pleasure of Wimble's company against the large dent his visitor was knocking in the liquor cabinet. Wimble was fat, no doubt, but much of his gut was an alcoholic's enlarged liver.

"It's not just me, Timon. You've gotten kinda famous from what happened and all."

Pardue snorted. "I saw the recall results. Anybody says there's no such thing as bad publicity is a damn idiot."

"I guess so, most times. But doors close. Windows open."

Pardue leveled an impatient glare at his former deputy. "Nice of you to visit, Sam. It's late. I'd like you to leave."

"Sure Timon. I like my bed at home as much as the next man." Wimble finally warmed to the reason for his visit. "But like I said, there're folks looking for you. They're hopping mad about you getting railroaded. Fed up with CBP saying they're going to do something, and not following through worth a crap, the way they shore up parts of the border, and leave us to fend for ourselves putting four or five guys where we really need fifty. We're in a choke point now. Cochise is the wide open hole in the fence, and all them illegals know it."

Wimble held out his cup again. Pardue did not want to refill it, but he did. The canteen was getting light. Curiosity, teamed with Jack Daniel's, was making Wimble almost interesting now.

After another deep swig, Wimble said, "These folks I'm talking about, they're mad, but they're not the kind to sit around the pickle barrel bitching. They want to take action." Wimble said *action* in a meaningful way, the way corporate recruiters told head-hunters they wanted a job candidate to be *well-spoken* when they really meant *not black*. "Timon, you been out here so long, you have no idea you're a bona fide hero."

"If nominated, I will not run. If elected, I will not serve."

Wimble looked confused for a moment, then he took on that conspiratorial look again. "Nobody's saying you should run for office again. This group of folks I'm talking about, they got no time for bullshit, any more than you do. Hell, half of them don't think there's any kind of political office worth having these days. Don't even believe in politics. They're proactive. They're self-determined."

Pardue could not help himself. He asked, "They *who?*"

"Ranchers, mostly. Even ones with spreads that don't front the border."

Pardue understood now. "Aw shit, Wimble. Those guys are pissed about illegals, but they just as much want to stir up a ruckus because they don't want to pay their back grazing fees. They listen to *America, Why I Love Her* over and over like it's the Gettysburg address."

Wimble puffed with righteousness. "Please don't make fun of The Duke like that, Timon. Not with these guys. I mean, John Wayne's a hero, too. But he's not here to lead anybody, God rest him. And it's not all guys. There's a woman on the committee."

"Adelle Congreve." Pardue spat into the fire.

Wimble looked surprised. "As a matter of fact."

Pardue knew Miss Adelle, as she affected to be known, quite well. A dynamic, wealthy, brassy, heiress to her husband Ricky-Ray Congreve's cattle ranch and oil lease holdings. Lurking somewhere in her fifties, probably forever, Adelle was a mainstay on the County Council. Before that, she was front row at all the meetings, with all her after-market augmentations and lifts, tugs, tanning, and suction work on full display. Wags called her Double-R ranch the *Double-D*. She knew it, and did not give a damn. The woman rode her fences, that's for shit-sure, mused Pardue.

Congreve always traveled from her ranch to Council meetings in Bisbee in a convoy of no fewer than three blacked-out armored Suburbans. Locals showed up before the meetings to lay odds which of the three trucks would disgorge her, since she randomly rode in a different one every trip to foil kidnappers she feared.

On nicer days, when Adelle Congreve felt like traveling to town with less of a parade, she flew herself to the Copper Queen Hospital Helipad (Airport Identifier 6AZ6) in her dead husband's Hughes OH-6 Cayuse Loach. It was a surplus version of the AH-6 attack type Ricky-Ray had piloted in Vietnam, and he had taught his wife to fly it. With Adelle's armed body-guard in the left seat, it was even more reminiscent of the Killer Egg her husband flew on his missions. She would descend to the hospital's new emergency department's rooftop pad, which she had paid for, to pick up her prescription of Oxycodone, which she used only socially, or when Ricky-Ray's absence weighed heavily upon her.

Prescription in hand, she always left the emergency department via one of the three convoyed Suburbans waiting there for her at the door. Adelle loathed the illegals that hiked across her property from the boarder. This struck many as hypocritical, since the mother of her beloved Ricky-Ray was from Chiapas. Upon hearing her name, Timon Pardue reflected, not for the first time, that Adelle Congreve was a complex, perhaps misunderstood creature.

"So what's she want with me?" asked Pardue.

"She wants to meet up. Her and a few others," said Wimble.

"I like it here just fine."

"So meet them here. Timon, they're serious. You're their man. Just hear them out."

Timon was bored and lonely enough for intelligent, sympathetic commiserating company to say yes at this point. Playing it coy meant keeping a thirsty Wimble around in camp long past his welcome.

"Sam, I really don't care what these folks are up to. If they want to troop out here to talk, I can't stop them. It's a free country."

"You're damn right it is, Timon. And we aim to keep it that way."

CHAPTER 5

BLACKSHAW HAD CHOSEN his seat on the bus with care, but it hadn't worked out. With all the windows taken, he ruled out the back of the bus, near the malodorous toilet. He declined to sit where larger passengers were likely to nod off, if they weren't already sleeping, and ooze elbows, hips and shoulders across the property line into his chair space. One can lean so far into the aisle for only so long.

After a quick assessment, Blackshaw sat down quietly next to a white kid who dozed against the window midway back on the left side of the bus. The guy was in his early twenties, with his head shaved, and a four-by-four gauze bandage on his right shoulder. The bandage was fresh enough. The kid's jeans and beater tank-top seemed clean. He was rail thin, and his feet, along with his angular knees and elbows, seemed to have caught in all the right parts of the armrest, the seat in front, and the lower wall AC conduit to keep him upright even though he slept deeply. Yes, Blackshaw noted the black-handled folding knife clipped into his front-right pocket, but that was standard issue for boys today. Finally, perhaps most important of all, this kid did not snore.

The bus pulled out of the station in Washington, D.C. on time, and headed to Los Angeles, but first Blackshaw would have to transfer in Richmond. There would be one other transfer in Oklahoma City, but that third bus would take him the rest of the way to the City of Angels. Blackshaw had recently experienced a fair amount of trouble hunting a serial sniper dubbed Nitro Express there in Los Angeles, but he felt drawn to visit the scene again. He recalled LA to be the opposite of Smith Island, even more foreign than he remembered New York City, where he had been dragooned into the Nitro Express business. Though it was urbanized upward in glass and steel nearly two thousand feet off the deck, the Big Apple was still an island, and Blackshaw was done with islands on principle.

Blackshaw looked out the window as the bus crossed the Potomac. He recalled that an airliner en route to Tampa had hit the structure in the early 1980s before plunging, passengers and all, into the icy river. Only five had survived from the plane. Four had died in cars on the bridge. As an island dweller, Blackshaw viewed bridges not only as roads over water, but as transitions to a wider world. For the Air Florida fatalities, they sure transitioned, but Blackshaw wasn't sure coffins and urns were the hoped for destination. Maybe there was a glorious heaven waiting for them. It all came down to how one regarded Tampa.

As the bus drove from the bridge into Virginia, intact and without mishap, the kid stirred, grunted, and woke. For a moment, his eyes had a sleepy, boyish sweetness. Then, as he came fully awake, certain deficits of personality clicked back in across his face, rendering him rat-like.

"The fuck you looking at."

"Just looking out the window. No offense meant," said Blackshaw evenly.

The kid assessed Blackshaw, took in his seatmate's size, and the complete lack of fear in his eyes, and nodded just once as if he were satisfied that the proper respect he was owed had been paid in full.

Blackshaw's mission welled into his psyche. He regarded the kid in turn, and determined that a physical confrontation was not in the cards. His travel companion had likely been bullied for much of his life. He wondered how deep the truculence ran, and figured this kid responded to his childhood suffering, not with kindness toward others like him, but with meanness. As there were few targets in the world who would actually bow down before a little shit like this, Blackshaw figured he got help dealing out paybacks. Some, thankfully a very few, joined the military. He had met guys like him. But for this fellow, maybe a gang had filled the bill. Now Blackshaw was curious about what lay under the gauze dressing.

"New ink?" Blackshaw asked.

"Color on one I had." The kid made a poor job of hiding his eagerness to display the work, but for some reason, he hesitated.

"I thought about a tattoo," said Blackshaw. "At first, I couldn't think of anything I'd stay happy with for the long haul."

"You ain't that young. Ain't got to be in love with it for too much longer." Relatively speaking, perhaps the kid was right. He was testing Blackshaw's tolerance for annoyance. Jerks so often traded on the politeness of the rest of the world. That ingrained social encoding was the first line of defense of caustic types to avoid serious trouble for themselves.

Blackshaw would brook only so much nonsense from this brat. Remaining calm, he offered, "That's true enough. But by the time I thought of something I wouldn't mind looking at for the rest of my life, my skin was too messed up to leave much room for the work. I did get one though."

The kid sat up, and paid closer attention to Blackshaw. "Messed up how?"

"Scars. A bad burn. Some bullets. My name's Ben Blackshaw."

His brag had the desired effect on the kid. "Rufus Colquette. Bullets, huh? What, like a shootout?"

"Like that. With Taliban."

Colquette frowned. That was not what Blackshaw had expected.

"You was in the Army?"

Blackshaw eased forward in the conversation, more damaged than embarrassed by most of his past. "Navy."

Colquette looked smug, as if he had caught Blackshaw in a lie. "Taliban got boats?"

"Navy has SEALS." Against his more subdued, unvaunting nature, Blackshaw briefly exposed his own shoulder tattoo of an eagle holding a trident, an anchor, and a flintlock pistol. Blackshaw sensed there was more to this kid than misery and bragging; something so needy that he was dangerous.

Now Colquette seemed angry, and his next words proved Blackshaw's intuition right. "Oh. So Navy's taking up for overseas sand-niggers, Big Ben?"

Blackshaw wondered if the flinch in the pit of his gut was evident in his face. "I think we were pushing Democracy that day."

Rufus Colquette snorted. Blackshaw guessed he had used too many syllables in one word and confused the kid.

After a moment, Colquette leaned hard left, and reached into his right front pocket. After scrounging his fingers around in a way that made it look like he had a rash, he finally pulled something out, though he kept it concealed in his grasp.

"Show you something, Big Bad Ben. Show you what I think—what I think's worth a good man's time to fight."

After a furtive check of his surroundings that was as broad and attention-getting as a silent film villain, Rufus Colquette slowly opened his hand.

Blackshaw was not sure what he was looking at for a moment. Colquette's eyes burned, watching for the response. The object, a ball of black, curled threads, was festooned with pocket lint, and other, smaller particles of dust. Blackshaw attempted to sort out what Colquette thought he should have recognized immediately; it appeared that Colquette had entered a barber shop frequented by at least one black client, and for some reason known only to himself, had swept up and removed a handful of clippings from the floor.

Colquette bunched the ball of hair, turning it in his hand. Then Blackshaw's stomach flip-flopped. He remained calm. As Colquette turned the hair in his fingers, working it like a curio shop fetish, Blackshaw saw that these were not loose hairs. A large portion of scalp underneath held them all together.

"I'm a soldier, too, Big Ben." Rufus Colquette eyed his trophy with pride.

Disgusted, Blackshaw was acting on his decision before he realized he had made one. He leaned forward in his seat, blocking the view of other riders. "Be careful with that, Rufus. Anybody else sees it—" He left the consequences up to Colquette's imagination.

"I ain't afraid." But Colquette wadded the grisly object smaller until it was concealed in his hand again.

"I guess not. Where'd you buy that?" asked Blackshaw, in hopes it would lead to more information.

"*Buy* it?" Colquette took umbrage. "You can't buy something like this. You *earn* it. You *take* it!"

"Oh. Okay, Rufus."

"I did, too! Look here!" Colquette worked a long grubby thumbnail of his left hand underneath the dressing's tape on his right shoulder.

Blackshaw leaned away to get a better look. As Colquette folded the gauze down, there it was. An iron cross, irritated, and freshly filled-in with red ink, with dark blue, or perhaps black bars crisscrossing the red fields after the pattern of the battle flag of the Confederate States of America. At the bottom was the figure **88**.

"I told you I'm a knight. Know what I mean?"

"I think so." Rufus Colquette was Klan, or something like it. Or maybe he was just a wanna-be skinhead collecting symbols of hate groups. Given the trophy, Blackshaw figured it was more likely this tattoo was the icon of a particular gang. He knew the **88** signified the eighth letter of the alphabet twice, or **HH** for *Heil Hitler.*

"Shoot, Rufus. I mean, that's some fine ink and all, and the hair is cool, but I mean, really?"

Colquette grew desperate to impress Blackshaw, to convince him. He pressed the dressing back over the tattoo, and dug into his left rear pocket. After a few moments of scrounging, or scratching, Blackshaw was not sure which, he extracted a cell phone. The phone was battered, smudged and grimy with poor care. This was a personal phone, not a disposable burner.

"Check *this* out, man." Colquette opened the phone's photo gallery. His finger swept back in time past the three most recent photographs. They went by quickly, but Blackshaw could see they were shots of Colquette with two other white men holding rifles. Heavily modified AR-15s. The kid stopped scrolling.

Once again, Rufus Colquette glanced around to be sure only Blackshaw could see. Then he angled the phone toward Blackshaw.

As a veteran, and a sometimes volatile civilian, Blackshaw had witnessed horrific carnage with his own eyes. Corpses, often fresh, and sometimes of a certain age. Once on a patrol, he had found an arm. Just an arm, disarticulated by a blast of some kind. But there was no body in sight around the limb anywhere. A simple group photograph should not have shaken him as much as the image Colquette revealed.

In the picture, Rufus Colquette stood with the two men from the other shots. One was a shorter, muscular man, perhaps in his fifties, with a burr cut of gray hair. He affected command presence by standing straight, but the set of his eyes was that of an underling, a flunky. The other was a shorter man, perhaps in his forties, with longer salt-and-pepper hair, and muscles turning to flab. There was a sepulchral emptiness in the taller man's eyes. Both men were wearing khaki battle dress uniform pants, and olive drab shirts, the sleeves neatly rolled and button-tabbed at the triceps. They were sporting their AR-15s in one hand, and large combat knives held over their hearts in some kind of salute.

Right of center, Colquette held a knife, likely the one that was now hooked into his pocket. The blade was unfolded, and it was bloody. There was a fourth person in the photograph. It was a boy who might have been ten or twelve years old but, given his condition, his true age was anybody's guess. The boy was black, naked, and tightly bound with his back to a tree in a thick wood. It must have been a very secluded place, because given the wounds on the boy's torso and groin, there would have been some very loud shrieking; yet the child was not gagged.

Blackshaw could not take his eyes off the young boy's head. There was some hair left on it around the sides, small tufts over the ears. The top of his head was a raw dome of bone and gore that bled into the child's eyes; terrified eyes that stared out of the photograph at Blackshaw. Utterly re-volted, Blackshaw realized the boy had still been very much alive when the picture was taken; there was no way the child had lived out the next hour.

In stark counterpoint to the abject misery on the victim's face were the shit-eating grins stretched across the visages of his torturers. Taking in one last look before averting his eyes, Blackshaw noticed Colquette's other hand in the photograph—in which he clutched the scalp.

CHAPTER 6

TIMON PARDUE BROKE camp the next morning despite the hangover racking his skull. He slowly loaded Popper with gear, then walked the animal down off the rocky hillside into the scrub in the ravine where the small stream snaked. He knew Wimble and his strange cadre might be looking for him, but if he sat tight and was easy to find, he felt it might make him appear pliable, or worse, eager to leap on the bandwagon.

Two hours into the easy walk, Popper snorted, shied hard against his lead, nearly snatching it from Pardue's hand, and stopped. Pardue was on the verge of getting angry at his horse when he saw the thick coil of the stirring diamondback six feet ahead, and heard its distinctive rattle. It was hard to tell how long it was, all wrapped around itself, but clearly it was enormous. Before he moved, Pardue studied the area around him and Popper to be sure he was on the edge of the snake's territory, and hadn't stumbled into the middle of the serpent's family affair.

The way back up the trail was clear. Pardue backed Popper up a good ten feet before wheeling the horse in place, walking him another fifty feet, and tying him to a lone California fan palm. The tree could have been a displaced refugee from the Kofa National Wildlife Refuge a hundred miles west northwest of here. Or maybe it was a holdover from the plantings of some stage coach company for a shady stop. An Indian or a bird might have dropped a seed. Pardue wondered at nature's workings as he drew his Henry from its sheath and moved back down the trail.

Pardue had been gone for only a few minutes, but when he returned to where Popper had shied, he discovered that the diamondback had surrendered the trail. Pardue followed a patch of sunlight uphill from the viper's last known, but this time, without Popper to warn him, he moved with greater care. And there it was, winding fat as a big man's arm toward higher ground it knew would be bathed in sun for the rest of the afternoon. This fellow was a monster, a good six-footer, with a head as big as a garden spade, or so it appeared to Pardue.

The former sheriff kneeled, and drew a bead on the rattler. A moment later, with the Henry's report echoing away in the hills, the viper writhed headless in Pardue's grasp.

As he coiled his kill and stuffed it into his field bag, his eye was drawn further up the hill to a tangle of brush. Something seemed wrong about it. Usually, Pardue could pick out the snag, the thing that had caused the weeds and sticks to aggregate in the first place. In a dry stream bed, it was often a log, or a piece of junk that formed the nucleus of the brush pile. In a running stream, back east at least, an old beaver damn might be the first blockage around which more detritus collected. In among this mess, there seemed to be tendrils, like kudzu. Pardue stepped closer. No, this was manmade crap.

A number of the tendrils trailed up the hill, pressed down by time, and perhaps the rare downpour, to take on the contours and colors of the earth and rocks. The tendrils terminated at a smooth, washed expanse. But for the snake, he never would have noticed, but now he knew what it was. An old parachute lay draped here, gathered there, across the hillside, but it was saturated in dust and grit, riven with rot, making the ground look smooth like dried mud.

Where the tan tones of the desert had not infused the fabric with new hues, the few exposed gores of the chute were pale, sun-bleached Army green.

Pardue let his eyes follow the tendrils, which were the parachute's shroud lines, back to the heap of brush. The sticks and dirt and, along with dead cheatgrass, thistle, and knapweed were wadded around something big. He went closer, peering among the shadows for clothing, boots, and bones, or more snakes. He didn't remember any sport skydiving operations, or jumpers gone missing. Perhaps this guy had been part of a long-ago training mission from Fort Huachaca. Maybe this poor bastard never made the papers because the operation was top secret, or he was part of some kind of foreign military exchange.

He picked up a rock, and tossed it into the clutter to flush any snakes. Instead of a viper's rattle, he heard a distinctive *clunk*. Another rock landed with the same distinctive sound.

Using the sight of his Henry rifle, Pardue slowly pulled back a layer of litter, and saw what looked like a canister the size of a large kitchen trash can. It was also olive drab in color. There was no corpse here. He exposed more of the container. There was a bound bundle of metal rods lashed to the side of the canister. In among the rotted canvas risers of the parachute rig, he noticed two other straps padded with cracked leather. One strap hung loose from a frame that would have conformed the roundness of the canister to the flatter contours of a soldier's back. The other strap was still drawn up tight, as if it had never been loosened for use. This thing had fallen from an aircraft and had never been found. No man lay with it; nothing but the parachute had borne it.

Then Pardue saw the faded, white letters stenciled on the canister's surface: **M-388VT**.

"Holy shit," gasped Pardue.

This was not a container of rations, or ordinary equipment. From Timon Pardue's time in the Army, he knew what he had. He wondered if he dared touch it.

Pardue remembered that in the early 1960s, the Los Alamos lab in New Mexico had developed and tested a low-yield battlefield nuclear warhead. The concept was for a device like this to be dropped on its own chute into the water with a two-man SEAL team who would place it where it was needed for remote detonation. It would clear a decent sized harbor of enemy shipping. Other variants were designed to be mounted on Walleye air-to-air missiles, the only such use of a nuclear warhead, to destroy an entire squadron of incoming Russian bombers with one blow at a time when conventional air-to-air missiles were still not very reliable or accurate. Unlike the W-54 backpack unit, which yielded about a kiloton, the Walleye variant was usually smaller. He figured an **M-388VT** was a warhead meant for the

Davy Crockett recoilless rifle, some parts of which were belayed to the canister.

Though Pardue wasn't sure he'd mention the nuke, now he smiled, anticipating this meeting with Wimble's bunch. He would look so badass offering rattlesnake meat around the fire. They would know they'd come to the right man, whether he told them to go to hell or offered to escort them there himself.

CHAPTER 7

RAGE WELTERED BLACKSHAW'S mind as Colquette
tucked his prize photograph away. At that moment, had the bus been pulling into a stop of any length, Blackshaw might have disembarked early from
his trip west leaving one rider with neck troubles forever quiet in the seat.
Instead, Blackshaw breathed slow and deep, quelling the gorge that had
risen in his throat.

"That's something," he said.

"My first," said Colquette in prideful remembrance, like a boy who
had lost his virginity by rape.

"Pretty brave. I admit, I'm surprised you showed me."

"You're a SEAL. I can see in your face you've spilled a drop or two.
Now you know I can. I proved it."

"That you did. You know, in DEVGRU we had a special tradition."

Colquette was all ears, half excited, half dreading to learn of some
hazing stunt he would have to perform, and all to fit in to some place of
strength, of domination.

"Can I trust you?" asked Blackshaw, with a worried tone.

"Hell yes you can trust me. We're comrades in arms, ain't we. What
tradition?" Colquette had committed a crime against humanity; perhaps it
was really a war crime. He would do anything to belong.

Blackshaw drew a breath and went on. "The tradition was to share
pictures of our first kills with our buddies. Now, back in the day, it was
actual photographs. Of course, we had our own recon operations dark

rooms to develop the shots ourselves, so they wouldn't fall into the wrong hands. You know. Folks who didn't appreciate what we were trying to do."

"Sure. I get it." Colquette sounded worldly, as if he understood the misunderstood.

"Did you keep the tradition with your friends there? Like you said," continued Blackshaw, "it's the proof. It's how anybody you meet knows you're the real deal. A stone cold killing machine."

Colquette was relieved, and charged. He had killed. He had witnesses. He had done what Blackshaw revealed as the way of a true warrior SEAL. He ticked off the chain of evidence on his fingers. "Nyqvist's got a picture 'cause it was his phone he took it on. He sent it to me. Oren's got it, too. Him, Nyqvist, and The Major helped me lay the trap, so you know The Major got him a copy. Nyqvist texted it around then and there, even before I cut that fucker's throat like a pig."

"The Major's the short guy? He's like your commandant?" confirmed Blackshaw.

Colquette's eyes got wide. "How'd you know that?"

"Like you said, Rufus. You can see it in the face. It's leadership. It's greatness. You have it, too."

Colquette smiled, proud. Never in his short life of humiliations had he been called a leader, let alone great. "You know, Nyqvist even sent a shot to headquarters for Malthys himself to see."

"They've got your number at HQ, for sure," said Blackshaw.

"They know my name out west. They know who the fuck I am."

"All the way out west?" Blackshaw made an effort to sound impressed.

"That's right. In Arizona."

"You're the man in Tucson."

"Bisbee."

"It's obvious they're grooming you for big things," said Blackshaw.

Colquette said, "Damn straight they are."

"Pretty soon, I'll be proud to say I knew you when. Of course," and here, Blackshaw looked chagrined, "nobody will believe I once rode a bus with Rufus Colquette."

Colquette swelled with righteous purpose, as well as an unhealthy largesse. "Yes they fucking will. You want me to send it to you, Ben? I could text it right to you."

Blackshaw kept his eyes from narrowing with satisfaction at this small deception. "You'd do that? I mean, it would be an honor, Rufus. Yes, I would consider that a real honor from a knight, and a friend."

Colquette punched in the number of Blackshaw's disposable phone. A few moments later, the burner chimed.

"Thanks, Rufus. Very cool," said Blackshaw, confirming the picture had come through.

And there it was, Rufus Colquette's grin from the photograph, stretching proud across his face, and not two feet from Blackshaw's white-knuckled fists. Los Angeles would have to wait. Here was a new mission, with death at the destination.

CHAPTER 8

PARDUE'S CAMPSITE WOULD not be big enough, and that was fine. It would be safe. It wasn't the site's capacity for a few extra people that concerned him. Plenty of room for a confab. On the other hand, if Adelle Congreve were involved, making an entrance was far more likely than just showing up. That is why he unloaded and staked out Popper, pitched his tent, and intentionally built a smoky fire about a hundred yards from a clearing large enough to serve as a helicopter landing zone.

He did not particularly like the taste of rattlesnake. It reminded him of fish meat that had gotten too wet somewhere in transit between its native waters and the table. His chili rub and a slower sauté would put some oomph back in the dish.

Pardue was just taste-testing the first bite of rattler when the rotor buzz and turbine whine of a helicopter reached his ears. It was not the iconic bass *thwop* of the two-bladed rotor of the Huey Iroquois used by many wildfire fighting services. And the Customs and Border Patrol had retired their remaining fleet of Loaches in 2011 in favor of Eurocopter AS-350s with their more rapid data-processing and multi-wavelength camera arrays.

Pardue grinned. Congreve was so predictable. Her Cayuse loitered for a few minutes farther back up the trail in the area where Wimble had first found Pardue. Then the helicopter transitioned back into cruise flight, bee-lining toward the plume of smoke rising from his campfire. He dropped five more snake cutlets into his iron skillet.

Adelle Congreve ably piloted her helicopter to the clearing Pardue had scoped out, and greased the landing with a certain amount of *yippee-ki-yay* flair. As he had planned, the rotor wash dissipated before it enveloped his campsite in dust and blew down his tent. Popper was not spooked in the least.

The Cayuse turbine spooled down, and soon, Pardue saw Congreve's blonde hair bobbing through the brush as she hiked in toward camp. It wasn't long before he could make out three men following close behind her.

"Hey Timon," said Adelle.

"Miss Adelle." Pardue stood and shook her hand. She tugged him hard into an embrace that was comfortably buffered by her Mentor breast implants.

When Pardue stepped back, Congreve made introductions to two ranchers he recognized and knew by reputation from around the county. She held her hand toward a tall, lanky white man in his sixties, and said, "Farrell Cutlip, this here's Sheriff Timon Pardue, retired."

Cutlip smiled, "I voted for you, sir. All three times."

"Last time's the kicker, but thanks. Flying K, right?" asked Pardue. "Nice spread. Good water."

Congreve presented the next rancher, a tanned bull of a man with close-set eyes and no neck to speak of. "You heard of Merton Dressler."

"Mr. Pardue." Dressler had a chilly smile, and there was aggression in his handshake.

Pardue said affably, "Call me Timon, please. Believe your foreman won bareback last year at the Tucson Rodeo."

Dressler gave a taut, satisfied nod of acknowledgment. "Two years ago."

The third man waited until Dressler stepped aside. The bluster left Congreve's voice, and became hushed as she introduced a gaunt, long-haired man in his thirties. Pardue knew him on sight, but not because of his resemblance to a cross between a post-card Jesus and Rasputin. "Timon, this is Malthys. His ranch is a few miles up the road."

Pardue said, "Good to meet you." Neither man extended a hand of greeting.

"Same," growled Malthys.

Calling Malthys's place a ranch was generosity bordering on delusion. Malthys was the Dean of the Pure Nation Comitatus which was housed in several dormitories on a hundred acre compound in northern Cochise County. There were rumors of polygamy bandied about, but not with underage girls, at least so far. The PNC fences were patrolled by armed guards, which alarmed a few nearby ranchers, as did the din of regular live-fire training at the PNC's shooting range. Pardue himself had made several trips to the compound to respond to complaints of loud music, but they had always turned out to be live concerts with lyrics roared in such a way as to be frightening, but otherwise unintelligible. Pardue had found the events' permits to be in order each time, and left with token requests that the bands tone it down. Being a crappy neighbor was not against the law.

Pardue gave supper to his guests, and everybody said the chili-rubbed rattler tasted pretty good; all except Malthys, who offered no praise but ate it anyway.

"Wimble couldn't make it?" asked Pardue.

"Oh Timon, you know him and flying," said Adelle Congreve.

Pardue knew Wimble did not mind air travel, even in light planes. It was Adelle's piloting that the former deputy did not trust. Still, Pardue's mention of Wimble did not have the desired effect of bringing the visitors closer to the real matter.

No one refused Jack Daniel's, which Pardue hoped would grease the ways of conversation, but unlike the rest of the party, Malthys was sipping his first round while the others were swigging their third. He was obviously bored, and more likely frustrated with unending chat about beef prices, fuel prices, feed prices, and any gossip that Dressler, Cutlip, and Congreve cared to bring up instead of the subject of the visit. Pardue didn't mind company, but this stretch of throat-clearing was getting on his nerves.

Coming up for air after an in-depth analysis of the dead cow that had blocked a slot canyon, and the many hikers' complaints about its horrific stench, Pardue noticed Malthys starring at the M-388VT canister and accoutrements lying with the other gear and supplies. Perhaps the gaunt stranger recognized what Pardue had found.

Finally, Pardue said, "You all came a long way."

Adelle Congreve nattered, "And you're such a fine host, Timon. I must have your recipe for chili rattler. But yes, here we all are."

Farrell Cutlip cleared his throat. "Timon, we are disgusted by what happened to you. And you, sleeping rough in the wilderness. You likely feel the same way."

"I needed a break," said Pardue, "after that whole deal."

Dressler put in, "We're not alone. My son looked you up on Twitter."

"I don't mess with that stuff," said Pardue.

"Who the hell does?" said Cutlip.

"Plenty," stated Adelle Congreve.

"Timon," continued Dressler, "my son says you're *trending*!"

"I'm doing no such thing. I've been out here the whole time." Pardue was not sure what trending was, but he did not like the chic, girly sound of it.

Now Malthys spoke up. "Mr. Pardue, you're more popular right now, right here, than you were after your first election, sir. There are at least eight sock-puppet Twitter accounts set up in your name, all of them claiming to quote you, to represent you, speculating on where you are, and how you feel, especially about the wets. A few of those accounts are international. You're hailed here, in France, and in Germany among certain groups, for thinking the correct thoughts about foreigners stampeding in and taking over where they just don't belong."

"Jesus Christ," muttered Pardue.

Cutlip said, "Now the question is, are you willing to leverage this popularity to make a real difference."

"You saw what happens when you try to do something about The Problem," complained Pardue.

"Maybe in regular channels, that's what happens," said Congreve, all sultry and coy.

"We're not talking about regular channels." Malthys got a gleam in his eye as he went on. "You're a sovereign citizen, Mr. Pardue. I'm not a hundred percent sure the government you tried your best to serve really has any say over you, or any of us, or any of your supporters. It's all Godless corruption in Washington. Customs and Border Protection has a burn rate. Did you know that? They fling cash all over, buying new choppers, or sending a bunch of guns across the border and then *losing* them in the name of law enforcement. I mean *come on*! If CBP doesn't blow their entire budget one year, even if it doesn't achieve a damn thing, they won't get the same, or more money *next* year. The entire incentive is for spending, not solving The Problem. It's a self-licking ice cream cone. One month, it's swarms of anchor babies—"

Cutlip interrupted, "My dog brought in a hunk of human afterbirth last month."

"Oh for Christ's sake," said Congreve, disgusted.

Malthys ignored Cutlip. "Next time it's unaccompanied minors by the tens of thousands. And they call it a *humanitarian* crisis instead of what it really is. A carefully plotted invasion of our sovereign lands."

"I did what I could," simpered Pardue.

"You did what *one* man could do," said Dressler. "You're not one man anymore."

"You're a leader, sir, on the verge of greatness. You're a general with legions behind him." And with that, Malthys stood, drew his combat knife, and held it over his heart. "I will follow you all the way."

"All the way where?" asked Pardue, befuddled by whiskey and the high-toned speechifying.

Malthys kneeled beside the former sheriff, bowed his head, and held his knife out to Pardue with both hands palm-up in a mawkish pantomime of surrender, allegiance, and obeisance.

Malthys's voice was husky with emotion when he said, "To the border, Mr. Pardue. To the border."

Merton Dressler, Farrell Cutlip, and Adelle Congreve struggled, after too long sitting and drinking, onto older knees with grunts, pops and crackles to rival the sounds from the campfire. Soon, they too were holding out some pretty fancy cutlery flat on their palms toward Pardue.

Pardue blushed, overcome with awkwardness, not knowing what he was supposed to do or say at such an important moment. Take the knives? Tap these wingnuts on the shoulders with his own blade and say *arise*? His native practical nature won in the end.

"Would you all relax, please? Now, Malthys, when you say legions, how many are we really talking about?"

CHAPTER 9

BLACKSHAW CLIMBED DOWN out of the bus into a warm Richmond night, leaving Rufus Colquette aboard and twitching in a fitful sleep. He noticed the stadium across the street before entering the big box bus station. Inside, it took only a moment to find the person he was looking for.

The black police officer was chatting with his white partner near the opening of the shadowy video arcade. Blackshaw waited, picking up a Snickers bar from one of the many vending machines lining the wall.

Finally, the white officer put down his soda, and ambled toward the men's room. Maybe the black officer had to go, too, but to maintain eyes on the terminal, one of them had to stay behind. The white cop went first. Blackshaw tried not to read too much into the order of things. He started walking toward the black officer before the other policeman was inside the restroom.

Assuming a worried look, he said to Officer Keene, "Sir? There's a man on the bus from D.C. He says he wants to die. Suicidal. He passed out. Said his name was Rufus Colquette. I think he took pills."

Keene started toward the door to the bus parking area. "What gate?"

"Sixteen," said Blackshaw. The officer shifted into a trot, but halted when Blackshaw shouted, "Hold on! He showed me his phone. A picture. Take a look. It's pretty bad. I thought you should see."

Officer Keene took the phone Blackshaw held out as if this could really wait. Then he saw the image. "Jesus Christ! He showed you this?"

Blackshaw pointed to Colquette in the picture. "I think that's why he's so upset, he's feeling guilty." said Blackshaw. "Left side of the bus, midway back by the window."

Keene ran for the door, shouting for his partner over the microphone clipped at his shoulder. A moment later, the white officer flew out of the men's room zipping his fly and adjusting his belt. Before Keene ran through the door to the lot, Blackshaw saw his right hand drop to his gun. Rufus Colquette was going to have an interesting night.

Blackshaw was in the back seat of the first cab in the taxi line before the driver was fully awake. "Train station, please."

The driver, a grizzled older man whose great bulk seemed to flow forth and merge as one with the entire front seat area, asked, "Main Street, or Staples Mill?"

"Union Station in D.C."

"That's a couple hour's ride. Not cheap. There's buses from right here. Not to mention we got trains."

Blackshaw pulled cash out of his cargo pocket. "Appreciate the advice. I'd like to go now."

The driver clocked the money and said, "Look buddy, it's not like I'm going to catch a fare back to here. Not from a train station in D.C. okay? Put's a hole in my day."

Blackshaw looked at the driver for a moment, then said, "Start the meter. Start driving. Double the meter when we get there."

The cab was pulling out as Blackshaw looked over his shoulder out the grimy back window. He could just hear sirens of additional police, or an ambulance, maybe both, responding to the bus station.

Then he saw Officer Keene and his partner run out of the bus station, looking up and down the sidewalk and North Boulevard. Where was Rufus Colquette? The cops should have been with him. They should both have that guy in cuffs, but there they were, empty-handed. There was no way they could have missed Colquette.

Blackshaw had passed Keene his own burner phone after purging the short call history and wiping it down. Maybe he should have taken Colquette's, but the kid might have woken and caught him in the act. Blackshaw had picked up his burner in a drugstore in D.C. It would not lead back to him. But how had Keene and his partner blown this arrest? It should have been a layup. And now these cops were gawking up and down the street for the one guy who had talked to them. They were looking for Blackshaw. Not for the first time tonight, he felt as though he should have handled Colquette his own way. Or minded his own damn business.

The cabbie caught the officers in the rearview mirror, decelerated, and said, "Oh boy. Police activity. Maybe I should slow down and ask 'em what's doing. See if I can help."

"You have a fare back here," reminded Blackshaw.

"Let's say quadruple the meter."

Blackshaw read the cabbie's name on his ID, leaned forward, and spoke low. "Let's say double, Thomas Jacobs, which is what we agreed. That's pretty good, right? And you take your money, be grateful, stay quiet, and you don't spend the rest of your life looking over your shoulder wondering when I'm going to catch up to you."

"Take it easy!"

"Or I could drive myself in your cab, and you can ride in the trunk until they pull this hack out of the Potomac."

Jacobs' eyes widened. "For fuck's sake, man!"

"It's a night full of options, TJ." Then, from nowhere, Blackshaw found himself shouting, "I need a lift to D.C.!"

The cab accelerated, and for the rest of the trip, there was no further discussion of money or death.

CHAPTER 10

TIMON PARDUE CHUCKLED as the Loach rose into the air. Their good-byes had been charged with a mordant, febrile excitement, though the handshakes remained formal. Adelle Congreve had done the right thing at their parting, pulling a fifth of Jack Daniel's from her over-sized bag, and handing it over with a suggestively wet peck on his lips. "See you tomorrow, big man."

Pardue followed the helicopter's path toward the horizon, and noticed that there was a haze in the sky. It wasn't weather. It was a big fire. Not a building burning. It was an entire countryside in flames.

CHAPTER 11

ENDLESS TRAIN CONNECTIONS, and the final cab ride from Tucson to Bisbee, had left Blackshaw uncomfortably tired, but not exhausted. He was enlivened by the work ahead of him. Before finding the cab, an hour's stop at the Second Amendment Exposition at Tucson Convention Center, where cash was still king, had fitted him with tools of his new trade. He could have flown here from Richmond or Washington, D.C., but TSA security checks would have cost him important items he wished to keep. The Bersa Thunder 380 he could have replaced easily enough. It was his satellite phone, of a make and model used only by a few government operatives, that he wanted to hang onto without explanation to authorities of any stripe.

In Bisbee, after a visit to a discount clothing store, followed by purchases at an electronics warehouse, Blackshaw was kitted-out. He took a room at the Bisbee Grand Hotel. Blackshaw was not one to be swayed by detective stories into lurking in dives and flophouses. They were the most closely observed lairs in any town. Alcohol, drugs, and desperation in bad neighborhoods kept the police attentive and busy. True unmolested anonymity was the purview of the wealthy. To have money, and to know precisely how and where to spend it, conferred privacy. Police departments wrangled the criminal, violent element. The wealthy were left to the FBI and grand juries. To be innocent and to be above suspicion were not the same thing at all.

Blackshaw entered the room, and limited his unpacking to charging the computer tablet and the GPS he had purchased. The sat-phone's battery was still good. After a shower, he lay down on the king size bed. When he woke, it was dark out. It only took a few moments to revive, align, and organize his rage and his fears into the personality that had drawn him to the town of Bisbee, Arizona.

CHAPTER 12

MALTHYS THOUGHT PARDUE was worth a second look as a partner. It might not work out, but of course he would do his damnedest to manage the situation if things went off course. It was possible that the former sheriff might be perfect, with his pouting in the wilderness. Glorious self-pity could be useful, just so he did not overshadow Malthys's control of his own followers. But what was the old man doing with his own army surplus gear? All of Pardue's other camp equipment looked only a few years old, straight from a chain camping outfitter.

All Malthys wanted was freedom to approach the U.S. Mexico border without getting shot at by a rancher. Pardue's situation was a godsend. Dressler, Cutlip, and Congreve were hot to create an occupation of sorts. As it was, the grounds of the Pure Nation Comitatus simply lay too far north in Cochise County to be useful for his current venture. But the land had been so cheap, and border ranchers weren't selling, no matter how they pissed and moaned about Mexicans. And now, because of his manpower, Malthys had everything but an engraved invitation to trespass. Cool.

The free labor provided by disaffected men, women, and even kids who flocked to Malthys's compound had been sufficient to start his operation off. He had welcomed only whites to give his following the proper Aryan Supremacist whiff. His first joiners had emptied their bank accounts into his without a qualm, as if that were expected, just part of the drill of dropping out of mainstream society into his radical cult's tributary. The problem now was that most of his recent applicants were broke, coming in and subjecting themselves to his doctrine willingly enough just so long as there were three hots and a cot provided.

Malthys had heard that many indigents in 19th Century New England suddenly, yet predictably, felt drawn to the hospitable Shaker faith at the first chill of November. When the weather thawed again in springtime, many of these Winter Shakers, as they were called, grew disaffected with the same sect that had fed and housed them through the coldest months, and wandered away again into the world where sex and alcohol were better appreciated. There were no temporary members of Pure Nation Comitatus.

Back at the PNC compound, Malthys tried to remember the faded letters on the side of Pardue's surplus pack. He should have written them down. He was pretty sure it was M-388V. A quick search on the Internet set him swearing under his breath in amazement. There was no way the fifty-year-old device was operable after all this time. He wondered if Pardue knew what he had. This put an interesting wrinkle in his plans.

He reached for the public address mic, and keyed it twice. Old Tannoy speakers clacked and clicked like rifle shots throughout the compound. He gave his followers two minutes to get their butts into the great hall for his announcement, the call to arms.

The message would be simple. In the morning, the men would be heading south to the border to ward off Evil Incarnate. He would include enough Biblical quotations in the diatribe to properly exhort them. Ephesians 6:11 would get their juices flowing. *Put on the whole armor of God, that ye may be able to stand against the wiles of the devil.* Maybe with a touch of Isaiah 9:5. *For every battle of the warrior is with confused noise, and garments rolled in blood; but this shall be with burning and fuel of fire.* In case of a challenge, which was highly unlikely, the men were so bored, and so ready to fight with purpose, he would include Acts 1:7-8. *And he said unto them, It is not for you to know the times or the seasons, which the Father hath put in his own power.* Anyone who shirked his righteous duty, after all the food and ammo Malthys had given, would be made an example, and expelled from PNC. A lone disaffected voice or two vying for media attention might cause a small public relations problem, but news outlets were likely to be focused on the ranchers involved. The PNC women would be busy enough back at the compound's SocMed shack rattling away at their computers, generating a flurry of social media messages to confound any truth that might emerge. Lord knows, once they moved south, there would be no reporters embedded with the Pure Nation Comitatus.

His Kryptovox phone buzzed on the desk next to him. He opened the line with a brusque, "What."

The caller was confident the line was encrypted. "Nyqvist. Seems the noob bragged along the way a few days ago. Attracted some attention. Maybe traveling separately wasn't such a good idea."

"Are you fucking kidding me? Did he get picked up?" Malthys stood and paced the office, his long hair, snatched back in a ponytail, flew out wide like a whip as he turned each lap.

"No. He was off the bus in Richmond grabbing a cigarette. Cops blew out of the terminal at a hundred miles an hour and went straight for the bus. He figured something was wrong and got the hell away."

"How does he figure the cops were looking for him?"

Nyqvist was quiet for a moment. "It was a gut-call based on some blabbing he did to a guy in the next seat on the bus to Richmond. When the kid woke up, the guy was gone. I mean, this guy was supposed to change busses, so his not being there could be no problem."

"What the hell did he say? Why did he say *anything*?" Malthys was amazed into stillness.

"He's a good-hearted kid. He just wanted to brag," offered Nyqvist.

"Is he with you?"

"Oh yeah. Not letting him out of my sights. The problem is, it wasn't just talk. You know that picture we sent you?"

Malthys's heart damn near stopped. "What about it?"

"He texted it to the guy."

"What the fuck!"

Nyqvist was abashed. "The guy said sharing pics of your first one with your buddies was how they did things in the Army or some crock of shit like that."

"Jesus Christ. Is the noob just telling you all this?"

"He ditched the phone, if that's what you're worried about. And no, I had to lean on him some."

Malthys was in full damage control mode. "Can he still travel?"

"No marks on him that clothes won't cover."

"Okay. Bring him with you. Now, who's the asshole he was talking to?"

Nyqvist said, "Ben Blackshaw. Oh, and he knows about Bisbee. And you."

CHAPTER 13

BLACKSHAW REACHED CYBERSPACE from his hotel room via actual space, using a modem in his sat-phone to ping his signal through a discrete orbiting government communications network. He did not have permission to do this, or authorization. He was an electronic trespasser surfing a beach dashed by breakers rolling in on private wavelengths, and all courtesy of his hacker friend, Michael Craig.

Though there was a haze in the night air outside his window, Blackshaw's first pass researching one Malthus in Arizona brought greater clarity to his prey. With the spelling he tried, he received the suggestion *Including results for **Malthys Arizona***. Since nothing had popped from the way he originally spelled the search, he okayed that prompt.

Newspaper articles and police blotters cited Malthys and his clan as nuisance offenders, mostly earning quality-of-life kinds of summonses. The Pure Nation Comitatus kept its collective nose clean, compared to the Branch Davidian lunatics of Waco, Texas. Beginning with the name of the cult, there was every reason to believe the group was organized with a white supremacist credo. The interesting thing was that Rufus Colquette had mentioned Bisbee, Arizona. All the hits on the net placed Malthys and his followers in Catalina, to the north of Tucson. Colquette had heard something, perhaps. His kill-buddies, Nyqvist, Oren, and The Major might have talked, though divulging any crucial operations details in front of Rufus Colquette seemed unwise.

Blackshaw cleaned-up, geared up, and took the stairs down to the lobby where the desk clerk who had checked him in was still beaming under the influence of a fifty dollar tip. Blackshaw had three sets of false identities, and a sheaf of corresponding credit cards that were paid automatically each month, so the clerk was not the least bit concerned about his generous guest. That wasn't always the case, as when Blackshaw had bulled his way into lodgings in Los Angeles with nothing more than cash only two missions back.

The identification held when he rented a Jeep from a major chain up the street. Blackshaw tossed his field bag in back, hopped in, fired up, and drove north to see what Malthys's idea of a pure nation looked like.

After traveling the highways rounding Tucson, the high desert countryside felt comfortable to Blackshaw as it gave way to the Santa Catalina range to his right.

He turned off State Highway 77 a mile before the GPS wanted him to, and tucked the Jeep into a ravine a half-mile up a rough dirt track. Short of a flash flood, the vehicle would be okay.

The two mile patrol across country felt good to Blackshaw. He heard a group of coyotes barking and yipping in the dark. The brightness of the stars at this elevation, with the crisp, clear air, was vivid, almost dazzling. The depth of space overhead made him think of his insignificance in the grand scheme, but it could not completely draw away his sense of mission; the urge to seek and quell a malevolent force remained strong. Glancing up from the ground out into the universe, or holding Malthys in his mental sights, was the best way to prevent looking too deeply inside. A small group of javalina peccaries scented him, stirred, and grunted away to his left. Any other night, he would have stalked them, and eaten well beside a solitary fire. Tonight, he maintained his slow advance on the Pure Nation Comitatus.

Unused to exercise, even this walk in the countryside left Blackshaw feeling a rare fatigue that was more like relaxation. He saw the loom of streetlights over the next ridgeline, and stopped. He lowered himself into a crouch, and rechecked his assembly of the VSS Vintorez *Threadcutter* sniper rifle. The Russian gun sported an integral noise suppressor which, when used with the 9mm armor piercing SP-6 boat-tail round, could quietly kill a Cadillac. Blackshaw had brought three twenty-round box magazines of SP-6 on his walk this evening. He could kill a dealership. Tonight, he had nothing against cars. Humans were another matter.

He studied the ridgeline through the weapon's NSPUM-3 (1PN75) night sight for pickets guarding the compound. His slow scan revealed no one, but that did not mean there weren't sentries lying low, dug in, and waiting. With a decent budget, Malthys's security detail might monitor the perimeter surrounding PNC's hundred acres with fiber optic ground vibrations sensors, but Blackshaw did not think devices like this would be in use. False triggers because of rampant nocturnal wildlife would make for a busy tour for any sentries on duty.

Blackshaw worked his way up the hill. From the crest, he scanned the compound below. It was ablaze with floodlights. Barn-like buildings, probably dormitories for PNC followers, were laid out in a square. A flagpole stood at the square's center, flying two banners. At the top was an inverted American flag, which was a signal of distress. Beneath that was another flag, mostly red in color, with a device Blackshaw could not make out. The night breeze was too still to unfurl this pennant in all its glory.

Blackshaw felt it was unreasonable to expect to see Malthys himself down there. The rifle scope would bring in enough detail for target recognition and confirmation. From Blackshaw's study of the known images of Malthys, and there were plenty, he had not changed his bearded Messiah appearance in many years. The issue soon became clear. Every male in that compound old enough to grow a beard had done so, perhaps in homage to his leader, perhaps in some throwback nod to the 19th Century Mosaic stylings.

The Pure Nation Comitatus motor pool consisted of a Unimog, and numerous other four-wheel drive trucks in all stages of filth and disrepair. There were lines of men and women streaming to the trucks with boxes and bundles of supplies. An expedition was being prepared.

Blackshaw heard a man approaching from the east, up the hill toward him. A sentry. Too noisy to be taking his job seriously. Blackshaw waited until the sentry came in sight, and carefully adjusted his own position to lie directly in the man's path. Slowly Blackshaw stood up at the ready behind an ancient saguaro cactus, its arms outspread and angled upward at the elbow joints. Abandoning the Threadcutter at the base of the cactus, Blackshaw carefully, silently shifted his position, keeping the massive barbed plant between himself and the guard.

Within a moment of the sentry's tromping past the cactus, Blackshaw had him face down on the ground, with his wrists zip-tied at his back. The stunned guard snorted and hissed, struggling to breathe through Blackshaw's massive hand enveloping his bearded face, with his other hand pressing a knife to his throat.

Blackshaw put his mouth close to the terrified man's ear. "Settle down, or you get a shave."

The sentry's convulsive bucking quieted.

"Good boy. Now, you want some air. I get that. If you promise to keep a civil tongue in your head, you might get to keep it. Nod if you agree. Shake your head, and you'll saw your own neck to the bone."

The sentry nodded. Blackshaw eased his grip on the man's face. The guard inhaled deep, like a free diver surfacing. That's all he got. Blackshaw cemented his hand over the guy's face again.

"What's your name, hairy boy?" Blackshaw gave the man enough airspace to answer.

"Lukas Malthys."

"Is *everybody* down there last name of Malthys?" This reminded Blackshaw of the hyper violent Move sect that was bombed in a Philadelphia firestorm. All the Move followers took *Africa* as their surnames.

The sentry waited for a chance to breathe and speak, but Blackshaw did not give him one. He nodded again. Blackshaw let him grab a quick breath.

"Catchy," said Blackshaw. "He must think a lot of himself. Where's everybody going?"

Blackshaw eased his grip for half a second, and Lukas Malthys gasped out, "Bisbee."

"Where in Bisbee?"

"Border," said Lukas, gagging for air.

"Okay Lukas Malthys. Been nice chatting. And goodnight." Blackshaw put the sentry into a sleeper hold. Lukas's struggles surged, then quickly weakened to nothing just as several engines in the compound motor pool below fired to life.

Blackshaw watched eleven trucks form up and convoy from the property with the Unimog in the lead. He collected his rifle, and exfiltrated down the hill toward his Jeep, not giving a rat's ass if Lukas Malthys woke up before the coyotes got at him. After a few minutes, he realized Lukas Malthys was safe. The pack of coyotes was following Blackshaw.

CHAPTER 14

LUKAS MALTHYS WAS discovered by his relief an hour after he failed to report. The zip-ties made it hard for him to deny the compound's perimeter had been probed. He was dragged before a PNC tribunal of inquiry, bound to a chair, and interviewed about his failure to keep the sacred PNC ground safe.

Before the beating at the hands of his interrogators became crippling, Lukas came clean. He admitted he'd revealed that the Pure Nation Comitatus convoy was en route Bisbee.

The shaggy members of the tribunal put their heads together for a few moments. It was decided that Lukas would be taken to the camp forming at the border, where he could disclose his failings to Malthys in person. Malthys himself would decide Lukas's fate.

Lukas was summarily thrown into the back of a van to take the long drive south.

CHAPTER 15

AS A RULE is usually followed by at least one exception, and plenty of excuses. In Blackshaw's Bisbee Grand Hotel room, the sun was threatening to rise and shed light on a bottle of budget rum gleaming darkly on the side table. The hooch was nearly the same color as the antiquated wood stain on the furnishings. There was a clean glass next to the bottle. This was as far as Blackshaw had gotten. As a rule, he never drank alcohol.

And yet this morning, things were different. Now the wildfire haze thickening around the town had its cousin in Blackshaw's mind. How had he gotten to this place? He had no idea of the right direction forward. His wife, LuAnna lay stricken and all but lost to him thousands of miles away on Smith Island. Blackshaw's closest friend was sick of him, and had turned his back. Blackshaw had failed to end Rufus Colquette, and even though the police had graphic evidence of the young man's crimes, there was no word in any paper, or on any news program, of his apprehension. Just hours before, Blackshaw had left a disaffected racist moron bound hand-and-foot in the wild without a qualm as to whether the man survived. Blackshaw wondered if something was wrong with him.

Blackshaw desired to break the rum bottle's seal, and twist off its plastic cap. He thought about what the liquid would look like sloshing into the tumbler. The booze would add something sweet, yet volatile, to the smoky scents seeping into the room from the fire scorching the land to the south. He half-believed that somewhere in the bottle, probably close to the turbid bottom, lay a sort of truth, or else oblivion. The liquor would either burn away his confusion, or cloud his mind past all caring. He was not sure which he preferred.

Blackshaw opened the briefcase containing the Threadcutter rifle's components. Though he had test-fired the weapon only twice in the desert the night before to check the sight's zero, he cleaned the weapon thoroughly. He glanced from time to time at the bottle as if it were a visiting friend with a lot on his mind, and a need to be heard by someone who cared. He wondered if this is what it felt like to consult oracles, to tend to the needs of household lares and penates upon whose protection he depended. How long was he supposed to politely wait for answers before following his own instincts? For the first time in many years, he did not trust his native leadings. Liquid spirits could either bolster a lack of will or corrupt his internal guidance, skewing the tests against which he usually gauged his important decisions.

A boy was dead. Savagely tortured and murdered. The society, which was governed by the Constitution that Blackshaw had sworn to protect, had failed that child twice. First, in allowing the circumstances for his or any hate-filled death to exist unchallenged. Second, in allowing a killer, his friends, and the radical subculture that spawned this murderer to persist, even thrive unchecked, after the crime was committed. Blackshaw believed that in Richmond, he had done everything he could to deliver this sadistic killer and his friends into the hands of the law and still retain a measure of his own freedom, along with the anonymity he craved.

Blackshaw unloaded, cleaned, and lubricated the gun's three ammo magazines. He wiped down all fifty-seven rounds of SP-6. He would not fill these old magazines to capacity, for fear of crushing and annealing the fatigued springs, which could result in a fatal failure to feed. The blue-tipped bullets weighed almost twice as much as a 7.62 NATO round, and would arrive to destroy a target at just under the speed of sound. Yes, words traveled faster, and sometimes hit harder than slugs like these, but today he liked the way a steel jacket ended any debate.

As Blackshaw carefully reloaded the bullets into the magazines, the rum bottle went on nattering at him. Even without taking a sip, Blackshaw knew that avenging this boy was a meager kind of compensation for his failure to protect LuAnna. Granted, the man who hurt his wife was dead, and by Blackshaw's hand. This knowledge offered him little solace. He realized life owed him no comfort, no ease with his past, his choices, or his actions. Right or wrong, they were his to bear into the field like a heavy pack. Today, he was the sum of all these derelictions. A wave of soul sickness overtook Blackshaw. There was no absolution coming to him. Not unless he were cleansed by fire, or drowned in blood.

CHAPTER 16

PERSHING LOWRY SAT alone in his Washington office staring at the horror on his computer monitor. The photograph of the tortured boy, and the animals reveling in the child's misery and destruction made him wretched with rage. There was a personal reason for his visceral disgust. Many years before, Lowry's nephew, Nathan, had been abducted from a church sleepover. No ransom was demanded. No remains were ever found. Lowry's extended family was still in tatters, some waiting for the little boy to come home, others convinced this would never happen, everyone staunching a psychic wound that would never close. And here was another young black boy taken and slaughtered. This made the impossibility of Nathan's return weigh heavier upon Lowry today. On other days, he held his nephew's memory and the unanswered questions of his fate in a place that was simply *not here*.

The child on Lowry's monitor, Sha'Quan Stewart, aged 11 years, had been reported missing last week. Tuesday. He had walked alone to his home in Goochland, Virginia from summer school, or rather, *toward* home. He had never arrived. Nothing had been heard from him. AMBER alerts yielded no solid leads, though tips were still being processed very carefully at the Bureau.

There was a gentle knock on Lowry's door. He recognized the rhythm the way eavesdropping British techs could recognize an individual German encoder's style of transmitting during World War Two. Lowry's heart sped up.

"Come in, Molly" he said. Lowry sat up a little straighter in his chair, and exhumed a smile from the crypt of his thoughts.

The bright brown eyes of Senior Resident Agent Molly Wilde from the Metropolitan office in Calverton, Maryland, appeared round the door. Lowry rose. Wilde enveloped him in her arms and kissed him hard. Then she leaned back to look him in the eye.

"Please don't be upset," Wilde teased. "Everybody here knows."

"It's not that," said Lowry. "You came a long way. You could have called. Or waited until this evening."

"I needed to see you. Sha'Quan Stewart. Are you okay?"

To any other subordinate, Lowry would have said *yes*. "It's difficult," was all he could confess to Wilde at first. Then he added, "We're nowhere yet. And telling Eunice Stewart there's no hope her son's alive without being able to return remains—it's awful."

Molly asked, "My God, she identified Sha'Quan from that photo?"

"A copy. And just a close-up of his face, of course. But she could tell her little boy was in hell from his expression. She joined him there. From experience, I doubt she'll ever come back, with or without remains."

There was nothing Wilde could do to help her beau. There were few aspects of their work more difficult than the sense of helplessness one felt delivering the worst possible news to a victim's family.

She said, "I'm so sorry, Pershing. I came to ask if you looked at the surveillance footage. From the bus station."

Lowry said, "Once, yes. What about that guy? Was he in on the murder? Only the officer's prints were on that phone. It was wiped inside and out. No prints. No call history. Just the one photo."

Wilde said, "He was in possession of that photograph. One hell of a strike against."

"Yes. But everything else says he was trying to do the right thing, showing it to the police," observed Lowry as he sat at his desk again.

"All except hanging out to give a statement," countered Wilde. "Or see if the guy he dimed was caught."

Wilde pulled a chair near the desk and sat down. "We tracked Rufus Colquette to his mother's place. He lives in her attic. She hasn't seen him in days. Said he packed for a trip, hit her up for money, and boogied. She didn't know where he was headed. That was the day before our stranger intervened at the bus station. He had White Supremacist pamphlets, and a brand new copy of Mein Kampf in his room."

Lowry suggested, "Maybe our guy didn't wait because, given the nature of the photograph, he was worried about a reprisal of some kind. Perhaps he wasn't looking for a reward."

"I'll grant your first point. But it's a bus station. Nobody's there because they're flush. Nobody there is above enjoying a windfall."

"But they enjoy greater anonymity. There's no ID check. No metal detectors. You can pay with cash."

Pershing Lowry was about to close the image on his monitor when Molly said, "What's that shadow?"

Lowry had been so fixated on the men in the picture that the shadow in the upper left corner of the frame had escaped his notice. "It's a finger. The photographer stuck his finger in front of the lens."

Molly smiled. "We can clean that up. We can get a hit with a partial."

"Let's do it," said Lowry. Then he clicked his way into another file. When the media player opened, he ran the surveillance footage.

Lowry narrated what he was seeing. "He waits for the white cop to go to the lavatory. He wants the black cop."

"Officer Keene," prompted Wilde.

"Does he want Keene because he's in the south, and isn't sure the white cop—"

"Officer Calloway," Wilde filled in.

"He isn't a hundred percent certain Calloway will do the right thing, or do it fast enough, because he's white—"

"And it's Richmond, in a low-rent area."

"Which is a cynical point of view, to say the least. He profiled the officers." Lowry rubbed his face, pondering.

"That's fresh." Wilde took over the narration. "He goes up to Officer Keene. See? He's wiping the phone as he goes. And he's got those gloves on. In summer."

"I checked on that. It was a cooler night, but not that cool," said Lowry.

"He's passing the phone. Stop there," said Wilde. "See? The gloves are kinda tight."

"Like driving gloves," said Lowry.

"Okay, but he's a passenger on a bus. Driving gloves have holes over the knuckles so they bend for a tighter grip on the wheel and shifter. And unlike his, they sometimes have an open back to stay cool. Now, tactical gloves—"

"—Have big carbon-fiber knuckle pads," finished Lowry. "Or they're smooth like those, so you can get a hand into cargo pockets without snagging or taking them off."

"Pershing, is there anything about this guy ringing a bell with you?"

Lowry considered Wilde's question. "He's big. He seems to be helping out. He's not in it for glory." Lowry clicked to another video file. "Here's the sidewalk camera out front. He arrives on a bus—"

"—And leaves in a cab," said Wilde. "Roll it back. See how he moves."

Lowry recued the video. "Relaxed—"

Wilde nodded and said, "But with intent to get to that cab. A bee-line. No moseying. And he's fit. Maybe even athletic. Not much luggage. Just that one bag. There wasn't anything unclaimed under the bus. That's all he had. And I guess there was just hand luggage for the missing suspect that our helpful stranger pointed to in the picture. I wanted you to see this."

Wilde opened a leather portfolio and withdrew a piece of paper. "The video's not so clear. Officer Keene sat down with one of our sketch guys." She placed a police artist's drawing on Lowry's desk.

"Yes, he does look familiar," admitted Lowry. "Blackshaw." Lowry took a few breaths. "Do you still feel indebted to him for saving your life taking down the snuff site? Are you seeing him everywhere now?"

"It happens. We assumed he died in the blast, like everybody else," said Wilde.

Lowry's memories of the case were still raw. "Not even teeth of some of the dead survived that inferno."

"And the death of Homeland Security Secretary Morgan at the scene was a big deal," said Wilde. "Not to mention the Who's-Who of philanthropists, industrialists, and a lot of others who should not have been there to burn up."

Lowry looked at Wilde carefully as he said, "Perhaps we assume Blackshaw died. What would you do if you knew for certain he was alive?"

Molly Wilde considered her answer. "Part of me would thank him."

Lowry was quiet for a moment, then he said, "I thought *you* had died in the fire. To find you alive, and to know Blackshaw had a hand in saving you, I would thank him, too. Despite evidence of his criminal activity, withholding information, obstructing justice, and God knows what else he got up to in that fiasco. But I think we've both operated with an understanding of what we owe him, and what he truly wanted if he survived."

Wilde said it. "To be forgotten. Like it never happened."

CHAPTER 17

GUNTER FOSS LED a motorcade of seventy-three handpicked Rot-Iron bikers southwest on Interstate 10. The wind parted his beard into two thick salt-and-pepper hanks, and whipped his unhelmeted braid a good two feet behind his head. The gang smelled like a herd of wet goats with a choking, sour exhaust-and-marijuana top-note as they rolled through towns along the way. If they were not already modified, all the bikes' mufflers had been drilled out with long cement bits to create the loudest possible fanfare in honor of this ride. Holding below the 88 decibel noise limit at highway speeds was the one area where no Rot-Iron worth his leather would compromise. Not on this trip. This was a war party, with the engines supplying the battle cry.

These gang members were fierce one-percenters, criminals who the American Motorcycle Association said besmirched the reputation of the other ninety-nine percent of fun-loving motorcycle enthusiasts. Today, they were traveling light, that is, without firearms. All that hardware was stowed in a rented pick-up truck traveling a much different route toward Bisbee.

The Rot-Irons had been founded in 1948 by Frank "Needlenose" Marsdan, with a credo that harked back a further three quarters of a century to a time when the Yavapai Apache were raiding the gang's current home turf of Wickenburg, Arizona. The mining town had been targeted for Apache attacks as much for portable goods to avoid starvation, as to harass white invaders of Yavapai lands. Attrition through the counter-raids of General Crook long ago brought the Yavapai to the San Carlos Reservation in Graham County, east of Phoenix, but Marsdan's festering hate, together with his flexibility with lucrative criminal ventures, kept the Rot-Iron gang roster bloated with angry men, roaring with their machines, and resounding with the ululations of the Amazons who marauded with them.

Even though the Rot-Irons passed through Tucson on the Interstate, the convoy had broken up into pairs, and loose pelotons of three to avoid citations for parades without permits, as if a lone officer on patrol would have the balls to pull anybody over. Stopping one Rot-Iron would bring a swarm of others from Foss's designated response unit who would shoot video of the stop, and bring the physical threat and harassment factor to the brink of arrest without crossing it. The Rot-Iron war chest was full to over-flowing. A blizzard of nuisance legal actions would be launched by the gang's team of expensive attorneys; this was regarded with as much fear by authorities as regular citizens feared Rot-Iron violence.

Foss was the Rot-Iron sergeant-at-arms. He was pleased with the ride from Wickenburg so far. There had been no arrests, and only one wreck. Sonny Manfredi had lost it in some sand, but at sixty-five, he was likely dead of a stroke before his bike went down. There would be proper Rot-Iron funeral rites for Manfredi once they got back home. If things went as Gunter Foss thought they would, Manfredi's would not be the only funeral.

CHAPTER 18

DEPARTING THE HOTEL room, Blackshaw went downstairs toting the Threadcutter's briefcase to the Jeep. It had been a long day, including a stakeout with chow brought up from the kitchen at appropriate intervals. Observation of the street from the room's window, interspersed with more wrestling with the temptations of the rum bottle, had left him tired. Though daylight was waning, he needed to get out of the room.

Despite the smoky air, he stopped on a bench in front of the hotel. After a few minutes, he noticed a convoy, but not the one he was expecting. This was an interagency wildfire fighting unit in heavy-duty personnel transport trucks marked **Geronimo Hotshots**.

A voice in the hazy dusk said, "Uh-oh. Must be bad."

Blackshaw glanced to his left at the dim form of the hotel manager, Louis, out enjoying a cigarette at the end of the porch. It seemed redundant to smoke downwind of a wildfire, but Blackshaw let it go. Instead he asked the elderly man, "The crew, or the fire?"

"No, the economy," chuckled the old man. "I'm sorry. Yes, the fire. Them Geronimos only leave the San Carlos Reservation when the other crews are in deepest shit."

"Is it close to town?" asked Blackshaw.

Louis said, "The wind and the hills will have their say on that, but it's been spreading generally outward from where it started down south of the border. It could get here. It ain't yet."

"You got a nose for these things." said Blackshaw.

The manager held up a walk-talkie. "I'm the Bisbee fire chief, and the only fire I'm working is on the end of this ciggy. We ain't toned-out yet, so I ain't too worried. I'm just waiting on the Gumball."

Blackshaw wondered if the miasmic haze was getting to Louis. "You're waiting for gum."

"The Gumball Rally. New York to L.A. on roads. Some nifty old cars run it. Should be along any day. I'm waiting for the Morgans."

Blackshaw was surprised. "I drove in a 3-Wheeler once."

"Then you, sir, have tasted of Heaven on earth," averred Louis.

"She was right quick. Won't this whole fire situation slow them down?"

"The organizers might put on a hold for a day or two, but Gumball drivers are bound and determined to drive. It's in their nature, smoke, or no smoke. Hellfire, or no fire."

Blackshaw sat quiet. Before long, another group of trucks, led by a Mercedes Unimog, snarled past the hotel.

"Aw shit," said Louis.

"Not firefighters," said Blackshaw. He recognized those trucks. Wondered what had slowed their drive from the PNC compound.

"More like to start fires," said Louis. "I know that truck out front. You know David Koresh from Waco?"

"Not personally."

"Those Branch Davidians were choirboys compared to these bastards. Them's Pure Nation Comitatus. Fellow name of Malthys runs that outfit. Hates the Mexicans, the illegals. Says they're carrying disease."

"Why is Malthys here?"

"County Sheriff got the boot 'cause he was stopping anybody with brown skin, checking immigration status. One of his deputies locked up a lady Latina judge for the weekend. Oh damn she was pissed!" Louis laughed. "That was months ago. Almost a year. Problem is, the former sheriff and some ranchers are making noise about locking down the border themselves. Ain't happy with how the Border Protection is allocating manpower. Malthys is joining the party."

"With the ranchers," said Blackshaw.

"Oh, it gets better. Heard tell a bunch of Rot-Irons are riding south, too."

"And by Rot-Irons, you mean—"

"Rot-Irons is an official, federally recognized Outlaw Motorcycle Club from up in Wickenburg. So they're likely coming in. All because of Timon Pardue's getting voted out of office because a deputy stranded a judge in the tank for a weekend. Every bigot with an axe to grind thinks that man's a hero."

"You don't think so?"

Louis considered for a moment that he was talking with a stranger, and a guest in his hotel, but soon he answered. "Don't get me wrong. Pardue was good enough at his job. A little zealous, because some big-money backers were pissed off about the illegals crossing their land, and he tried to do something about it. It was the deputy who busted the judge, not Timon. But now—"

Blackshaw waited.

"Now," continued Louis, "there's what you'd call a groundswell. Angry citizens. Timon's been sulking out in a cave or some such, camping south of here. Powerful folks are trying to turn his head, to make him thinks he's still doing something important. Clamoring for him to lead a movement. He's been a general without an army for too long, and worse, without his accustomed enemy."

"And Malthys is going along?"

"Yes and no. Yes, Malthys's here, and doubtless making all the right noises, chiming in, kissing ass. And no, he likes a crowd, he likes press, but that one's always got an angle. I mean, that man don't take a crap lest he's got use for the shit."

Blackshaw said, "So they're going to seal the border. Is this Pardue still going to abide by the law?"

"There's the rub, friend. Before, when Pardue was on the job, he needed the law a lot more than the law needed him. Now, I don't know. I think him and a bunch of folks believe the law's plum smack in the way of doing what they think needs to be done. What's in the briefcase?"

"Paperwork," said Blackshaw. He rose from the bench and strolled into the thickening haze toward where the Jeep was parked.

"You're here on business." Louis called after him.

"Reckon I got loose ends to tie up, yes." And the haze swallowed Blackshaw.

CHAPTER 19

TIMON PARDUE HATED his new campsite. It was in the middle
of a caldera bowl, or maybe it was an old meteor crater, he wasn't sure. The
scrub, with the Guajillo trees and various acacias were nice enough. There
was plenty of water in several holes, and he could still see mountains. What
he did not like is that he had not chosen the location himself. It had been
decided by the committee of Congreve, Dressler, Cutlip, and that venom-
ous freak, Malthys.

The site was also surrounded by a loop of West International Road to
the west, north, and east. The border with Mexico ran east to west a thousand yards to the south. The road was key, the committee told him,
providing easy access for anyone who wanted to join the movement, as they
called it, even for a day. Congreve had kindly offered Pardue a helicopter
ride from his old camp, and the ranchers had offered him a lift in one of
their trucks, along with Popper in a horse trailer, but he had declined. He
wanted the walk. He wanted the time to think.

When he arrived at the new site, it was swarming with people. He
counted at least twenty tents already pitched, and many more in the process
of being erected. There were vehicles, expensive dually pick-ups, from the
ranches of Congreve, Cutlip, and Dressler. There were other trucks, filthy
and dented, with **Pure Nation Comitatus** on the doors. There were so
many Harleys he could not count them all in the few minutes he enjoyed
before he was spotted.

Pardue had been led to expect that the time it would take him to walk Popper to the new spot would allow a few folks to get there ahead of him. He had no idea. Popper whinnied, and heads turned. A lot of heads.

Then Pardue was surrounded by a throng of well-wishers. Hands stretched toward him, pulled at his clothes, dislodged his hat, stroked Popper, who took it pretty well. When Pardue noticed folks touching his rifle, he drew it, and carried it himself. That brought a thunderous cheer from everybody.

Pardue had no idea what kind of reception Jesus received upon returning from the wilderness where the Devil had tempted him, but this was nuts. And it was pretty cool, he had to admit. Adelle Congreve pushed through the crowd, and gave Pardue a hug and big kiss that earned even louder shouts of joy.

CHAPTER 20

TEDDYBEAR CHOYA WAITED. He was pissed. He and his crew had been ready for two days. Gunter Foss said to expect a time, and a place; a signal via text message. Choya had been persuaded to forego the usual human mules in favor of this new way to carry cocaine across the border. The method he had agreed to try was supposedly cutting edge, foolproof, and would defy the usual arrest and interrogation of anybody who was caught. *Okay* he'd said. Give it a shot. The human factor was a costly, risky pain in the ass.

Now that he had a big box truck loaded with all these *pinches* gadgets sitting in the middle of the Sonora desert; he felt vulnerable. Time was wasting. He had product to move. Grabbing his AK-47, he eased his bulk down from the cab of the truck, and went to the back where Paolo Estrella y Castro was burning his way through a pack of Camels.

Estrella y Castro was in his thirties, a rail thin brilliant workaholic who had departed the Massachusetts Institute of Technology when he realized the hard truth, that a guy from Mexico, with no connections, was never going to run his own lab, anywhere. It was not so much a function of racism, as it was a simple fact that there were only so many labs in the States, dwindling money all around, and Estrella y Castro was an impatient man with big ideas. He had called his cousin Teddybear Choya, and several months later, here he was, about to revolutionize the drug trafficking industry through a radical autonomous-swarm concept of robotics.

Choya said, "You're sure about this."

"I need a latitude, a longitude for the center point of a sixty foot circle over there, within five miles of here."

"And that's all," confirmed Choya.

"Yes," said Estrella y Castro. "I promise you, you're going to be a legend. On the other side, all you'll ever need is somebody with four-wheel-drive, opposable thumbs, a strong back, and big balls."

Teddybear Choya smiled.

Estrella y Castro went on, "It's going to be manna from heaven, my friend. I'll even get you video. You're going to be the only *narcotraficante* with his own YouTube channel like this."

"They'll take it down," complained Choya.

"Not before it gets pirated. It'll go viral. The world's going to see it. They won't believe it. It's going to be like a plague of locusts over there. You'll see."

For a few more minutes, Teddybear Choya believed all this, and he beamed.

CHAPTER 21

BLACKSHAW PATROLLED INTO the wilderness south of Bisbee. After abandoning the Jeep in an arroyo off the main road, as he had when reconnoitering the Malthys's Pure Nation Comitatus up north, he assembled the Threadcutter, pulled on his pack, and disappeared. He was satisfied he was moving in the right direction. The smoke in the air might have been unrelated to the human clinkers about to flare to life, but it seemed like a trail, the way the smoke from burnt offerings of ancient tribes made a visible link to a remote god residing high in the Firmament.

As evening fell, Blackshaw continued walking. He was waiting for fatigue to cleanse him, and to tell him when it was time to stop. As Blackshaw topped ridges among the foothills, he began to see the glow of actual wildfires in the distance. They seemed far enough away to not be worrisome. What did concern him was a storm building with a fair amount of lightning. There might not be a drop of rain from it, but in this tinder-dry terrain, any lightning strikes would make more work for the firefighters.

The last ridge set Blackshaw back on his heels. The light blazing into the sky was no fire. It looked like a town, with floodlights obliterating the brilliance of the stars. As he gazed down on the make-shift encampment, he recognized the vehicles from Pure Nation Comitatus, a number of other trucks, and a collection of motorcycles worthy of Sturgis. Must be the Rot-Irons that Louis had spoken of. They had arrived here by some route other than the Bisbee road Louis had been monitoring. The old man had missed the parade he'd been hoping for.

Blackshaw turned the night scope of the Threadcutter on the crowd, assessing the gathering beyond the crosshairs. The assemblage fell between Burning Man, and Woodstock without the rain. The crowd was in a full swing party mode.

In the middle of the throng, he observed what was clearly a confab of the six leaders. The command area had both military surplus and modern tents, and a campaign table covered in maps. Various underlings highlighted their poohbahs by their deferential behavior, whispered conversations, and orders dispatched to eager, trotting runners. Camp was still in the making. There was even one horse there, strangely out of place among the humanity, the vehicles, and the tents.

Among the leadership, one man stood out. An older fellow. All the mucky-mucks were raising beer bottles to him in toasts. He had to be Timon Pardue, the recalled sheriff. Blackshaw also recognized the man who had to be running the biker contingent by his Rot-Irons colors. Most of the others close to the map table were the ranchers and their lieutenants.

Then Blackshaw spotted the man he had crossed the country to study. Thin. Mid-thirties. The cultivated appearance of The Messiah, properly commercialized for the American market, meaning non-Semitic looking, with long, flowing light-colored hair and beard. In the available light, Blackshaw could not tell if this fonny boy had blue eyes, but it would not come as the least surprise. That was Malthys. That was the man to whom Rufus Colquette and his friends had texted proof of their monstrous act.

Then Blackshaw noticed something that had escaped his attention before, likely because it had blended in with the few other pieces of military surplus gear. As a matter of training, he was assessing the materiel along with the personnel before him. Supply lines for this party were robust enough. This site was close to Bisbee grocery stores. The canister pack struck Blackshaw as unusual, but somehow familiar. He lay his rifle down, and pulled out his spotting scope. There were faded letters stenciled onto the canister. **M-388V** was all he could make out with certainty. In the 1960s, SEALs had been issued powerful ordnance like this for clearing enemy harbors. But this was not nuclear in nature. The **V** told the real story. It was *viral*. Biological. Here was a new problem to contemplate. Were these jackhats planning to do more than blockade the U.S.-Mexican border? Maybe they were going to contaminate and close it with a wall of bugs.

Blackshaw gathered his rifle, and eased back from the crest of the ridge. When he could stand fully upright without skylining himself, he started exfiltrating down the hill. He walked for several hours, but not back to the Jeep. He went deeper into the hills.

Only when many arroyos, shallow crevasses, and two box canyons lay between him and the assembled mass in the wilderness did he stop. He ate a protein bar, and then rolled himself into his shiny space blanket. In his dreams he saw a barren, empty world. No one lived in it. Blackshaw walked the ruined wastes alone.

When he woke an hour later, the world around him was on fire; a phalanx of flames was burning across the face of the hill toward him. He had nowhere to go.

PART II
THE BEAST

CHAPTER 22

THE BEAST DEVOURED Ascensión Huerta's family. With her husband murdered in San Pedro Sula, Honduras, Ascensión had decided to take her three boys and two girls to the United States to look for her brother. It was a decision born out of desperation. No one tried to board the Death Train, or the Beast, without giving serious thought to what one might meet in its belly, or on its back; the Zetas back home wanted her sons as fighters, and her daughters as whores. Ascensión knew the dangers of this train. Her cousin had been exhausted by his third day riding *La Bestia*, and had fallen asleep on top of a grain car. He rolled off, losing both legs beneath the wheels before he bled to death. Ascensión's aunt had disgraced the family, buying her tall cousin a child's coffin, because his legs were never found, and it was cheaper.

They were two hard weeks into their journey. Gangs had attacked one of the trains, and ripped her oldest daughter from her arms, because after earlier robberies, Ascensión had no more money to hand over. In another town, a man who claimed to be from Grupos B, a Mexican government aid agency that provided food and medicine to train migrants, had lured them to a brothel with promises of rest until the next leg of the journey. There, her children had witnessed her violation by many men over the course of one night. She had escaped with her children early the next morning when assailants and captors alike were passed out. Her babies looked at her differently now.

Ahead, through the dust and haze, Ascensión saw Mexico City. She shook her children, who slept on a cattle car with arms linked for safety. Bleary-eyed, they looked where she pointed. They went back to sleep. They had no strength left to care.

CHAPTER 23

MALTHYS WAITED IMPATIENTLY for all the welcoming tributes to be paid to Timon Pardue. Listening to the ranchers gush at the old man was one thing. When it came Malthys's turn to hack up encomiums and a call to arms like so much phlegm from deep in his throat, he could barely manage it. Watching Gunter Foss chafe and squirm under the weight of the bullshit was Malthys's only compensation.

After a few hours of this, Pardue gathered everyone around the camp table to pour over maps of the area. Dressler, Congreve, and Cutlip were soon marking out the most common routes that illegal aliens took across their properties.

Malthys complained that the beer was going through him, and he was going to check how the latrine construction was coming along. Gunter Foss said he would go along to give the privies a practical test of his own.

When the two men were out of earshot of the command tent, Malthys asked Foss, "How we looking?"

"All good. My guy's blowing up my phone saying everything's ready. We just need an LZ."

Malthys had another question. "You've got distribution set up?"

Foss stopped Malthys with a hand on his arm, and turned him for a look straight into his eyes. "I could sell this shit three times over if I wanted. Getting me in on this gig here is fine, and thanks for that. And cleaning up the money is yours to handle after we collect. Cool. But if you have anything else to ask me, keep it to your fucking self. Maybe we'll grab a beer afterward. Maybe go plinking niggers and 'skins for a hoot. Meantime, you fucking stand down, shut up, and let me do my job. Got it? You'll get your cut, but I'd sooner burn your head off with a blowtorch as hear you question my methods again. Do you feel me, Jesus-Man?"

Malthys recalled the unusual package Timon Pardue was carting around with him, and imagined tying Gunter Foss to it before setting it off. The picture helped quell the rage Foss's words had stirred in his belly.

"We're cool, man," said Malthys. "Just doing my bit for the team. No offense intended."

The two men continued to the latrines at the edge of camp, and pissed in silence. They exchanged no words on the walk back to the command tent.

When Pardue saw Malthys and Foss approach the campaign table again, he asked, "This isn't a goddamn Chautauqua out here. Any of your people sober enough to assign patrols and set up pickets? We have a nation to protect."

CHAPTER 24

SENIOR RESIDENT AGENT Molly Wilde did not return to her Calverton office. Instead, she created a satellite workspace in the conference room of Pershing Lowry's D.C. office. Blackshaw's possible involvement joined Wilde to Lowry on the case. Sha'Quan Stewart's abduction and murder was a hate crime. The case felt as though it would generate a full blown task force. Molly wanted to be involved from the start. Lowry had no objection at all.

He put his head in at the conference room. Molly said, "We've got priority time on the FacRec mainframe. We tapped surveillance video from that night from nearby bus and train stations. I got possible facial recognition hits on Blackshaw at Union Station in Washington, and again at Chicago, but we need the images to be cleaned up to verify."

Lowry was impressed. "Molly, we're not sure it was Blackshaw. And do you think the Washington hit is good? Why would he double back where the bus he was on came from?"

"Because the other guys in that photo might not think to look for him there. That's if they thought he was worth the effort," said Molly. "And if Chicago's good, then we know Blackshaw, or someone who looks and behaves very much like him, is on the move. And after handing over the picture, he may be avoiding authorities."

"Okay. I know finding this person could be useful," agreed Lowry.

"Persh, he's more than useful. Remember when we ran into him last time? He came in, or acted like he was stumbling in. Then he gave us his two cents. And then took his head start, and sprinted all the way to the finish line himself where everything went boom. If that's a pattern with him, we need to know where he is, where he's going, and why. Then maybe we can keep things from getting out of hand."

"Like multiple fatalities, including dead government officials, and catastrophic damage to our energy infrastructure? Is that what you mean by *out of hand?*"

"If you like."

Lowry stood in the doorway for a moment, thinking. Then he said, "You've got a meeting in ten minutes with Davis from the Richmond office. Brief him. Let him take over on FacRec, the canvasses, everything. Let him run it from Richmond."

Molly bridled. "You taking me off this? Persh, this kid—"

"No, Molly. When you're done with Davis, sit down with the artist. Work up your own sketch of Blackshaw. And then do another with the black man who was with him on that boat on the last case. I trust your recall better than mine at this point. When you've got those, get FacRec working on *your* Blackshaw sketch, and the other guy as well, just in case. Then we'll go to Smith Island ourselves. See if we can find his friend. See what he might know."

Molly's expression was crestfallen. "Not in the helicopter." She absolutely hated to fly.

"Sorry, Mol. We don't have time to drive and then take a ferry. Now, how about Rufus Colquette? His last knowns."

"We've got FacRec working every face in that photo. No hits so far, but the images are clear enough. Starting with Virginia, West Virginia, and North Carolina motor vehicles. We'll get something. Colquette's mother isn't cooperating at all. A canvass of their neighborhood got us nothing. A lot of closed mouths."

Lowry mused, "But we've got possible hits on a maybe-Blackshaw."

"I know. It's working backwards," agreed Molly. "I want to support local police on the canvass with additional Bureau personnel. Maybe two more, just so they know we're serious."

"Approved," said Lowry. "Add six agents. Sha'Quan's mother is doing her best not to go public until we have our unsubs better figured out, if not in hand. But she called to say certain family members feel our request for media silence is a cover-up to save face. Some want Sharpton involved, or even Jesse Jackson himself. I persuaded her we have leads, and to give us forty-eight hours so our unsubs get bold, maybe crow a little, and perhaps don't burrow into hiding. But she's starting to think that having as many folks as possible looking would be better. It's hard to argue with her."

Molly said, "But we're sitting on the suspect list, right? At least 'til we have names for all the faces."

"No," countered Lowry. "I've decided we're taking the initiative to go public this afternoon ahead of Sha'Quan's family."

"But we know Sha'Quan's dead."

"You and I do, Molly. But you also know as well as I do that no media implies no action and no effort to some folks."

Molly said, "For Christ's sake! I've got three expert witnesses from National Parks Service examining every tree and shrub in the background of that shot to narrow down where the crime scene is. It was secluded enough. It's likely Sha'Quan's remains aren't far from there."

"All except his scalp," said Lowry.

CHAPTER 25

MALTHYS ENDURED THE speechifying, and choked down the chow that his first PNC wife, Lilith, had prepared with his second wife, Eve, from his personal stores. They cooked well enough usually, but removed from the Pure Nation Comitatus kitchens, they struggled.

Lilith brought him a second Coors from the cooler which he traded for his stew-stained tin plate and fork. Her slight sigh said what her strong, impassive features did not betray; the PNC dream was letting her down mightily.

As he tilted the can up to drain it, he saw a PNC elder named Marcus walking into camp from the parking area. Marcus was pulling another man along with him, and the guy looked weary, and sore. He recognized the second man, but could not dredge up a name to go with the haggard, bruise-mottled face.

Malthys rose and strode to intercept Marcus and his companion. Marcus shook hands with his commandant, and said, "This is Lukas."

Lukas put out his hand. Malthys stared at him, arms crossed. Lukas lowered his hand, and his gaze.

"What's up, Marcus?"

Marcus explained, "This'n was on the fence two nights back. Didn't report. Didn't come in on time."

"Lukas, you go AWOL? Take a run into town for some tang?" asked Malthys.

Lukas only shook his head a few degrees.

Malthys examined Lukas, tilting his swollen face upward by the chin. "Seems you handled it, Marcus. What the hell are you doing here?"

"Tell him," ordered Marcus.

Lukas remained mute, so Marcus said, "We found him all trussed up in the dirt like a damn hog. Zip-ties."

Malthys's anger surged. "What happened, Lukas? You get anal-probed by an alien?"

"Shit no!" bellowed Lukas.

"That's good," said Malthys. "So who tied you up?"

Now that embarrassment had overcome fear, and Lukas had found his voice, he said, "A big guy. Snuck up on me, and choked me out."

"Just for the fun of it?" asked Malthys.

"He asked me where you were going." Lukas's fear of Malthys was reasserting itself.

"What'd you say?"

Lukas blustered, "He was choking me. I nearly passed out. I did pass out."

"So you told him. So what?" Malthys's mind was working hard now.

"It sounded like he had business with you," said Lukas.

Marcus-the-Elder said, "He was asleep on guard duty. We figured you had final say in what happens."

"That's correct, Marcus. I have final say in everything. What kind of business would he have with me, do you think?"

"Not bringing no flowers." Lukas was desperate to defuse Malthys's anger, even with humor. No one laughed.

"Lukas, do you think he was planning to come here to do us harm?" asked Malthys.

Lukas nodded.

"Would you know him if you saw him again?"

Lukas nodded again.

Malthys gestured that the two men should stay put. He returned to his tent. Somehow, the call from back east about the kid who had bragged about his kill seemed related to this assault of his guard at the compound, though many miles separated the two events. Forces outside the usual annoyance of police and federal agencies were at work. Someone had a beef with him. After a moment, Malthys rejoined his men. Now he was carrying a canteen and two hatchets. He gave these things to Lukas.

"You've brought shame on us all, Lukas. But you can redeem yourself. Trial by combat. Go into the wilderness, and find this infidel. Bring me his scalp, or don't come back."

Lukas looked crushed. "What if he's not out there?"

Malthys's eyes turned to granite as he stared at his man. Without another word, he walked back to his tent.

CHAPTER 26

MOLLY WILDE KNOCKED on the door of Knocker Ellis Hogan's old Smith Island saltbox for the second time. There was a fresh breeze bending the reeds that grew on the hummocks of this Chesapeake archipelago. The air was redolent of the mud exposed by a low tide close by.

Pershing Lowry strolled toward the door after shading his eyes and peering through the window of the one car garage on the property. He said quietly, "I swear I saw the car in that garage on *Top Gear* once."

"Those guys destroy a lot of cheapies. Looks like fun," said Molly.

"On the contrary. It's a supercar. Like a Bugatti."

The front door opened, and there stood Ellis. He was brusque. "What do you want?"

Wilde and Lowry held their open identification folders up where Ellis could see them. Wilde said, "I'm Senior Resident Agent—"

"I know who you are. Hold on." Ellis stepped out to the garage, opened the door just enough to reach inside, and came back with an empty fuel can. He held it out to the agents. "Thanks for the gas. From last time. Guess I should have returned this. Saved you a trip."

During their last encounter, Blackshaw and Ellis Hogan had borrowed this same can filled with fuel for their boat. Borrowing fuel had been a pretense to cover their real purpose, gaining intel from the feds for their mission, and leading them toward a suspect.

Lowry said, "We're not here about that."

Ellis set the can down on the stoop. "State your business. I don't have all day."

"May we come in?" asked Wilde.

"Hah! You got no warrant, or you wouldn't be asking. You're like vampires without one, and I'm not inviting you in," declared Ellis stepping outside. He made a show of closing and locking the saltbox's front door with a set of keys. Then he strolled over to a lovely set of cast aluminum chairs placed around a matching table in his garden, and there he sat down, admiring the marsh.

Wilde and Lowry followed him and took chairs without invitation. Lowry inquired, "How have you been, Mr. Hogan?"

"You don't give a rat's fuzzy ass how I'm doing. Ask your questions, or take your damn fuel can and get the hell off my property."

"Where is your friend Benjamin Blackshaw?" asked Lowry.

"Now you're getting to it," said Ellis, with a sardonic grin. "I have no idea where that one is. And frankly I don't care. Is that it? Who wants to know?"

Molly Wilde opened her portfolio, and after a few swipes at her tablet's screen, she angled it toward Ellis so he could see.

"Jesus Christ!" said Ellis in revulsion. "What in God's name is that mess?"

"Take a good look. Do you know any of the men in that photograph?" asked Lowry.

Hogan turned away from the picture and looked out across the marsh. "No. No I goddamn well do not, the sonsabitches."

"Has Blackshaw been in touch with you in the last few days?" asked Wilde.

"Oh please. You people been all up in my phone records before you come here. You ever ask questions you don't already know the answers?" Ellis tipped the tablet screen facedown onto the table.

It was clear to Lowry and Wilde he was repulsed by the image.

"No," continued Ellis. "No way Ben Blackshaw had anything to do with that. Jesus God. Who's the child?"

Molly picked up the tablet again so Ellis could see it. "Sha'Quan Stewart. And Blackshaw might well be involved, and in some danger. A man fitting Blackshaw's description passed this image to a Richmond police officer, and identified this man." She pointed to Colquette on the screen.

"Mr. Hogan, the informant, whom we believe to be your friend, said this man's name is Rufus Colquette," said Lowry. "Did you notice Colquette appears to be holding the victim's scalp in his hand?" Lowry pointed. "Right there. Cut while the child was still alive, obviously, like these other injuries, here, and here. And here, too. Any one of them fatal."

Ellis was furious. "Then don't sit here yammering with me. Go get those bastards!"

"Mr. Hogan," began Wilde, "I assure you we are making full use of every resource at our disposal to locate these men. But we think it's possible, like last time, that if we could speak with Mr. Blackshaw, we might be able to move faster."

"We couldn't save Sha'Quan," said Lowry. "But we don't want this to happen again. Mr. Blackshaw might have additional information. No matter how insignificant he thinks it is, it might help."

Ellis touched his gut at the sight of that nauseating trophy photograph, but he said nothing.

Wilde asked, "Does Mr. Blackshaw have a cell phone? A number? An email we could reach out to?"

Lowry cleared his throat. "Under the circumstances, we would be willing to forego an in-person meeting with him."

Ellis shook his head. "Ben's got burdens. Even a cell phone would break that camel's back. I don't know where he is."

Wilde took out a business card. "That's my mobile. Text or email. If he does call, please encourage him to contact me."

Lowry and Wilde stood.

Ellis remained seated, and said, "I thought we were done with that."

"Done with what?" asked Wilde.

"The killing. The lynching."

Lowry said, "We both know better, don't we, Mr. Hogan? Thank you for your time."

Wilde and Lowry left Ellis leaning heavily on the arm of his garden chair. They strode purposefully over the footbridges and winding paths back toward the Smith Island helicopter pad.

As they walked, Wilde checked in at the Richmond office and was disappointed to learn there were still no hits returned on the FacRec system for any of the unknown faces in the photograph, or from the sketches. "Now what?" she asked.

"We keep working. Do you believe Ellis Hogan doesn't know where Blackshaw is, or how to reach him?"

"Of course not. But he was telling the truth about one thing," said Molly. "There haven't been any calls whatsoever to or from his phone."

Lowry said, "To any phone we know about. There are other ways. All the boats would have radios."

"Citizens band, too," agreed Wilde. "And marine radios often have single side band mode. We got all that covered?"

"The drone's been on station overhead since before our helo' took off to bring us here," said Lowry. "Every side and carrier frequency is being scanned every second. If Hogan or anybody else reaches out, we'll snag it, trap and trace. There aren't that many people on this island. We can analyze transmissions fairly quickly."

"Did it seem to you that Hogan was angry at Blackshaw, and not just upset we dropped in?" asked Wilde.

"You picked that up, too. I wasn't sure. If they're at odds, this trip might be a dead end."

Wilde countered, "When I came here before, there was some hostility. Remember? Just the helicopter coming here would fire up the grapevine."

"That's true. Just as well we're monitoring all signals from here, not just Ellis Hogan's."

"Getting a warrant to reap an entire town's call/com data must have been difficult," said Wilde.

Lowry hesitated to answer. "I have no idea, but I'll let you know if I ever try to get one."

Wilde was astonished. "Feels like I'm working for the NSA."

They walked together in silence for another minute. Then Wilde said, "Before we get on that damn chopper, let's do the obvious thing."

"What do you mean?"

"We've been so focused on Hogan," said Wilde. "While we're here, why don't we go knock on Blackshaw's door?"

Lowry said, "Makes sense."

Wilde stopped on the path and said. "Wait here for me. I'll be right back."

"Molly?"

"Just wait here, please?"

She turned, and marched back along the pathway to Ellis Hogan's place. She found the old man where they had left him seated in his garden. He didn't look up as she went to the stoop of his house and retrieved the fuel can.

He did take notice of her only when she stood next to his chair, and said to him, "If you ever speak to Ben Blackshaw, please tell him I owe him my life. And thank you."

Ellis looked up into her eyes and nodded once.

CHAPTER 27

MALTHYS AND FOSS, each armed with rifles, patrolled the border as a two-man team. Only Pardue and the ranchers' men had looked askance when the unlikely pair formed up and waived off more volunteers. There were plenty of other known coyote trails by which footsore, dehydrated immigrants might come in tonight. All these routes required close watch, so no one was put out if two of the movement leaders felt like hanging around in the brush for a few hours. That was good leadership initiative in Pardue's view.

Foss consulted a map with his flashlight, and directed their steps away from the well-traveled arroyo they had told the others they'd watch. Instead, they made their way up toward higher ground.

After an hour of scrambling through low scrub, Gunter Foss yelped in pain. He pointed the flashlight at his left foot, and saw as well as felt the spiny lobe of a cactus clinging to the thick leather of his boot.

Malthys asked, "Got a comb?"

Foss glared at Malthys from beneath his tangled thatch of hair.

Malthys pulled a long-toothed comb from one of his pockets. "Hold still, tenderfoot." he ordered. Then he slipped the comb's teeth among the spines between the flesh of the cactus and Foss's boot. With a flick of his wrist, the cactus, spines and all, leapt away from the boot, landing in the darkness.

After grunting in a way that was supposed to pass for thanks, Foss walked on. A half hour later, they topped a rise, arriving at a plateau.

Foss said, "There's flat enough ground here, and an easy grade on the other side, about a quarter mile. From here, the road's close."

Malthys surveyed the area as if he shared Foss's unique understanding of the project's requirements. "This is the place?"

"Tonight," said Foss. "Now. Different spot every night. Don't want to get predictable. Okay. Let's do it."

Malthys said, "Wait, I thought we were just scouting now."

"And we're done. Now we roll." Foss rested his gun against a tree, and pulled a GPS from his light pack. "No telling how long the party's going to last before the Feds break up the camp. We gotta do *what* we can *while* we can."

Foss walked farther out into the plateau's clearing. It was really a wide wash, veined with narrow, dry rills. After feeding coordinates from the GPS into his phone, and hitting send, Foss sat down on a rock.

Malthys asked, "That's it?"

"Our truck's coming in from the north for the pick-up," said Foss. "Goods are coming in from the south. Yeah. That's it." Foss pulled a joint from his pack, and sparked it up. Contrary to custom, he did not offer Malthys a toke.

Malthys got nervous. "What about ground sensors? You don't think the Feds have this place wired? Who's hauling it?"

Foss laughed. "Not *who*, Jesus-Man. Relax. The border's almost half a mile to the south. We're cool."

CHAPTER 28

PAULO ESTRELLA Y Castro was out of Camels. He would have lit one if he had any left, since the Federales would likely miss the tiny ember's glow amidst the wildfires. Even then, it was even money whether any cops that found them would follow through with a bust, or demand a piece of the action.

He could barely see the stars through the haze. Poor visibility wouldn't matter. He would get this load across the border.

Teddybear Choya hustled back to the tailgate. He'd been pestering Estrella y Castro several times an hour all day, but this was different. The boss was moving fast.

"Here," said Choya, jamming a mobile phone in Estrella y Castro's face. "I got the numbers. Let's go!"

Fifteen minutes later, the parcels of cocaine were unloaded. The area around the truck looked as though it had been infested with giant spiders each with a small cargo of coke wrapped in black plastic and latched under its thorax.

Estrella y Castro fed the latitude and longitude information into a laptop. Dim red LED lights, like eyes, winked on the top of each spider, to show the coordinates had been loaded. When all the spiders showed a light, he pressed ENTER on his laptop.

The spider lights went out. The air was filled with a buzzing whir, as if a hundred giant bees had converged on the clearing around the truck.

Teddybear Choya watched in awe as the spiders rose slowly into the air. As they climbed, they channeled small swirling downdrafts of hazy air toward the ground, where it rebounded toward the two men. The whirring hum receded as the spiders swarmed north through the night sky toward the border.

CHAPTER 29

BLACKSHAW PROBED THE fire around him. He had slept through the thunder that followed each of the storm's lightning strikes. He had slept through much worse while operating forward overseas. One brilliant jagged fork must have struck the earth downhill, igniting this fresh blaze. The fact that he lay in a slight depression slowed the fire's spread just enough to save him.

He cloaked himself in the reflective space blanket and started scrambling up through loose scree, trying not to slip and bash the Threadcutter's scope out of true.

He had managed a few yards when he saw the glowing eyes to his left. Then he heard the snarls, and the yipping barks. A band of coyotes. There is no way this was the same lot that had trailed him as he left the Pure Nation Comitatus so many miles to the north. When he stared at them, they fell silent.

Blackshaw brought his rifle around to bear, and eased his way more slowly up the scree. The dominant male coyote barked, and howled. Blackshaw stopped. The big animal dashed toward him. He raised the rifle, but the coyote circled downhill from him, crossing the scree with sure-footed four-legged ease. Then the creature took a position to his right, not ten feet away, and crouched for a leap, teeth bared. With fire below him, the big male coyote to his right, and the rest of the band to his left, Blackshaw figured uphill was still the way to go. Then he glanced to his left. The glowing eyes of the band were now farther away. They had retreated no more than fifteen feet, so that the smoke all but shrouded the firelight reflected in their eyes.

The big male bounced, howled, and lunged at Blackshaw, digging its forepaws into the scree, and stopping short just five feet away. It growled again. Blackshaw stepped toward the pack to the left. The animals wraithing in the smoke yipped and fell further back. Blackshaw sensed he was being herded.

Then he looked uphill as a gnarled old tree burst into flame. The scrub around the tree caught. Had he climbed up that way, he would have been engulfed. He stepped again to his left. The coyotes that had been there an instant before were gone. Blackshaw looked right, and like the others, the big male had vanished. He stepped to his left and made his way clear of the flames, which dropped away in a line to his left down the hill.

Over the roar and crackle of the fire, Blackshaw thought he heard a whining hum in the sky. Ducking low, he looked up and saw dark, fantastic, multi-legged shapes swarming overhead. Thirty, maybe forty shrieking, flying bugs whizzed from the south to the north, and then they were gone.

Blackshaw kept moving. He saw no sign of the coyotes, but was almost certain he had not imagined them.

As if to confirm that he was patrolling through some kind of Boschian hell, a bearded man loomed up in his path. He was in bad shape, eyes swollen shut, his nose beaten flat. Blackshaw was on the verge of offering help until he saw the man carried a hatchet in each hand, and they were both cocked for murder.

"You!" shouted the specter, who started a low dash at Blackshaw.

Blackshaw got a jolt of recognition. "Lukas?"

It was the unlucky sentry from the PNC compound. Once again, Blackshaw regretted an act of mercy that had rebounded to curse him. The hatchet blades spun in the low light in some kind of martial artist's Viking-head-fake-before-the-strike. Blackshaw figured the noise of a suppressed gunshot would not make his night any worse. He fired from the hip.

Lukas staggered with a round in his shoulder, and dropped a hatchet. In shock, he stumbled backward, regrouped, and started forward again, his injured arm streaked with blood.

Blackshaw fired again, taking his attacker square in the chest. Lukas Malthys's legs worked a drunkard's backward jig for several steps. Then, to Blackshaw's utter consternation, Lukas disappeared.

A river of fire flowed uphill toward Blackshaw. With the notable exception of meeting Lukas Malthys, the coyotes seemed to have the best predictive intel on the blaze. He slung his rifle and pack, unwadded the space blanket, and lurched on across the face of the hill, but the flames were gaining on him. Roughly where the hatchet man vanished, Blackshaw felt the ground slip out from under his boots. In a welter of sparks and searing heat, he dropped to the front door of Hell.

CHAPTER 30

ESTRELLA Y CASTRO watched the laptop's screen while Teddybear Choya drove the truck toward the recovery site. Choya asked, "How they doing?"

"They're all fifty still flying. All on course. A little headwind, but we're cool."

"Beautiful! Amazon was onto a good thing my brother." Choya beat the steering wheel with glee, then slugged Estrella y Castro in the shoulder in painful celebration and comradery.

"FAA told them no," said Estrella y Castro.

"We aren't asking permission," said Choya.

The fifty octocopter drones were Estrella y Castro's brain children. Every unit sprouted eight high efficiency electric motors turning propellers thrusting downward. The motors were controlled by onboard processors, which were directed with GPS guidance. The real genius lay in his swarm software that allowed all the units to fly autonomously, yet in close proximity to each other with the precision of a flock of birds. They were homing in on the position Gunter Foss had sent to Teddybear Choya's phone. Every drone except one carried a kilo of cocaine. The last one bore a very different, more deadly cargo.

CHAPTER 31

THE EUROCOPTER CREW saw the flock of birds as it crossed the border into the United States. But something seemed wrong to the Customs and Border Protection pilot, Nan Greenway. For one, the flock, likely of night migrating cliff swallows, seemed big. The other problem was that it was late in the migratory season. These birds were usually nesting along the western reaches of the States and Canada by now.

Greenway radioed in the sighting as unusual, but stayed on course along the U.S. side of the border. One bird strike could ruin your whole night. Her crewmate, Francine Eckhart, monitored the Forward Looking Infrared screen for the ghostly image of illegals on the ground. Their work was as much humanitarian as it was service as aerial sentries. Hopeful migrants were often abandoned by their guides in the desert without water. Last night, they had vectored a CBP ground unit to six Mexican men near death from exposure and thirst. Once again, the Nan & Fran Show had saved the day.

Checking her radar, Greenway said, "Looks like those birds are following the border. I got 'em at seven hundred feet MSL. A mile a head, going west like us. Damn shame. Windfarms and cell tower guy-wires hack 'em up by day. Light pollution from cities throw off their navigation by night."

"No cities out here," said Eckhart.

"Except for that crowd south of Bisbee," said the pilot. "They're going to be nothing but fun."

"Vigilantes," agreed Eckhart. She worked hard to discern between living creatures and patches of fire on the ground. "I don't care what Incident Command is telling folks, these wildfires aren't even close to contained."

"That flock's still bee-lining. Can you point the FLIR at it?"

"You got it," said Eckhart. She rotated the FLIR array on the Eurocopter's chin to point forward and angle down toward the target birds. "I got nothing yet."

That was about to change.

CHAPTER 32

TEDDYBEAR CHOYA DROVE half off the road before wrenching the truck's steering wheel and regaining control. Paulo Estrella y Castro had muttered, "Shit," and that was enough to make Choya crazy.

"What the hell is wrong?"

"A helicopter. Or a plane. Behind our flock. I think it's border patrol," said Estrella y Castro.

"How the hell do you know?" demanded Choya.

"I put a TCAS sending unit on one of the spiders. Anything with a transponder shows up, like that plane or whatever, it registers here." Estrella y Castro pointed at the screen. His pride was justified. A Traffic Collision Avoidance System was a stroke of genius.

"How much does that TCAS thing weigh? Did you have to leave some product behind?"

Estrella y Castro said, "I think you should pull over. You need to know something. You need to make a choice."

Choya directed the truck to the roadside. "What's going on?"

"You already know about the security system on the ground."

"Of course." Choya did, and he thought it very badass. Each flying spider was burdened with less cocaine than it could actually bear. The rest of the useful payload on forty-nine of the units was a small fragmentation grenade, with its detonator rigged to a keypad. Anyone who tried to separate the drug packet from the spider without first entering a three-digit disarming code into the keypad would die in a cloud of shrapnel and coke.

"One of the spiders is different. My Tarantula. No product on board. But it's got the TCAS, extra batteries, and a Claymore mine."

Choya grinned. "No!"

"Oh yeah. It's got enough juice to stay in the air instead of landing with the others. Like a baby sitter. Then it follows the other forty-nine back home to the recovery site for the next trip. If somebody messes with the goods, that Claymore's got seven hundred ball bearings, four thousand feet a second. Nice kill radius. Somebody you don't like comes near the swarm while it's on the ground, you can let the fragmentation grenades take them out. But you lose product. Probably more than one spider. The Tarantula can take down somebody before they even get to the swarm. I can cut the Tarantula loose form the group and target it myself."

"Oh my God! That's fucking *sick*! I love it!"

Estrella y Castro grinned as he said, "I know! But man, the thing is, I think the Tarantula can work air-to-air, too!"

Choya got the idea. "You sure that's a border patrol following my babies?"

"We can take a look. Tarantula's got a real-time camera feed." Estrella y Castro pointed to a black square on his laptop screen. "We could change the course on the swarm and see if the plane follows. I think it's a helicopter. CBP planes are faster. They would have caught up by now."

"Change the course. Same landing zone. Just crank in an extra couple turns."

Paolo Estrella y Castro worked the keys of the laptop. They waited, while the swarm obeyed the new instructions. "Still following. If it gets too close, I'm telling you, a chopper's downwash could be bad for the spiders. They're so little."

"Shit!" shouted Teddybear Choya. "Take that fucker down!"

CHAPTER 33

THE EUROCOPTER PILOT, Nan Greenway, monitored her radar, while Francine Eckhart looked for the weird flock of swallows on the FLIR.

Eckhart asked, "What's the range now?"

"Three hundred yards. Eleven o'clock. You don't see them?"

"Not yet. Weird," said Eckhart, adjusting the FLIR range. "You think our patrols will ever get replaced by UAVs?"

Greenway said, "Some Xbox-and-Hot-Pockets kid in a trailer cannot do this."

"They've shot a bunch of hellfire missiles okay."

Greenway was silent for a moment. "A hundred yards. I'm climbing." She raised the helicopter's collective.

Eckhart gave a satisfied, "Got 'em. Christ! They're as big as geese! Swan maybe. And did one just separated from the flock?"

"Is it—" began Greenway.

"Coming toward us—*yes*! I got it! I got it! Like an intercept. Look at that thing climb! Not a goose! It's going overhead!"

Greenway was lowering the collective left to avoid a collision with the strange object. She said, "Got it. We're under—"

The explosion slammed them from somewhere aft of the cockpit, and it was loud. The scream of shearing metal accompanied horrendous vibrations threatening to shake dental fillings loose. Greenway immediately lost yaw authority over the helicopter as the fuselage wrenched to the right beneath the main rotor, and kept spinning. She fought hard to stop the gy-rations, but the bird did not respond.

Eckhart radioed the mayday call and their position in a cool profes-sional tone, and joined Greenway standing on the left anti-torque pedal. This was catastrophic tail rotor failure. Damage in the drive train, and per-haps to the main rotor itself added shake to the shimmy. The sink rate was far faster than textbook autorotation. If the helicopter slammed into the earth with more than a brief peak force of fifty g, they would not be walk-ing away from the wreckage. Less than fifty g, and burning to death was still an option.

Greenway said, "We're going in."

"Kinda figured," said Eckhart.

In eleven seconds, it was all over.

CHAPTER 34

MALTHYS AND FOSS kept watch in the haze, disappointed that the lightning storm's winds did little to sweep the smoke from the air. Fresh fire starts and restarts from lightning strikes made the visibility even worse with a confusion of flares through the smoke.

The two men were expecting a flock of small, autonomous drones to whirl into the clearing before them. They were completely unprepared for a full scale helicopter shattering into the earth fifty yards up the hill behind them. The ground rippled from the impact. They turned in time to see the fuselage shed its skids, which were whipped back into the air by impacts from the disintegrating main rotor blades.

Foss shouted, "What the hell!"

"Look out!" screamed Malthys. He tried to run, but he stood transfixed, watching the fuselage career down the slope toward them, with fractured rotor stubs like a buzz saw, gouging up the earth as it came on.

The fuselage stopped five feet from Malthys.

Foss reappeared from where he had run for cover. "You got balls, pal. I give you that."

Foss's recovery truck, a filthy Chevy Tahoe, pulled onto the edge of the plateau. The driver jumped out, and swore, laughing at the downed CBP helicopter.

Malthys looked into the wreckage. "I think the crew's still in there."

In comparison, the arrival two minutes later of a million dollars of co-caine, humming out of the sky aboard a swarm of alien craft, and gently settling across the plateau, seemed anticlimactic.

Foss told the driver, "You got the code. Get the goods off those bugs and in the truck. They take off again in ten minutes, with or without my shit."

The giggling driver stared at the wrecked helicopter. "Its CBP! Fucking CBP!"

Foss drew a pistol and pointed it at the driver. "Get on it!"

The driver stirred from his hebephrenic reverie, trotted to the nearest drone, and went to work entering the disarming code to free the kilo packet of cocaine.

Malthys still peered into the wreckage. He said, "Shit! They're moving!"

Foss looked at the shattered crew still strapped into their seats. Smiling, he took out a long hunting knife. Leaning into the wreckage, he said, "Let's see if we can help 'em out."

CHAPTER 35

THE FIRE RAGED on the mountainside below him. Delshay Goyathlay was trying his damnedest to regroup with his squad on the fire line farther down the crag before dark. The light was already failing. He knew he was lucky to be alive, but he was still cut off. The Arizona woodland wildfire ranged down into desert scrub. Del and his men were struggling to contain the blaze, but it had hopped sparking through the trees across the firebreak that they had cleared of its tinder-dry undergrowth and ground cover. He should have seen that flashover coming.

Del could hear his squad boss yelling intermittently for him over the walkie on his chest, but it was plain his replies were going unheard, either because of signal blockage from the mountains, or from the walls of this crevasse, or because of damage in the fall he had taken. The battery meter was still in the green, if on the low end.

He wanted to rejoin the crew as much to get back to work as to stop his friends worrying about him. Del would never hear the end of this. If he wasn't back on the line soon, manpower would be yanked from the real work to locate him. Getting separated had been stupid, but he was on the line's end closest to that stream up the mountain, knew the way better than anyone, and all the water bottles needed a refill. That was another problem. Except for the camelbacks built into the three newer packs down with the crew, Del now had all the squad's canteens. He had to get back to the guys or it would be a long thirsty hike back to camp with a fair amount of cussing, and most if it directed his way.

When the flashover had ignited the trees downhill from him, their trunks had blown up bright in an astounding roar and rush. It was like some kind of thermal bomb had gone off in his face. He'd staggered back involuntarily from the heat, and tumbled down twelve feet into this crevasse in the rock. Many decades' accumulation of tree litter had recently burned down here, and the ash and charred branches had broken his fall. Now he was choking in the smoke of the flashover and the fine ash he'd kicked up on impact.

Del's right knee was twisted and hurting from the tumble, but other than scrapes, that was the worst of it. He retrieved his clear-lensed goggles, and swept his black braid on top of his head before replacing his red fiberglass helmet. The drip torch for lighting backfires seemed sound, so he lashed it onto the pack for the climb. One less thing to get hollered at for busting or losing.

He scrambled a jagged path over the steep uphill face of the rock fissure as handholds and footholds allowed. The rock was still warm through his leather gloves. As he climbed, he managed to recover his Pulaski axe out of a tangle of roots.

Toward the mountain's peak, he hoped he could catch a quick breather without fear of immolation, and figure out his next move. Lightning from a storm two months before had already scorched at least three hundred wooded acres to black stumps in that direction. There was no fuel left.

Del kept climbing. His knee loosened up a little bit, though it still hurt. Five feet below the lip of the fissure, Del noticed a smaller crack in the rock about two feet wide. Despite his problems, anger surged in his chest. The glint of metal, like part of a buried aluminum soda can caught his eye in there. He could not fathom who would hike into this country to be one with nature, and then leave trash behind to foul it.

He reached in for the can, but it folded like fabric in his grasp. It wasn't metal at all. This was an ash-covered, scorched space blanket, and it flexed, then crumbled and tore in his fingers. He pulled a few more silvery fragments out of the rock gash, and tucked them into a pocket in his yellow brushcoat. Del sure as hell wasn't going to make the trash problem worse by dropping crap into the crevasse. He wondered if a hiker had lost the blanket. Perhaps a firefighter attacking the earlier blaze had lost it.

A larger swatch of the blanket ripped away in Del's hand all at once, and that's when he saw the human head. It was very well-preserved, likely from the dry elevation, with short bristling hair; it was gray-black with soot. *Oh hell*, he thought. This is exactly the kind of niche, in just this kind of crevasse, for an ancient native or prehistoric burial. Del wondered if he was disturbing an ancestor.

The head opened its eyes. Del shouted in shock, lost his footing, and slid down the crevasse's slope a few feet before he caught himself. The eyes stared down at Del.

Then the mouth opened. "Got any water?" The voice rasped.

"A little," Del said. He still had to get to the stream, but he unscrewed the top of a water bottle and passed it up toward the head.

Lower in the niche, blackened fingers jutted through the tatters of the space blanket in a puff of ash, seized the bottle, and tipped it to soot-caked lips.

The voice, a little less raspy than before, asked, "What day is it?"

"Wednesday," answered Delshay.

The dark face seemed puzzled. "*Wow.* Okay. I need to get moving."

The cover of detritus in the niche shifted beneath the blanket as the very big cinder demon bent to extricate himself.

Del climbed to assist the specter. "Man, for a minute I thought you were a dead mummy."

"Me, too. I'm okay. But this guy wedged in here beside me is for sure a gonner. What's your name?"

Another body, this one confirmed dead? The firefighter could not speak for a moment, but he soon said, "Del."

"I'm Ben. Now Del, if you could help me out of here, we might-could save a couple-two-three million folks before breakfast."

"What?" asked an incredulous Del.

"You're probably right," reflected Ben. "By tomorrow supper at the latest."

CHAPTER 36

SENIOR RESIDENT AGENT Molly Wilde, and Section Chief Pershing Lowry were at the office late after the junket to Smith Island. The trip had netted no additional leads. At best, Molly thought she had impressed upon Knocker Ellis Hogan that the connection she felt with Blackshaw was one of personal gratitude, and not merely as a source of critical information on an ongoing case. They had left the door open as wide as possible if Blackshaw wished to reach out. But odds on, the Bureau had seen all the help from him that it was ever going to get.

Stopping by Blackshaw's home had been interesting. On her last visit to speak with her source, a local man had insisted that Blackshaw was dead, shown her a grave that was quickly proven to be unoccupied. Then he misled her to a property that Blackshaw had never lived in. Today, with the correct address in hand, but no warrant, their knock on the door had been answered quickly enough by an efficient woman who had the air of a nurse, or a home health aide. The nurse declined to admit them into the house, and refused to answer any questions. Over the nurse's shoulder, Lowry, who was taller, thought he caught sight of the back of a hospital bed in the parlor, with several intravenous bags and a feeding pump at the head. With the bed angled away, Lowry did not see the patient. After their brief inquiry, during which the nurse denied knowing Blackshaw, the door was closed in their faces.

Special Agent Davis phoned Wilde as she was hanging up her Armani Collezioni jacket on the hook behind the door in Lowry's office. She opened the line on her cell phone without greeting or preamble and asked, "What have you got?"

Davis said, "FacRec cleaned the surveillance image from the Chicago train station. Three Chicago agents canvassed employees there and, paired up with your sketch, a ticket agent confirmed this person purchased a ticket with cash two nights ago."

"To where?" asked Wilde.

"We synced ticket office surveillance of his buy with cash sales time stamps. He went south," said Davis.

"To *where?*" repeated Wilde.

"Tucson, Arizona. But that might not be a stop. Could be a way point. Yes, we're pulling the footage from Tucson to be sure. And we got a hit on the finger in that picture. It's a partial, but it belongs to a Timothy Nyqvist. Six priors for assault. All his victims were black. Three pressed charges at first, then dropped them."

"Get Nyqvist's face out there. Call me when you know about Blackshaw," instructed Wilde, and she broke the line.

Then she said to Lowry, "Got a hit on the guy who took the picture. And they have Blackshaw buying a train ticket Chicago to Tucson. Let me see it again." She did not have to explain what she meant.

Lowry brought the gruesome picture of the lynching-in-progress up on his screen. Wilde leaned close. Then she zoomed in on Rufus Colquette.

Lowry said, "Nobody's seen him."

"Maybe we haven't either." Wilde zoomed in again on the upper area of Colquette's sternum. "See that? Sticking out of the top of his beater? I always thought it was a shadow."

"That's a tattoo. Three letters, or numbers maybe. Hard to tell with just the top half."

Wilde said, "Take a sheet of paper, and cover only the top half of a line of type, and it's hard to read from the lower parts of the letters. Take that same sheet of paper, slide it down a little, and cover the bottom half of the letters, and you can still get the meaning. Most of the important information in a letter, the part we register, it's in the *top* half of the letter's shape."

Lowry studied the enlarged image. "Okay. I see what you're talking about. Is it BNG?"

"Maybe," said Wilde. "Pull in the context you know."

"Oh. PNC. Did this little shit rob a bank, too?" Lowry was getting there.

"Not the bank, Persh. Think *hate*. It's PNC, yes. Think Tucson, or Arizona. But I think it's Pure Nation Comitatus."

"We need to call Tucson."

"Persh, we agreed somebody at Blackshaw's last known is sick. Like downstairs, in the living room, in a hospital bed, long-term kind of sick."

"But we couldn't see who it was," said Lowry.

"No. I wonder if we should do something about it," said Wilde.

"You want to send a fruit basket?"

Wilde shot Lowry an unappreciative glance. "I mean follow up. If we know who's ill in his house, we might know more about what going on in his mind."

"Could be a sick friend," suggested Lowry. "If we do have Blackshaw placed in Chicago en route to Tucson, whoever's in his house isn't that important to him."

"My gut says different," countered Wilde.

"Do you think it's worth another trip?" asked Lowry. "Right now?"

"Maybe not. Still, I can't help think home is important to Blackshaw."

"Even though he's never there." said Lowry. "He's Odysseus, or something? Always homeward bound. Always tragically side-tracked."

"Everyone wants to go home," declared Wilde. "To *be* at home. Which means to me that anything that keeps him away from there is—"

"Much more important than a fishing expedition," finished Lowry. He and Wilde had been completing each other's thoughts for weeks, now that they were an item.

"A *hunting* expedition, I would have said."

A secretary knocked hard and fast as she put her head in at the office door. "I just heard. There's a CBP helicopter missing in Arizona. Near Bisbee."

Wilde said, "Oh no. I told you those things aren't safe."

The flustered secretary continued, "The pilot used to fly for us. Nancy Greenway. She transferred to CBP two years ago. Jeez, I went to her son's eighth grade graduation. They got out a mayday, but—"

"Any survivors?"

"No word," said the distraught woman. "They haven't gotten to the crash site. Search and Rescue's homed in on the ELT, but they're not there yet. There's a bunch of White Supremacist skells hanging out in the search area. Protesting undocumented immigrants. Hunting them."

Lowry said, "Thank you. Molly, in light of the circumstances, the linkage to our case, I think we're going to need a jet."

"Circumstances—" asked Molly.

"I know Nancy Greenway," said Lowry. "She's black."

CHAPTER 37

THE WILDFIRE FIGHTER, Del, helped Blackshaw pull himself out of the narrow crevasse. Together, they climbed the fire-heated rock wall up to ground level. Del stared briefly at the dead man they left behind, but his gaze was pulled back to Blackshaw's rifle. Blackshaw swayed, took in his wobbly state, and tried a few steps.

Still parched, Blackshaw pulled a water bottle from his pack, and held it out to Del. "Want a refill?"

"No, you'll need it." answered Del quickly. Looking over the edge of the crevasse, he asked, "Who's he?"

"Name's Lukas. He's Pure Nation Comitatus."

"Are you?" Del changed the grip on his Pulaski ax, and backed a step away from Blackshaw, wondering if he had just helped a bad one.

"Hell no." Del found the disgust in Blackshaw's tone reassuring.

"What happened to him?"

"He overbalanced."

Studying the dead man, Del said, "You're lucky he tripped. Neck broke his fall."

"If you say so," said Blackshaw, surveying the blackened, smoky landscape.

"Hold it. It wasn't an accident?"

"Gosh no, Del. I shot him. Twice, if it makes any difference. He was coming at me with a hatchet in each hand."

"I guess you had your reasons." Del masked any surprise by checking his radio. The unit appeared to be working, but he couldn't hear his boss now.

Blackshaw asked, "What outfit are you with?"

"Geronimo Hotshots. At least I was. Flashover must have driven them back a ways," explained Del.

"Good luck regrouping, Del. Thanks for the help." Blackshaw started a slow walk down the hill.

"You don't want to go there," said Del.

Blackshaw stopped. "I have business, remember? Everything's all burnt now. I need to get back."

"I wouldn't. Keep going that way, soon you're walking into some real dry stuff. The lightning storm was crazy. Feel the wind? Up here it seems okay, at your back. Down that hill, and the valleys have it all turned around. Tricky stuff."

"You're saying I should stay at this elevation for a while."

Del took a map out of his coat pocket and began tracing circles with a soot smudged tip of his gloved finger. "These flares were not contained even an hour ago. The smoke will hide the trouble, and you could get stuck in another flashover with no hole to jump in. There's no lines dug there yet. We were working on that. What I'm saying is turn around and go the other way."

"That's Mexico."

"And it's on fire, too, just not as involved yet."

"I don't have a passport."

"The fire isn't checking passports. Ben, my dope's more than an hour old, and I'm cut off from my team. With the lightning, it's nothing but surprises waiting for you."

Blackshaw continued his survey, folding Del's informed caution in with his own drive to connect with Malthys.

Del waited quietly for a moment, then asked, "What did you mean about saving a few million people? You talking about the fire hitting Bisbee? There's not that many there."

Blackshaw tried to walk his pronouncement back. "Never mind. I spoke out of turn. Must've been the heat."

"You still look half-dead," observed Del.

"The better half, I'd like to think. Got an extra map?"

"Got extra smoke. Some extra fire. Extra fuel to burn where you're headed. But not a whole lot of *extra* in the map department." Del took his map back.

"I hear you. Thanks again." Blackshaw's stride was short and bound by pain, but it was clear to Del that he was determined to go back toward the gathering, against advice.

After a frustrating tussle with his common sense, Del caught up with Blackshaw. "You need help."

"I'm okay." Blackshaw kept moving.

Del clarified. "I'll see you down the hill, but then I've got to find my team."

"Negative. Not necessary."

Del caught Blackshaw as his foot slid into another smoke-wreathed cut in the hillside. "Have to disagree," he said.

Blackshaw asked, "You didn't save my life, Del. Is this some kind of obligation you think you have? Like you're responsible for me from now on?"

"Like an Indian thing?" asked Del.

Blackshaw went on, "Because, truth be told, I can't think of a bigger pain in my butt."

"No, Ben. I put out fires. You got other ideas, I see, starting with yourself." Del went on, "You're going to leave that guy back there."

"He seems safe enough." Blackshaw stumbled in a patch of scree, but caught himself before he went down.

Exasperated, Del asked, "Why are you doing this?"

Blackshaw took a few more steps before answering. His legs were loosening up. "A kid is dead, Del. It was a lynching; a hate crime, if you'd rather. Either way, Pure Nation was involved. And somehow, they're hooked in with some Rot-Irons up at that get-together, along with a bunch of other folks who think we're at war with Central American civilians. They aim to act all on their own about what they see is wrong. Now, here's where the millions of people come in. Somebody there hooked into a weapon. God knows where they got it. I didn't get a good look at it, but I've seen the like before. Odds are good it could kill a lot more than Bisbee. If you follow me, and it's like you said, you're walking into a big fire."

It was easy for Del to keep pace with Blackshaw while he digested the stranger's words. In the end, he simply repeated, "I'll see you down the hill."

CHAPTER 38

TIMON PARDUE WOKE before the rest of the camp. He drew in the morning air, and found the smoke thicker than he recalled. Sunlight washed out with the haze. He brought the fire outside his tent back to life, got some water heating in a pan for coffee, and went to check on Popper. Cutlip had brought hay for his mounts, and dropped a bail off for Pardue's horse. Two thin flakes made for Popper's breakfast.

Pardue was brushing Popper down when he saw Malthys and Gunter Foss returning out of the scrub from their patrol. Foss had bloodstains browning from scarlet on his pants. The men weren't talking. Fatigue might account for the silence, but Malthys seemed pissed.

"You boys made quite a night of it," said Pardue. "How'd it go?"

Foss said, "Thought we were trailing wets, but they might have been wild pigs. I took a shot."

Pardue said, "Your pants are a mess."

"I think I got one," said Foss. "It must have bled on some brush, and I ran into it."

To Pardue's trained eye, the blood on Foss's pants appeared to be more of a through-soaking stain than a swipe in passing. He asked, "You took a shot at something you couldn't see?"

"It's the wildfires. Smoke's choking up the ravines," said Malthys.

"We're here to apprehend illegals, Gunter. No pig ever took a shot at you, though I couldn't blame one if it did. You might've hit another patrol."

Foss looked like he had a few choice replies to spew, but after a moment, he mastered his temper, and with it, his tongue.

"Sorry, Sheriff. Won't happen again," he promised.

CHAPTER 39

MALTHYS STUDIED MAPS on the camp table in front of Pardue's tent. Breakfast fires and Coleman stoves were radiating bacon aromas which for once went well with the heavy scent of mesquite becoming charcoal in the fires of the surrounding countryside. Malthys's concern this morning was not so much where he and Foss would patrol tonight, as it was a review of where they had been. It took only a little bit of review to figure where the helicopter had crashed. Somehow, viewing the site on a map made the events of the night before more real than the near miss the aircraft had made in person.

Malthys was interrupted by someone calling his name. He turned and saw three men and a teenager approaching him along the path from the parking area. It took him a few moments to recognize them. Seeing the younger guy, whose slouching demeanor lay a few ticks below abashed, sent Malthys into a fury he could barely contain. The three older men were tired, on edge, and wary of their reception. Malthys pointed to a clearing well away from Pardue's tent.

The Major, the shorter, muscular man with the close-clipped haircut said, "Hey Malthys. Is that coffee on the fire?"

Before the newcomers could even grab mugs, Malthys stabbed a finger toward the clearing again, and marched that way. The four guys followed.

The Major muttered, "Shit," under his breath, and joined Malthys.

Oren, a plump man in his fifties, with his head shaved down to the wood, griped as he passed by the aromatic coffee pot, "We've been on the road for four days."

"I don't give a crap," said Malthys. He got right in the face of the youngest guy, Rufus Colquette, and demanded, "What the hell are you trying to do?"

Colquette made a game reply. "*Fourteen words*, sir. No use us doing the right thing if nobody knows we done it." He was invoking the slogan of the dead Aryan hate monger David Lane, whose credo was *We must secure the existence of our people and a future for White children.*

The Major said, "Ease up, man."

"Shut up, Major!" Malthys was incensed, shaking, his face blanching white. "This was *yours* to oversee. Every photo of a take-down has just the animal in it. No hunters. Then I manage when and on what site the images are released."

Oren wheedled, "It was his first hunt. Give the kid a break."

"I'll break his damn neck!" Malthys preferred to control everything to do with the Pure Nation Comitatus's public relations, so he could twit the authorities as well as astound existing followers and recruit new ones. Few of Malthys's flock realized that he sold his gruesome collection of pictures on the internet for enormous sums of money to the right buyers. Colquette had spoiled that option by linking the image directly to PNC.

"Have you seen any papers? Any news?" Malthys was pacing now. He jabbed the air with gestures he had copied from Leni Riefenstahl's propaganda films of Hitler addressing his mobs.

Nyqvist, a skinny, shriveled cracker in his sixties, spoke for the first time, repeating Oren. "We been driving four days straight. Took us a round-about ride like you said."

Malthys seethed, "Your pictures are all over the news."

"Not mine," said Nyqvist, sounding defensive and smug all at once. "I wasn't in the picture."

"Because you don't have a damn selfie-stick? You idiot, they got you, too!" said Malthys.

Nyqvist looked confused and worried. Rufus Colquette stifled a chuckle. Malthys punched the killer on his weak chin. Colquette went down hard on his ass, his eyes wandering before regaining focus a few seconds later.

"You're fugitives. You're wanted men," explained Malthys. "The four of you are worth two hundred thousand dollars in reward money."

Despite the dire news, the weary travelers swelled with a corrosive pride.

CHAPTER 40

DELSHAY GUIDED BLACKSHAW down the hill as prom-
ised, helping only when the recently exhumed man teetered on the verge of
slipping. Blackshaw's gait was improving, but hours parching in a rock oven
had taken their toll.

Del asked, "The people that hurt the kid—"

"Killed him," corrected Blackshaw. "Tied him to a tree, cut him, and
scalped him."

"They're PNC?"

"Yes." Blackshaw eased down over an outcropping of rock.

"And they're sitting up there with those others? The ones looking for
Mexicans?" Del hopped down off the rock Blackshaw had just scrambled
over.

"They know how to party."

"And you, Ben. You're going back there. To get after them with your
gun."

"I tried to do the right thing, Del. Reported the killer to the cops. He
should be in jail now. But they missed him."

"So, it's going to be a turkey shoot at that camp," said Del.

"I couldn't save her. I have to do something."

"Her?"

"What?" asked Blackshaw.

"You said you couldn't save *her*," said Del.

Blackshaw took a second to digest that. "I meant *him*. The kid. Anyway, I have to secure the weapon. It's a WMD. It could kill a lot of people if they use it."

"What kind of WMD?" asked Del.

"You ask a lot of questions for a guy just making sure I don't fall on my head," said Blackshaw. "Sure you want the answers? If I tell you much more, you'll be an accessory." Then a thought struck Blackshaw. He stopped and faced Del. "Or are you going to dime me?"

Instead of answering Blackshaw's question, Del asked again. "What kind of WMD? Is it like the ones in Iraq? Really scary, but not really there?"

Blackshaw said, "Biological."

"You mean like a bunch of blankets with smallpox all over them. Yeah. Maybe I know what you mean." For the first time, Del sounded derisive. "Let's say you secure it. Then what?"

"I don't know yet. My track record with things like this isn't the best."

Del sounded incredulous when he said, "You have a *track record* with WMDs? You know Ben, you wouldn't be the first wingnut I've run into wandering around a desert with a complex."

"I'll take my history over yours any day."

Del went on as if Blackshaw hadn't spoken. "Guys like you. Dime a dozen. Mescaline salad messes them up. Sun does the rest. Listening to Everlast, coming here for a whitey vision quest, going home dehydrated, with a sunburn, and story they can't remember. If they go home at all."

"I'll be okay from here, Del. Maybe it's time you go find your crew—"

"And get out of Dodge."

"It's a good plan. Domestic terrorists have killed a lot more folks stateside than overseas ones."

"Domestic terrorists. You mean middle-aged white men."

Blackshaw said, "Del, you've got a chip on your shoulder big as a Buick."

Del stared. Blackshaw heard himself, and looked as close to sheepish as he ever would.

Del forgot Blackshaw for a moment, his gaze focused down the mountain. "I told you."

Blackshaw tried to see what Del was looking at. "Told me what?"

"Fire, Ben. Look around you. Fresh fuel. Scrub. Trees. It's down in that ravine. Now, I figure you're about out of water. Looking pretty beat up. Can't hardly walk straight. What's the plan, Ben? You can't shoot your way out of this, let alone into anything else."

Blackshaw was stymied. "Got any ideas?"

"Keep going downhill," said Del.

"Toward the fire."

"Exactly," said Del. And he led the way.

CHAPTER 41

DEL STEADIED BLACKSHAW as they moved down over a
steep karst of rock.

Blackshaw coughed from smoke as he said, "Getting worse."

"Sure is," agreed Del, with an unruffled tone.

"Aren't you the guy who said not to walk into fire?" Blackshaw's trust
of Del waned with every step.

"Aren't you former military?"

"Reckon," admitted Blackshaw. He stopped his descent.

"So you're used to being in a tight spot," said Del.

Blackshaw did not answer. *Tight spot* covered a lot of emotional territory, most of which reminded him of the desert terrain he was walking now.

Del went on, "You're not dead, because you don't walk *into* fire. But
you get damn close. Come on. A few more steps."

"You aren't helping me, Del. You think you are, but you're not."

Del glanced down at the ground for a moment. "Don't move," he told
Blackshaw. He removed a thick, red plastic bag from his pack and kneeled.
Using a small stick, he worked to scrape a large green pellet, like the stub of
a piece of oversized chalk, into the red bag. Then he dropped the stick into
the bag as well, and sealed it. Then he replaced the bag in his pack.

"What was that?" asked Blackshaw.

"Ten-Eighty," explained Del. "Sodium fluoroacetate. Pest poison.
Ranchers used it to bait and kill coyotes and wolves. Some places, they
spread it from helicopters. Potent stuff. But it kills everything. Looks like

somebody might have tried it around here, and that one dropped out of the hopper. Just a pin-prick's worth would kill a man. Nasty way to go."

Blackshaw sat to rest for a moment. "I saw something fly by last night. A bunch of them. Couldn't see them in the haze and dark, but it looked like spiders."

"We talked about peyote, Ben."

"I saw what I saw," insisted Blackshaw.

Blackshaw looked into the ravine. He thought he could see a yellow flame licking in the smoke. When he looked back at Del, he was gone. Blackshaw got to his feet and peered farther downhill. Del hadn't fallen. Where the hell was he?

Del's head emerged from around the rock. "Okay. Let's go. Take off your pack and hand carry it. You won't fit otherwise."

Blackshaw eased his way toward Del. Around the smaller outcropping, he saw the firefighter wedge himself into a jagged crevice.

"Again?" asked Blackshaw.

"This one's different."

Blackshaw hesitated.

"If a flashover's coming, you're about out of time," Del warned.

With his pack and rifle in hand, he pressed himself between the rock faces. From the twilight within, he felt Del grab his arm and pull hard, nearly dislocating his shoulder. Blackshaw scraped deeper inside. Without any warning, the constricting stone walls widened, and Blackshaw fell to his knees on a cool rock floor.

Del flipped on his light. They were inside the small vestibule leading into a larger cavern.

Del said, "When I got split up from my crew, this is where I was headed. To get water."

"Water's not getting me back where I need to be," said Blackshaw.

"Maybe it isn't. Maybe it is. If you can't go through a fire. And you can't go over, or around it, what's left?"

With that, Del turned away, rounded a corner in three steps, and was gone again. *Under* thought Blackshaw. He picked up his pack and the Threadcutter, and followed the receding lamplight into the mountainside.

CHAPTER 42

AFTER THE FLIGHT to Bisbee Municipal Airport, Lowry and
Wilde had been picked up by a perturbed Wanda Van Sickel, the CBP's
Assistant Commissioner of the Office of Air and Marine. They had been
expecting their counterpart from the Tucson FBI office to meet them.

Before they rolled off the ramp at the field, Van Sickel was firing
questions. It was a backward kind of briefing.

"Fill me in," said Van Sickel. "Greenway is a former colleague?"

"Yes," said Lowry. "She worked with us at the D.C. office. How is she
doing?"

Van Sickel ignored the question. "We appreciate your interest, of
course, but it seems a long way to come for a pilot."

Wilde replied, "Our Senior Resident Agent from Tucson should have
been here, too. You must've worked with Mike Haberman before."

"Many times. We had coffee last month. I was talking to Mike through
the night. He decided he wanted me to meet with you first. He's coming in
soon." Van Sickel was being cagey.

"You met on the Joint Terrorism Task Force," said Lowry.

"Yes. Among other things, we're working together on new protocols
for the cross-border threat."

"Anything in particular?" asked Molly.

Van Sickel looked weary and distracted as she answered. "Not so far,
to be honest. But Senator Pile, from New Hampshire of all places, is

convinced Al Qaeda will be weaponizing unaccompanied Mexican children with ebola."

Wilde asked, "But no cases like that? No chatter?"

"That's not the point." observed Van Sickel. "We must prepare for that which Washington *believes* we must prepare, to safeguard our budget for the work we *know* we have to do. We haven't exactly war-gamed Pile's notion, but you get me."

Lowry said, "So Haberman briefed you that we have a person of interest in a hate crime, and that crime is connected to Pure Nation Comitatus."

"Malthys," sneered Van Sickel. "The Sha'Quan Stewart case."

Wilde said, "Yes."

"Mike forwarded the photo. What they did—*animals*," spat Van Sickel.

Lowry explained, "Rufus Colquette, one of the suspects, has a PNC tattoo."

"Right about here," said Van Sickel, tapping a few inches below her collar.

"Exactly," said Lowry. "We didn't have an east coast PNC cell on our radar, so we need to learn more. Understand what we're dealing with."

Van Sickel said, "Malthys's M-O is to cast his net as wide as he can on social media, on Reddit, but the final call to action for a recruit is usually to come to the compound here. And bring your checkbook. But first they have to make their bones. Sometimes, it's with a kill. Does Colquette have money? A rich family?"

"Far from it," said Wilde. "May I call you Wanda?"

"I'll answer to it," grudged Van Sickel.

"The helicopter crash. Wanda, there's almost nothing about it on the wires," said Wilde.

"You'll see. It's a remote desert site. Not accessible. We're still examining the debris field," Van Sickel hedged. "Why do *you* want to see it?"

Lowry said, "Mike said the PNC is part of an unusual gathering that happens to be within a few miles of the crash site."

"You think there's linkage to the Stewart case." asked Van Sickel.

Wilde said, "They've joined with a group of ranchers, and a cadre of the Rot-Iron Motorcycle Club there. Strange bedfellows."

Van Sickel sounded defensive. "That would be my back yard. I know about it. We're monitoring the situation."

Wilde challenged, "What aren't you telling us about this crash?"

"I'd rather show you." Van Sickel slowed the truck at an Arizona State Police checkpoint on the highway near a low hill. She rolled down the window, and held up her identification in front of the officers overheating in their Kevlar vests, and after a nod from them, bounced at low speed along fresh vehicle tracks into the hills.

Thirty minutes later, she stopped. There was already an assemblage of NTSB crash investigation trucks, along with personnel in white helmets. But there was no helicopter in sight.

Van Sickel got out of the truck. Lowry and Wilde followed her up a hill to a plateau that lay at the foot of another hill rising from the level ground. There was the fuselage of the downed chopper. It seemed unevenly rounded in some areas, flattened in others, as if it had rolled and crumpled on the ground.

To Wilde's eyes, the debris field appeared contained in comparison to an airliner crash, or even a wreck of a small fixed wing plane. Then she noticed that more wreckage, the main rotor, and other twisted sections of exterior aluminum skin, trailed halfway up the hill.

Lowry was concentrating on the plateau itself. "Wanda, there's an area that looks swept here. All the natural litter under a certain size seems blown away. Did the helicopter hover there before it climbed and hit the hill?"

"Thank you," said Van Sickel sincerely. "That is one of the weirdest things about this."

Wilde commiserated, "It's early in the investigation."

"Not that early," said the CBP official.

Van Sickel's radio hashed, and a man's voice on it said, "We got it. Is Wanda on scene yet? She's going to want to see this."

Another voice answered, "Affirmative. I'll get NTSB as well."

Van Sickel keyed the mic and said, "I'm here. Go to three."

Van Sickel changed channels, keyed the mic on her unit again, and reconnected with the original caller on the new frequency. Then she said, "I'm here. Where are you?"

The voice on the microphone replied with a bearing from the crash site. Van Sickel said, "We're on our way."

"What is it?" asked Lowry.

"See anything else wrong with the fuselage?" quizzed Van Sickel.

Lowry studied the wreck. It was Wilde, who hated everything about choppers, especially flying aboard them, who quickly said, "The tail thing. The propeller, or rotor. The whole thing. Where's that?"

"Come on." Van Sickel led off again across the face of the hill. "Watch your step. Diamondbacks."

Lowry and Wilde followed Van Sickel. After twenty minutes hiking through difficult terrain made up of loose scree careering them down toward waiting cactus spines, they saw a man from the shoulders up, waving from a distant arroyo.

Ten more minutes brought them to the lip of the arroyo. Van Sickel introduced them to one of her officers, Eric Rymon, a tall man with a dark desert tan on his hands and face. He took off his hat, revealing a pale forehead when he shook hands. He was worried. For Rymon, finding something important had been trumped by learning something terrible.

The tail rotor, and several feet of the boom assembly and its drive shaft, lay at the bottom of the arroyo.

With the quiet monotone of anger in his voice, Rymon asked, "You see what I'm seeing?"

"For Christ's sake," said Van Sickel.

"All those holes," said Lowry. "Looks like a shot gun blast."

"But a lot bigger," said Wilde. "It was hit hard."

Van Sickel said, "But the entry holes are along the top surface. A few exit holes on the bottom. See how those're puckered outward on the bottom?"

Lowry said, "Was it hit by ground fire? Was it in a steep bank?"

"Maybe *after* it was hit, and the tail rotor came off," said Van Sickel. "The preliminary read from the black box says it was transitioning from a steep climb to a steep descent when it came apart. But it was level in the roll axis."

"Still, it sounds like evasive maneuvers," said Wilde. "This helicopter was avoiding something, but this wasn't a collision. It was definitely shot down."

Van Sickel said, "That's how I'm seeing it. Unless it was completely inverted, which we know it wasn't, it was fired on from *above*."

No one present said anything for a long while.

"Let's go look at the fuselage," said the Assistant Commissioner.

They hiked back to the crash site. Van Sickel led Wilde and Lowry around the perimeter of the cleared area of the plateau to the fuselage.

"No fire, at least," observed Lowry. He stepped closer, and looked into the mangled cockpit. There were bloodstains, mostly on the seat and floor, as best he could see. "You never told us about the crew."

Van Sickel looked hard at Lowry and Wilde, with an angry sadness in her eyes. "Because I don't know. Nobody knows. They're missing."

"Excuse me?" asked Wilde.

Van Sickel explained, "The SAR team that found the fuselage said it was empty. No crew aboard."

"Were they ejected on impact?" asked Lowry. Then he amended his own thoughts, adding, "There's a lot of blood in there. Right there. No, I guess they rode it all the way down."

"Look closer," said Van Sickel. "Take your time."

Wilde and Lowry each produced the small LED flashlights they carried, and scrutinized the cockpit, squatting from time to time for a better angle.

Wilde said, "That harness, the right one—Greenway's I guess—that was opened at the buckle. The other—"

"Francine Eckhart's," Van Sickel filled in.

Wilde continued, "Eckhart's harness—that one was cut. They carry hook knives, right? To self-extricate if the buckle fails."

"Yes they do," said Van Sickel.

"Jesus," marveled Wilde. "Did they walk out?"

"Maybe Jesus could have, but look at the blood in there," said Van Sickel. "Put it like this, we held onto the Loaches for so long before we ordered the Eurocopters because the things were so damn survivable in a crash, ever since they were deployed in Vietnam. We went with Eurocopters because they're even better, and with more useful load."

Lowry said, "If they walked out, there would be blood elsewhere. It would leave a trail. And how far could they get, injured that badly?"

Van Sickel said, "We found the blood trail. It was minimal, compared to what you'd rightly expect given that mess in the cockpit. Traces on brush, on the ground, leading that way. The thing is, there are two sets of boot prints."

"Okay. That's what you'd expect," said Wilde.

"But single file, not side-by side, like one helping the other. And one of the tracks is walking *backwards*," said Van Sickel. She let that sink in before adding, "Both sets of prints are size thirteen or bigger. *Men's* size thirteen. And they lead to vehicle tracks over the plateau's edge in that direction." She pointed west, away from the tracks she had made with Wilde and Lowry coming in from the northwest. "Greenway wears women's ten. Eckhart wears women's nine wide."

With hope in her voice Wilde said, "Maybe an ambulance crew saw the crash. The services jump each other's calls all the time in D.C. We've had patients die while EMTs slugged it out for the right to transport and bill."

"Saw the crash how?" asked Van Sickel, hoping against her common sense for some credible possibility she had missed. "From where? You saw how long we drove cross country to get here. This site's invisible from the road."

"But somebody saw the crash," said Lowry. "Two men saw it. Hunters. Good Samaritans who came to help, and—"

"Greenway and Eckhart are not in any area hospital. We're checking everywhere, including quack shacks statewide every fifteen minutes, in case there was some kind of confusion in admissions. Even veterinary hospitals. Nothing. Agent Lowry, they're just gone."

"My God," said Wilde. "They're abducted? They're hurt, *and* abducted?"

"How about the vehicle tracks?" asked Lowry.

Van Sickel said, "We've got them out to the road. We've got impressions, checking tire databases, checking the boot prints, everything."

"Can we help?" asked Wilde.

"Mike's got his lab working on the castings now. But thank you," said Van Sickel. "Now let's talk some more about Colquette."

CHAPTER 43

NANCY GREENWAY SWUNG in and out of consciousness. She lay on her back, unable to move. From that position, when the black of her vision receded to shades of twilight, all she could see was the stained overhead of plastic or fiberglass, and the cracked convenience light of the ambulance in which she was being transported.

The surreal moments before the tail rotor failure rebounded into her memory. Then she caught flashes of the catastrophic loss of yaw control, and the sickening spin. There was Eckhart straining on the left anti-torque pedal with her left leg, then stomping down hard on the pedal with her right foot as well. The altimeter unwinding in a blur. The horrendous shaking. She remembered trying, with no outside references, to gauge when to complete the emergency autorotation landing, and transfer kinetic energy from the main rotor into slowing the descent. That's it. It came back to her. She'd used the FLIR. The fact that she was still alive was testament enough that *something* had worked.

She tried, but could not remember the landing at all. Pain throughout her body signaled it was a crash more than a landing. Turning her head left sent a spasm of agony through her neck. The sight of Eckhart lying next to her, pale and still, confirmed their return to earth had not been gentle.

Somebody rasped, "Fran?" Greenway did not recognize her own voice.

A bearded face loomed into Greenway's view. From somewhere inside the whiskers, a graveled voice said, "Save your breath, nigger. That bitch died an hour ago."

And with that, Greenway knew she was not in an ambulance.

CHAPTER 44

BLACKSHAW FOLLOWED DEL through a narrow, low corridor that soon angled downhill.

"Best sit and scoot on this part coming up," said Del.

Blackshaw took the advice. The cavern's corridor floor was steeper here, and loose grit had almost cost him his footing. This far, his only view of the space came through the jumping light on the front of Del's harness. The light's angle left the spaces overhead shrouded in unmeasured darkness. Echoes bounced confusing information into Blackshaw's ears. Alone, he could have *heard* more from his surroundings, but Del's scraping footsteps and the clatter of gear kept Blackshaw concentrating on sight, on what his hands told him about the walls, and the deck angle he registered through the soles of his boots.

"Del, where are we?"

"On a map? Not sure."

"That's not good enough," said Blackshaw.

"It's got to do for now. This system has a few entry points, but like I said, they're not on any map."

"No surveys."

"Not like latitude and longitude," said Del. "Folks don't know about it."

"You mean white people don't."

Del chuckled. In the dark, the sound was creepy, the way the walls made a crowd's roar out of the laugh of one man. "Some have come here, but none alive today."

"You know where you're going."

For an answer Del just tapped his helmet.

"I don't like it," confessed Blackshaw.

Del stopped, and turned back to Blackshaw, careful to keep the light in his harness from shining directly in his eyes. He said, "I don't know where we are. I know the next step. I know the next turn. The next chimney climb. The next drop into nothing. I told you, maybe I could mark a map with the passable entry points, but that's all. And I won't ever do that. We're just, I don't know—*between*."

"Sacred ground?"

Again, Del's laugh was muffled and redirected by the limestone walls. "There's folks born here. Folks have died here. It's *all* sacred ground. Show me someplace that isn't holy."

They continued without speaking, letting the cavern echoes mark their progress ever downward. Blackshaw's world was one of recorded surfaces and features, places where others he could understand and relate to had traveled before, and marked out on maps, or in stories. Watching Del's silhouette loom and fade, rise and fall, and bereft of coordinates he could relay, or even remember, Blackshaw felt he was moving through a state of mind more than any singular place. Despite Del's company, Blackshaw felt a growing unredeemable dread of being utterly cut off and alone.

CHAPTER 45

GREENWAY WOKE TO severe pain again. The silence and stillness of the truck were new. She carefully turned her head to the left, and felt a grinding crackle in her neck. Eckhart still lay there next to her. With hope for her co-pilot's survival gone, Greenway could see death taking up residence in the remains like a filthy, unwelcome squatter who would never leave, could never be driven away.

Then Greenway heard the rhythmic scrape. She counted four, nearly five of her own heartbeats between each grinding, metallic punctuation of the quiet. Then she realized what she was hearing. Someone was digging into hard earth. She wondered if digging a grave made a different sound from other labor, other holes or trenches made with a shovel.

The digging stopped. A moment later, Greenway watched with a wrenching sense of loss as Eckhart's body was pulled along the truck bed toward some door, maybe a tailgate. Eckhart's head lolled loose on a neck with no muscle tone, and her jaw gaped. Hiding from her grief and fear inside dispassionate analysis, Greenway figured they had been on the ground either less than two hours, or much more than twenty-four hours, the usual window for the onset and dissipation of rigor mortis, particularly in neck and jaw muscles.

No, Greenway tried to shout, to protest as Eckhart disappeared from view. She made no sound. Her mouth and throat were sticky dry as if she had eaten paste.

She heard a man's voice. "Get the jumpsuit off."

Another voice, that of the man whose face she had first seen, complained, "Zipper's jammed. All the blood."

There was a sound of tearing fabric, and another complaint. "Fucking Nomex." More tearing noises.

The first voice said, "I'll take that thong. At least she trimmed."

These animals were stripping Eckhart's body! Greenway struggled to get up, but her limbs defied all commands.

The first voice said, "Prop up her head. Good. Now give her a cigarette. No, man. Light it, you asshole! Do it right! Okay, get in close. Now say cheese!"

Nausea welled from deep in Greenway's gut. They were taking pictures. Gray overtook Greenway's consciousness; light drained away to obsidian.

CHAPTER 46

TEDDY BEAR CHOYA beamed with a new sense of power and pride as he drove the truck back to his base of operations. Word had come from north of the border that the weird delivery of cocaine had been recovered by Malthys. Paolo Estrella y Castro's plan had worked. It had actually come off, even though his flying spider drones sounded like so much science fiction.

Adding to his happiness over the successful delivery was the exalting fact that the swarm had defended itself, and brought a CBP helicopter down. That was amazing! The radio was reporting the incident. Granted there was something missing for Choya, because he had not personally pulled the trigger, but he was the author of the crash. Estrella y Castro had thought of everything. No one would mess with his stuff!

There was one small problem. Though forty-nine drones had delivered their cargo, one of them had not made it back to the LZ south of the border for pick-up, inspection, and reuse. For all Estrella y Castro's diabolical innovations, there was no real-time diagnostic telemetry coming back to his laptop to analyze in order to figure out what happened to the wayward craft. The loss was a very small cost in the grand scheme, far less than losing the cargo en route to the drop, but the mystery rankled both the rogue designer and his boss. Estrella y Castro cross-checked the recovered drones' serial numbers to figure out one which was missing. Now he knew who on their assembly crew had built the lost drone. It was Manuel, a known goof-off.

Choya drove the truck past the sentries guarding his base, and through the gate in the high cinderblock walls. He parked next to the five other trucks being packed by his men with freshly laden drones.

Estrella y Castro left his boss to crow with his men, and marched straight over to the drone assembly area. To contain an accidental detonation of the fragmentation grenades during the build process, a worker constructed only one drone at a time. The assemblers worked alone in small, windowless cement block cubicles. Completed drone units were placed just outside the cubicle doors, and collected by other workers for loading with one kilo of cocaine each. The builders could not take the drones to the loading area personally. They were all chained at the ankle to the back walls of their cubicles. The shackles were small. The senior builder on the team was a nine year old girl named Rosa with quick little hands.

At a signal from Estrella y Castro, one of the guards overseeing the builders entered a hot, cramped cubicle, and soon emerged again dragging Manuel, who was small and skinny at eight years old. Estrella y Castro kneeled down so he could look the boy in the eye. Manuel squinted in the morning light. He had not seen the sun in days. The designer shook his head, and walked back to his shop.

The guard dragged Manuel behind a shed, which had walls thick enough to stop a bullet. A few moments later, two gunshots rang out. Quality Assurance was serious business in Teddy Bear Choya's compound.

CHAPTER 47

A DEMON FOLLOWED Del through the stone warren. At least that's what it felt like, having this guy Blackshaw trailing him down here. And what was Del doing, guiding this fury down into the earth? Was he escorting a fiend back home? Not for the first time, it crossed his mind to leave Blackshaw in the darkness. There were numerous spots along this winding path where Del could slip into a side chamber, and make his way back to the surface alone, with or without a flashlight. Blackshaw would get himself turned around and lost in no time. Del would have no blood on his hands. Not exactly. The cave would do as it always did for unwary intruders, binding them in confusion and fear and squeezing until the life went out of them.

Del meditated on his choices. He had found Ben in one slash in the earth. He could leave him in another. To abandon Ben down here would, in a very real way, condone the murder of the boy that Ben had come to avenge. To return Ben to the surface would unleash more carnage, if that rifle were any indication. The gun seemed to be a part of Ben, as much as Del's axe was an extension of his own mind. He had only to think, and trees toppled before him.

The time had come to test Ben, to see if he were to live or die down here.

Del said, "We're coming to a place we should stop."

"I'm not tired," said Blackshaw.

"It's not about how far you've come," countered Del. "It's more about how far you still have to go. You'll want to stop for a bit."

The corridor widened into a broad, high chamber. Del waited for Blackshaw to play his small flashlight all around the space. That took time. Every surface begged for scrutiny.

The stranger's jaw hung open. "Oh my blessing. It's beautiful."

Del was pleased his companion found it so, and had to agree. The chamber was girded with hundreds of astounding natural formations, lime-stone stalactites and stalagmites, molten-looking cones of dripped calcium bicarbonate that met in the middle space at their apices high overhead. Some of the formations did not yet touch one another. Only inches apart, they would not meet for another thousand years.

Blackshaw asked, "Who did this?"

Though much of the conic stone remained in its natural state, there were forms that had felt the hand of an artist. These were carved into mythic animal shapes, and human caryatids supporting ton upon ton of vaulting weight. Many of the astonishing carvings lay well beyond the reach of the tallest man. Blackshaw trained his light throughout the space, whirl-ing faster whenever he caught glimpses of startling stone faces emerging from the base material to peer at the intruders.

"I don't know," answered Del.

"It's incredible," marveled Blackshaw. He moved closer to the cham-ber wall to examine a gargoyle bear, its head and left shoulder struggling into the open air from the rocky matrix behind. "These are so old," he went on, more to himself than to Del.

"That one you're looking at. It wasn't there when I was a boy," said Del. "The mountain lion next to it? My great grandfather remembers that one."

Blackshaw stared at his guide in disbelief. "It's a work in progress."

Del could see that it took a few more moments for Blackshaw's racing mind to fall quiet enough to hear the slow knock-and-ring of a mallet strik-ing a metal chisel into stone; it seemed to toll through the cavern from a hundred miles away.

CHAPTER 48

ADELLE CONGREVE FOLLOWED Pardue into his tent. She had things on her mind. Things she preferred not to reveal in front of the other leaders of the Movement Against Immigrants, or MAIm as it was called among the rank and file with knowing half-smiles.

"Timon, we gotta have us a talk."

Pardue spun from his beeline to the liquor locker.

As Congreve zipped the tent flap, Timon was wry when he said, "Make yourself at home, Adelle."

"I've always had a high regard for you," she began. "But I'm not so sure now."

"Get in line," said Pardue.

"I think MAIm is in trouble."

"Wasn't trouble the intent from the beginning?" Pardue lowered himself onto a folding camp stool and pointed to another one for Congreve. She sat, and leaned in close.

Congreve bridled. "*Action* is the intent. *Results* are the intent. Everything the CBP *isn't* doing."

"Fair enough. But this isn't a sit-in," said Pardue. "We have unauthorized, armed men and women patrolling our nation's border. We're a paramilitary assembly. A militia. You knew that going in. What's changed in thirty-six hours?"

"What's changed is you haven't offered me a drink," griped Congreve. "It's five o'clock someplace, isn't it?"

While Pardue set about correcting his oversight, Congreve continued, "I'm worried. This wildfire's getting closer. The damn CBP lost a chopper overnight, and how long will it be before they show up here?"

"Helicopters crash. We have nothing to hide," said Pardue. "But our patrols would be more effective if everybody wasn't farting around out there on ATVs. They should walk, or sit a horse. All that engine noise will drive the immigrants to ground."

They clinked glasses and sipped. Congreve hoped her perfume together with the redolent whisky scents would make Pardue more pliable. She said, "What do you think about Malthys bringing that biker along?"

"You can't pick up a turd by the clean end," said Pardue. "Seemed odd to me when a lady of your stature, you and Dressler and Cutlip, would bring Malthys in."

"I've had second thoughts on that," disclosed Congreve. "He keeps getting visitors from his compound, and they all look mangled, like drunk sailors rolled on shore leave."

"I noticed," said Pardue. "But I suppose he brought his own muscle to the cause, and that's something. Now, that Gunter Foss is bad news."

"That's what I was thinking. PNC is a freak show, but Malthys's nose is clean enough. Foss is a *criminal.*"

"I'm not sheriff anymore."

Congreve warmed to her complaint. "Foss puts a bad smell on our cause. I mean, MAIm is first and foremost a show of strength by a group of concerned sovereign citizens. If we catch illegals, that's good, too, but where the hell is the press?"

"Covering the fire. The crash, maybe. We're just a big bunch of wingnuts in the burning wilderness now."

Congreve was crushed to hear this, but in her heart she knew it was true. She sat up with stiff-backed resolve. "We have to get trending again. Everybody with a smart phone has to tweet their balls off. Hashtag-MAIm."

"Is calling it MAIm a good idea, Adelle?"

"Bad ideas *trend,* Timon. For God's sake, get with the program. And you need to eject Gunter Foss's ass on out of here. Today. He smells like a sour ass-crack. All those Rot-Irons do."

Pardue asked, "Are you here for Dressler and Cutlip?"

"They agree completely. Foss is out," proclaimed Congreve.

"And Malthys?" asked Pardue staring into his whisky.

"He wasn't consulted on this particular point."

Pardue puffed out his cheeks. "Still, I guess that makes four of us."

Congreve grinned and clapped her hands together. "I'm so glad to hear you say that."

"Don't want this blowing up in our faces," said Pardue. "You let me think on the best approach."

Congreve was slightly disappointed. To conceal it, she rallied and kneeled close to Pardue, straightening his collar, pressing fifteen thousand dollars' worth of saline against his arm. "You do that, Timon. You'll come up with something. Meantime, let's you and me give them something to tweet about."

Even in the throes of complete surprise, Pardue managed to kiss her in return, and then some.

PART III
DUENDES

CHAPTER 49

BLACKSHAW WANTED TO stay, to examine every carving, every figure. Some of the works made use of the natural whipped cream shapes in the limestone to accentuate mythic animalian muscles, or wry expressions. In addition to the creatures, many of the designs were enveloping decorative motifs, like spirals, Greek keys, Celtic knotting, and patterned Native American textiles fluttering around the chamber; so many influences, clearly, but all with unique treatments and innovative twists of a single visionary mind. Yet, as Del had indicated, these works represented a deep-time labor expended over the lives of many brilliant artisans.

The duet of mallet on chisel, and chisel on stone rang on slowly for a few moments more. Then it stopped. Blackshaw checked Del's face. His guide had heard it, too.

"Who else is down here?" asked Blackshaw.

"No idea. Never seen another soul. We just see the changes. The new things put in. And sometimes we hear it happening, like there's a duende, or mountain spirit working down here. Maybe Crow Spirit has a prisoner again," said Del. He regarded Blackshaw for a while, and then went on, "You're lucky. It's quiet most of the time when I've been here. Whoever or whatever it is must be okay with your coming in. You an artist? You make things as well as destroy?"

"Been known to dabble." For Blackshaw, this modest statement felt like the worst bragging.

Del smiled. "That must be it. You're a kindred spirt to whoever's down here."

Blackshaw observed, "Which means there's another side to this artist."

"There's another side to everybody," said Del. "We have to go. Don't want to wear out our welcome."

"I want to come back," said Blackshaw, in a rare wistful moment. "There's a lot going on here."

"Maybe you could stay," suggested Del. "Quit on the vengeance."

Blackshaw shook his head, but he was not above considering life in a strange, rare tomb like this.

"Then follow me," said Del.

The next hour was difficult for Blackshaw, and the hardship went beyond scrambling through caverns cut by waters that did not respect the human need for easy footing. These walls had also received the mysterious artist's ornate, macabre, lyrical, often soaring carvings. A part of Blackshaw wanted to linger in every gallery, pore over every figure, and study more of this weird subterranean creator's hand. He willed himself onward.

After a long period of quiet travel, Del said from up ahead, "Don't freak out."

That put Blackshaw on notice. They rounded a bend to the left, and climbed a short wall on all-fours to a wide, flat area.

"I think we're a little late to help," said Blackshaw, taking in the scene.

Del gave a wide berth to the three desiccated bodies sitting up against the far wall. Blackshaw trained his own light on the dead men. Their skin was hard, like yellowed rawhide. The tatters of clothing suggested the stylings of another century, likely the early 1800s. Their pistols were flintlocks. One of the men was wealthier than the other two. His boots were finer. His pistols gleamed with gold inlaid designs.

Del squatted, looking at the bodies from a respectful distance, and said, "It's a little weird, seeing them for the first time."

Then Blackshaw noticed that the wall carvings in this gallery passed completely behind the dead men. The work there was done before these intruders had arrived and died. Unless the mysterious underground artist had placed the bodies here, this was another testament to how long the cavern project had been under way. Then he noticed one of the dead men held a small pick. The delicately carved stone head of a deer lay on the floor, broken from its body in the wall. Blackshaw wondered if a rumor of the carvings had drawn the men in to their doom.

Blackshaw asked, "What happened to them?"

"One time, when I was full of myself, I took a closer look. Not a mark on them. Maybe they starved."

"You ever light a fire down here?"

"Never," said Del.

"Good. Because if you did, carbon monoxide could take you. Happens sometimes when kids go caving where they shouldn't, and light a fire to party."

"There's no sign of any fire here," said Del.

"I'm not saying *they* lit one," said Blackshaw. "But *somebody* might've. If these boys came hunting for souvenirs, it might've ticked somebody off. It would me, if this were my life's work."

"But wouldn't that kill whoever lit the fire, too?"

"Might could, if they lingered."

Del was in no humor to ponder the question anymore. "Let's keep going."

"You said you came here for water for your crew, Del."

"That was a long ways behind us. But trust me, you'll get some water. Plenty."

With a final glance at the dead men, Del moved across the mausoleum gallery, and disappeared into a low opening. Blackshaw followed, and found Del at the bottom of a rock chimney shining his light on a series of footholds carved in the wall like a ladder. Blackshaw scaled down.

Ten minutes walking brought them to a gallery bordered on the far side by rushing torrent. The water emerged from the chamber's wall to the left, and dashed in a misty plume into the wall on the right.

Del had to shout to be heard above the echoes. "Okay Ben. I hope you don't smoke. Big, deep breath."

Blackshaw stared at the millrace before him. "You're not serious."

"If you want to get where you're going, I'm dead serious," yelled Del.

"How long's the ride?"

"To the end." Del was grinning as if he'd said something funny.

The wildfire fighter sat on the stone bank of the stream, and lowered his boots into the water. His legs jerked as if they'd been hit by a wide open fire hose. He bellowed, "You want to stay as much to the right side of the stream as possible."

Del slid into the stream up to his waist. Water battered his torso so hard, he had to seize a small outcropping of rock with both hands to keep from being swept away.

Blackshaw shouted, "Why to the right?"

Del's face became serious. "My brother and I went in together a long time ago. He went left. I went to the right. Haven't seen him since."

With that, Del let go of the rock and sank out of sight. The cavern was plunged into twilight. All Blackshaw could see of Del was the glow of his flashlight as it rushed toward the right hand wall. An instant later, the light was gone.

With mistrust and terror constricting his chest, Blackshaw grabbed the same jutting rock that Del had used, and lowered himself into the water. The pack was torn from his shoulder and swirled away under the stone wall. Somehow, he maintained a grip on the Threadcutter. Part of Blackshaw's mind registered that the rock from which his hand was slipping was carved with the face of a laughing frog. The water's roar and lashing cold was horrendous, firing his limbic brain ever closer to panic. He took as deep a breath as he could, and let go, spinning down into the cold stony maw.

CHAPTER 50

PERSHING LOWRY LOOKED up from his phone's screen at Molly Wilde. He was also trying to juggle three mugs of coffee back from the break room to the empty office Wanda Van Sickel had lent the Bureau so they could work locally for the duration. Senior Resident Agent Mike Haberman from the Tucson FBI office was squinting and clawing at the screen of a small tablet on the desk. Wilde felt the tension in Lowry's body as much as saw it.

"What? A text?" she asked him. Wilde rescued Lowry, taking the coffee cups from him.

"It's Davis in Richmond," said Lowry. "The UAV over Smith Island."

Wilde said, "Ellis made the call to Blackshaw."

"I don't know," said Lowry. "Davis says every single phone on the island made a call. Every number. Every landline, every cell, even the marine radios. They all dialed or radioed out at once eight minutes ago, for a duration of one minute."

"I don't get it," said Wilde. "Did Ellis make a call, or not?"

"Probably. No way to know," said Lowry.

Haberman offered, "It sounds like a very low-tech denial-of-service attack on your surveillance."

Lowry agreed. "The drone we had over the island relayed maybe a few bits of data, but then the circuits overloaded, just cooked. We got nothing."

Annoyance mixed with admiration when Wilde said, "Damn that's clever. And sneaky."

Lowry said, "We thought the drone would have to surveil only a few calls, maybe a dozen or two at most. This was a tsunami."

Wilde thought for a moment, sipping her coffee. Lowry knew she preferred it white and sweet these days, more like warmed up coffee ice cream. A recent brush with death had changed her greater character hardly at all, but this urgency over small, simpler pleasures was new.

Haberman asked, "Did any calls the UAV managed to grab get answered in this area?"

Lowry said, "We won't know until the drone lands, and we can get inside the onboard server. It might have stored data it just couldn't transmit."

"How can somebody like Blackshaw have this kind of pull over an entire island?" asked Haberman.

Wilde said, "Picture everybody dialing out all at once." She was still impressed.

"Blackshaw is a native son. He's embedded there," said Lowry. "And maybe Ellis is the one with the juice. Remember that super car I saw in his garage? The people there are supposed to be middle class, some of them really struggling."

"Remember, that makes twice we've looked for Blackshaw on Smith Island and not found him," observed Wilde.

"Once is an anecdote. Twice is data. The last time, he was right under our noses," said Lowry.

"Out ahead of us, if we're honest," amended Wilde.

Van Sickel tapped on the door frame. She answered their question before they asked it. "Still nothing on Greenway and Eckhart. The tire imprints trace to Chevy Tahoes sold from 1998 through 2002. They're pretty worn, and might have been bought second hand. No idea what they're mounted on today. Maybe a Yukon. We're checking. On the boot impressions, one pair is Bates. The other is Galls' house brand."

"Law enforcement," said Haberman.

"Or military," countered Van Sickel. "But everybody wears them these days. Solid gear, with a badass look."

Lowry said, "Wanda, there may be another person of interest out here."

"Other than Malthys and Gunter Foss and all the good people of MAIm?" asked Van Sickel.

Lowry said, "Molly, would you please show her your sketch of Blackshaw?"

Wilde passed her tablet over to Van Sickel, who said, "Oh my. Too much to hope he's one of the good guys, I suppose."

With a proprietary air, Wilde said, "Married. And even though his heart seems to be in the right place, his methods in the past have been—"

"Draconian," finished Lowry.

Haberman chimed in, "That's half the vigilantes out there."

"Which leaves us nowhere," said Van Sickel, the hope ebbing from her voice.

CHAPTER 51

WATER SLAMMED BLACKSHAW into a rock wall. He was tumbled over and over with no clue which way was up, let alone which wall was on the right side. It was as if Poseidon were beating him to death in the dark. His light whirled out of his grasp, followed immediately by his rifle. He tucked his head and wrapped his arms around it as defense against the next turn in this tortuous subterranean flume. Whenever he opened his eyes for a second, a dim bioluminescence cast a sick green pall over the next turn, the next stone, the next blow.

Blackshaw was strained like baby peas through a series of stalagmites that might have formed eons ago when the present streambed was once dry. As he jetted through this natural high pressure water main, the mammalian dive reflex slowed his heart against the adrenal surges of fear. The smaller blood vessels in his fingers and toes closed; then his arms and legs began to cramp. Blackshaw's attempt to relax and remember that water flowed *around* obstructions and not *through* them was belied by impact after blunt impact. The battering ride felt endless. A stalagmite raked his ribs as he was swept past it, driving precious air from his lungs. Now he struggled to quell the urge to inhale. In the tumult, it crossed Blackshaw's mind, *this would be one hell of an ugly death*. Then his head slammed a stalagmite, and after a splash of stars exploded inside his skull, he blacked out.

CHAPTER 52

MEXICO CITY VANISHED over the horizon behind the rattling jolt of the train's last three cars. Ascensión Huerta had found an actual Grupos B representative, and though her four remaining children were now grabbing any handhold they could find on top of the car, at least they were fed, rehydrated, clean, and refreshed with a few hours of sleep.

And there was the Grupos B man himself. Eduardo was Ascensión's age, was almost handsome, and not a priest. He treated her, and her wretched children with compassion, and respect. Ascensión was so grateful to Eduardo for helping her. Her kids did not want to leave his side. She thought she could love an almost-handsome man who was kind to her children, but when she allowed her heart to dwell on Eduardo, she felt dirty. She had been raped. Her children had seen it go on, hour after hour. More than any man's love, she wanted an HIV test before she could even hope to be touched again. For now, she clung hard to *La Bestia*, which was always trying to obliterate her family.

Looking forward again toward the locomotive, Ascensión first noticed the skinny, needle-pocked arms poking up through the hatch in the car roof. Like a filthy spider, the face, body, and legs of the addict followed. She knew that bankrupt look in his face. This creature reaching out toward her small bag of treasures from Eduardo, the bread, the cheese, and the water, he had no soul anymore. He was crazed with longing for his fix. He would take her precious bag and sell it to a black marketeer on the train. Then he would squander the pittance he received with a drug dealer somewhere else on the train, get high, and come back when he was no longer sick from withdrawal to steal her children. There was a self-contained, mobile economy of misery aboard this train preying on the hopes of northbound immigrants.

Ascensión reached into her bag and felt for another important gift from Eduardo, the knife. Her children had witnessed her shame. Now, God help them, they would see her kill.

CHAPTER 53

GUNTER FOSS BOLSTERED the spirits of his Rot-Iron contingent of the MAIm occupation. During his walk-through among the ranks, he and many of his most reliable soldiers seriously wondered if you could call it an occupation when you held ground nobody gave a damn about. Everybody he spoke with gazed at him with eyes rimmed in red from the thickening, acrid wildfire smoke. Occasional coughs were growing more frequent. Only a trusted few knew the real reason for the Rot-Iron presence here.

Foss could not argue with those whom he sensed questioned this mission. He agreed that an outlaw motorcycle club's power lay in its mobility. Like the Mongolian horde of old, sweeping through fresh territory, striking fear into sedentary hearts, ravaging the countryside and swiftly moving on, these were the true signs of any real invading force. He was aware, but scratched out of his grade-school recollection, that the hordes he admired had eventually settled into dynasties lasting centuries and holding more than two million square miles. For him, the ride was the true invulnerability, even though he knew in his heart that it never extended past the distance he could wring from a single tank of fuel. Foss's ferocity was bound by gas stations and their owners who were willing to sell to him. This thought lurked like a rabid dog in the back of his mind. An outlaw survived praying on the productivity of others, and died when solid citizens banded together in their intolerance of him. How Foss hated walking this fine line! His Mad

Max fantasies were shattered whenever he remembered that he was, in the worst sense, little more than a politician now.

Foss was finishing his walk among the Rot-Iron road kapos and thinking about a beer when Timon Pardue called his name. Foss turned and waited for the putative leader of the MAIm camp to walk over to him.

Pardue stated the obvious. "Smoke's getting worse. Fire's burning closer."

"So what?" said Foss, dismissing the old man's opening chit-chat.

"We're thinking about regrouping after the fire dies down," said Pardue. "No illegals in their right minds would try to walk through that inferno."

This was the kind of cowardice Gunter Foss loathed. "Suit yourself. Rot-Irons are fine to see this through. You go home. We'll hold the fort. Your smarter Spics would love to make a run under this kind of cover. Their coyotes sure don't give a crap, and neither do we." Foss was only too happy to conduct his smuggling operation without a righteous ex-cop breathing down his neck.

Foss wasn't sure he had heard correctly when Pardue said, "I'm thinking you and your bunch should head north first. Lead the way, like. You could save a lot of civilians if you showed 'em there was no harm in living to fight another day."

Foss spat. "Are you crazy?" That was when, through the haze, Foss noticed Dressler, Cutlip, and that bitch Congreve, not to mention a dozen of their ranch hands, watching the conversation just out of earshot.

"Maybe," said Pardue. "But I'm not stupid. Discretion is the better part of valor. You know about picking your battles, don't you, Foss? You pick the ones you can win, just so winning doesn't cost you everything."

Anger thundered in Foss's chest, pulsed at his temples. His hands tingled with the urge to close hard into fists. He took an easy glance around, and saw that several of his own lieutenants were observing the parley. He was sick of the smoke, the same scenery, the fake bonhomie with all the non-Rot-Irons, but if he relented here and now, his own people would eat him alive. "I thought we wanted the same thing, Timon."

"Oh I'm sure we do. But there's a time and a place, Gunter. You could take Malthys with you. The border will always be there. The bigger problem's not going away."

"Neither are we," snarled Foss, stepping closer to Pardue.

The former lawman smiled. "No reason to get testy. Lots of ways this can go. Say you get word of important business someplace else. Tell folks that you and your people will be back. I'm sure you have interests all over Arizona that need your attention."

Foss said nothing, and did not move.

Pardue went on in calm tones, still smiling. "Or I could call it. Congreve, Dressler, Cutlip and I up-stakes with our folks, and roll out. We say we'll be back after the fire's contained. Like as not, we will. That leaves you and Malthys explaining to your people why they're still sitting here choking on the smoke, waiting to burn up if the wind takes a turn, and all pretty much for nothing."

Foss looked into the depths of Pardue's eyes. The old man wasn't kidding. After a moment, the Rot-Irons' chief said, "Follow me." With that, he turned, and entered his big tent.

Foss waited, watching from within. It was plain that Pardue was uncertain of his back-up, but knew enough not to look around to check. He did as Foss directed, and ducked his head into the dim space. Cigar smoke, with a tang of marijuana, made the atmosphere inside as acrid and murky as the wildfire's mesquite fuel did outside. A few sheets that hung from the frame served as partitions.

At a signal from Foss, four of his brother Rot-Irons cleared out. They were slow, their limbs heavy. Stoned. Foss knew all this time in one place was sapping Rot-Iron morale, despite their being in camp for only a day, a night, and a morning.

Foss stared at Pardue again, measuring him with a sick grin on his face.

"You're staying," Foss declared, as if it were his decision alone. "All of you."

"We've been over that," said Pardue patiently.

At the back of the tent, Foss moved to one of the sheet partitions, drew it aside, and watched Pardue's face. It was plain the former sheriff could not understand what he saw bundled onto the folding camp cot. The tan flight suit was stained in the browns of dried blood.

Pardue stepped closer. Close enough to recognize the CBP Office of Air and Marine insignia patch on the uniform's shoulder. The horror and disgust on Pardue's face was a glorious sight for Foss to behold.

Pardue moved to the side of the cot and knelt down. "Goddammit, she needs a hospital. Are you completely crazy?"

"Like a fox. See, she's been here since this morning. In a camp run by *you*."

"I didn't—I didn't know!" said Pardue, incredulous.

"Tell it to the judge," said Foss, grinning. "Pal, you're an accessory."

"To what?" Pardue squared off with Foss. "The helicopter just crashed."

"No. It had some help, Timon." Foss was enjoying the hell out of this. "Like I said, you're not going anywhere."

"There's always two. Where's the other pilot?" demanded Pardue.

Foss could imagine the dread metastasizing in the pit of the sheriff's gut.

"Long dead, and deep buried," confided Foss. He took a pull on a bottle of cheap vodka. "Ain't a soul on earth going to believe when you found that out."

"I have an alibi," said Pardue. "Adelle—"

"You weren't ten minutes in the sack with that bitch. We all heard you. What about the rest of the time? Now, on the other hand, I got an ass-load of Rot-Irons and PNC who could put you right at the scene. And what a scene it was. Welcome to my world, Timon. You're staying put. Say one word, and you'll be my cellmate."

Smiling, Foss held the vodka bottle out to Pardue. With bewilderment on his face, and a defeated slump in his shoulders, the old lawman took the bottle and drank. He had just been patched-in as the newest Rot-Iron.

CHAPTER 54

BLACKSHAW OPENED HIS eyes to find himself lying on a narrow ledge of rock. One wrong move, and he would plummet, thrashing again into the torrent that rushed past the ledge four feet below. His sob wet pack, his rifle, and his light lay on the ledge just past his boots. The flashlight was off. The eerie bioluminescence from the streambed's algae threw just enough of a glow for Blackshaw to discern the confines of his crypt. Whether he had climbed out of the flume by dint of instinct or by ingrained training, he was grateful to be alive. He coughed up a gout of water. Make that grateful to be living, and surprised. He could not recall recovering his gear, or getting up onto that ledge. Del might have helped him, but now his guide was nowhere in sight.

The shadows revealed no way out of this chamber. Blackshaw considered the possibility that, after catching his breath, he might have to return to the cold water and see where it might lead. The stream's dash and roar obliterated any organized thought of options. He did a clean sit-up, almost knocking his head on the low rock ceiling, and reached between his feet for the flashlight. It still worked.

"Del!" called Blackshaw. The growl of the stream damped the echoes, and hugged his shout too close to do any good.

He played the flashlight beam around the chamber. Except for the stream's entry to the left, and effluence to the right, the small stone cell was sealed. On the cavity's longer, far side, immediately over the stream, a carving of a serpent leapt sleek curls of its body up out of the water and down in again. To the right, near where the water disappeared beneath the wall, the tapering serpent reared again, and was finished off with a human head trailing a thick mane of hair. The carving was rich in detail, yet it read like the simplest signpost indicating the last direction Blackshaw wanted to go, but the only path he could hope to take. Even stripped down with no gear, and in his best fighting form, clawing his way upstream to the left through the tumult, and back the way he had come was impossible. The rush of water was too swift to overcome.

He was not sure how long he had been contemplating the grim options of a quicker death by drowning, or a dragged out end by starvation, when he heard a distant voice shout his name. The cavern walls and the din of the water confused any effort to triangulate the sound's place of origin. Of course it came from Del, but where was he? Blackshaw wondered if Del's cry had been sluiced downstream with the subterranean water.

He heard Del's call again. This time it sounded as though it came from a much closer place, almost as if Del was somehow inside the chamber with him, but invisible. The cavern's acoustics were perverse, unreadable. A beam of bright light distinct from Blackshaw's own danced on the water's roiling surface. The source of the light seemed to emit from below the ledge on which he lay.

Taking care not to tip himself into the stream, Blackshaw squirmed onto his side and peered over the edge. The rock beneath the ledge was swallowed in darkness. Then a ray of light stabbed Blackshaw straight in the eyes. He flinched, and almost rolled into the water.

"There you are." Del shouted over the stream's noise, though their faces were only a few feet apart. He redirected the light, and Blackshaw saw the recessed duct in the limestone wall right under the ledge.

Blackshaw swung his pack down to Del, then passed him the rifle. It required Blackshaw to execute the maneuvers of a contortionist to lower himself off the ledge, and get a foothold on the lip of the tunnel mouth below. Del helped Blackshaw regain his balance in the new, lower chamber. Blackshaw started scrambling down the dry flume in the same direction of the adjacent stream's travel.

Realizing Del was not with him, Blackshaw turned back and found the firefighter studying the serpent carving on the opposite wall, playing his light along the creature's length, and at last fixating on the head. Down here, the stream's surface was only a foot below this new chamber's threshold. This lower vantage point brought the artist's use of the chamber's surface into full glory. The serpent's striated, spotted skin (there were no scales) gleamed as if lit from within from the moisture frothed up by the rushing stream. Del was mesmerized.

Blackshaw understood wanting to drink in the work of a fine sculptor, but he gave Del a rough rap on the shoulder. Del pulled himself away from the rock veranda opposite the creature, and followed Blackshaw into a new chamber in which they could both stand, and more importantly, hear each other speak in nearly normal tones. Only here did Blackshaw realize how cold he was in his wet clothes.

Blackshaw said, "I thought you were dead."

"Me too you. I got out of the water about thirty yards past where you did. Down that way," said Del, pointing ahead. "I heard you yell."

Confusion must have shown on Blackshaw's face. "You hauled me out."

"No. You got out on your own," explained Del.

"You saw me do it?" Blackshaw knew that could be the only explanation, but still, he wondered.

"I assumed—" said Del, now baffled. "I've never seen that little room before. And my gear was hauled out, too."

"Let's get moving," ordered Blackshaw. "We've killed too damn much time down here."

Del took the lead again, and after ten more minutes of scrambling through a series of low conduits connecting larger chambers, he started to climb up through a narrow chimney.

Finally, Del said, "It's what my father called him."

Blackshaw brushed loose grit from his face, granules that had fallen from the treads of Del's boots up above. "What do you mean?"

Del did not stop climbing. "My brother."

"The one who died in here?"

"My *only* brother. He was the fastest swimmer on the San Carlos Reservation. My father called him Black Eel."

"Could have made a good SEAL," offered Blackshaw, not knowing what else to say. "Sorry I never met him."

Del kept climbing. He said, "Don't mean to get weird, Ben, but I think we did."

CHAPTER 55

THE VOICES RECEDED, and Greenway knew she was alone. Every time she surfaced from the void of unconsciousness into twilight, her first thought was that she was waking from a nightmare, the kind that lingered with the weight of foreboding, and would stick with her well into the day. After a few more moments, that eerie sensation burgeoned into her most heartfelt prayer, that this truly was nothing more than a bad dream, and Franny Eckhart was really at her home, slugging back strong coffee while she got her first weather briefing before their next flight—but then the waves of pain rolled in from all over Greenway's body, some sharp, some dull, and all real. Her helicopter had in fact crashed. Eckhart was actually dead, and even after death, her remains had been obscenely desecrated and tossed into a grave like garbage.

And Greenway was a prisoner.

She opened her eyes again, and tried to piece what she saw together with what she had heard. For a moment, her memory looped her back to a field hospital in Iraq when she had visited a wounded comrade. The fabric walls and the overhead all moved in the breeze. The way sound played around her head, this tent lacked the interior volume of the Army hospital as best she could determine. She was sequestered from the rest of the space by a fabric partition. Turning her head still hurt, and improved her understanding of this place very little. Her nose worked. The sour tang of marijuana, horse manure, and body odor hung in the air assaulting her nostrils with every breath. It crossed her mind that she would want to postpone any drug test at work until the contact high metabolized out of her blood-stream. Then she almost laughed when she realized how long it would take her to be in good enough shape to pass her flight medical again. That's if she lived.

Greenway listened with a hunter's care for a long while. She could hear distant conversations through the tent walls. She could not discern words, but the boisterous tones, the bellowing laughter impelled by machismo and bravado recalled the men who had transported her, and who had misused her friend.

The full picture formed. She remembered she was an injured black woman in the hands of white supremacists. The throbbing of heavy motor-cycle engines erupted. The thunder bludgeoned her aching head. Bikers. This kept getting better and better.

Yes, as best Greenway could determine, she was alone in the tent. That helped her sort important information. Her captors believed she was hurt badly enough not to require constant oversight. More likely, there was someone, a guard, outside the tent. The conversation she had overheard earlier led her to think her presence here might not be common knowledge to the entire bunch of bastards outside. Then she heard a man clear a wad of phlegm from his throat. It sounded close by, and came from the direction where she guessed the tent's entrance might lie. The sentry. He was likely charged with keeping others out, even more so than he was worried about keeping someone as injured as she was confined inside.

Pieces of information, what she could detect now, and what she could remember from the pre-flight briefing, fell into place like pins in a lock. *Don't buzz the encampment of those border vigilantes. The ranchers might not take a shot at you,* her boss had said, *but the bikers might.* These weren't just any bik-ers. They were *Rot-Irons.*

Given the size of the crowd she heard outside, she was now inside that vigilante camp. There might be somebody with a sense of human decency close by who would help her, if only they knew she was here. Maybe the ranchers. If she were strong enough to scream loud enough, somebody might come. If no one rallied to her aid, that sentry would make sure she'd be gagged from then on, or worse.

Why were the bikers holding her? Maybe she was a bargaining chip to be tossed into a negotiation. Her immediate safety lay in her captors' belief that she was too hurt to move, yet her long-term survival depended on getting medical care as soon as possible.

Greenway continued her self-triage. She tried to move again, starting with her toes. She could feel them. Even they hurt like hell. She craned her neck and looked at her boots, and was relieved to see them sway side to side with her effort. Ankles seemed okay. She wasn't paralyzed. Always a plus, but she wasn't going to win any races for a long time. Add lower extremity sensation and motor function to her meager list of assets.

Next, she lifted her left arm. Agony. She nearly vomited from the lightning bolts of pain as bone ground on bone in her upper arm, maybe her shoulder. Not good. She was left-handed. She took time to calm her breathing. Then she tried to move her right arm. It rose from her side as if it were independent of her commands. Numbness. No doubt she had caromed hard off her door more than once during the crash. She flexed it. God knows it hurt from the buffets, pulls, and strains of dropping out of the sky, but she could move this limb a little. She made a fist. In the most primitive way, she was now armed.

Then it struck her. She was still in her khaki flight suit. From when she had looked at her feet move, she remembered her abdomen and pelvic area were stained with blood that was drying brown. One hell of a lot of blood. She might have a bad laceration, or—and she hated even thinking this—the blood might have come from Fran's injuries.

After listening for a sentry's approach, and determining from another wet, roopy cough that he was still outside, Greenway inched her left hand down her left leg. Her fingertips brushed the flap closure of a long thin pocket still tacky with blood. The pocket had Velcro tabs keeping it closed. To avoid the signature ripping sound of Velcro's hooks and loops separating, she eased the pocket open over the course of what felt like hours, though it took no more than a minute.

She pressed the blood-drenched flap open flat, and snaked her fingers into the pocket. Her heart nearly flew out of her chest with joy. There it was. Her rescue knife. It had serrated edges to slash through a seatbelt with a jammed buckle that failed to release for an emergency egress from the helicopter. It could cut other things. These bastard Rot-Irons had kid-napped her, and let her pilot, her friend, die. But they hadn't patted her down carefully because she was covered in blood. Too icky for the big, bad bikers.

Greenway managed to squeeze the two tabs on the plastic sheath and, as advertised, the short hilt hopped a half-inch into her palm on a light spring load. After drawing the knife, she tucked it out of sight under her thigh. It was then she heard the flap of the tent unzip. She closed her eyes and played dead.

CHAPTER 56

THE FBI LOANER office at CBP was quiet. It was still early. Even though half the CBP staff was already at their desks throughout the floor, the ambient noise in the place was as somber as parishioners waiting for early mass.

For appearance's sake, Agents Wilde and Lowry had two adjoining rooms in the local motel, but after the few hours they had spent there, only one bed was disturbed. Their affair was still heating up. They had only recently discovered their affection was mutual, and ran deep, despite caveats throughout the Bureau about intra-office romances. As Wilde's superior, Lowry had requested a transfer out of the Calvert office where they had worked together for several years. Lowry's new posting in the D.C. office allowed them to observe all the proprieties prescribed by Human Resources, and preserve both their careers, while giving their love room to breathe and grow after hours. They had come back to the office this morning without having slept for a second.

Lowry's phone burred.

Van Sickel's voice was brusque. "Search and Rescue found a body."

Lowry's thoughts went to the missing helicopter crew. "Oh no. Which one?"

Wilde and Haberman stared at Lowry, waiting for him to pass along Van Sickel's answer.

"Neither," said Van Sickel. "But you should come. Given what you've told me, I want your eyes on this."

* * *

An hour later, Lowry, Wilde, and Haberman were deep in the desert hills waiting at the edge of a rock crevasse. The agents were better shod and dressed for work in the field than on their first visit to the distant helicopter crash site. The night's chill had not yet given way to any warmth, though the hazy red disk of the sun lay barely revealed on the eastern horizon. Crime scene technicians cased the immediate area for evidence. The surrounding hills had been badly burned in the wildfire. The scent of charcoal rose out of the earth. Charcoal, and pemmican. Deep in the cut, which opened into a larger arroyo, the scene techs were collecting thin flecks of scorched silver Mylar.

A pale medical examiner, who seemed comfortable enough with Van Sickel's group that he answered only to Doc, had clambered down in the arroyo, and was looking at a body wedged upright in the stone rift.

Doc shouted up to the waiting agents, "He's like meat stuck to a pan. Getting him out's going to be fun."

Haberman asked, "Okay. What can you tell us from there?"

"Like I said to Wanda, I can see at least one gunshot wound, through-and-through. Left shoulder." Then Doc muttered to himself, "Interesting. You're going to need a rifle box, please. And two ties."

One technician pulled a flattened Arrowhead Forensics evidence box out of his truck, and a pair of plastic ties to secure a weapon and prevent its shifting around. He quickly folded the cardboard box into shape.

Another technician asked, "Rifle?"

Doc answered, "Make that *four* ties. No. Not a rifle. This guy was carrying two hatchets. They're under his feet, consistent with his dropping them, intentionally, or as a result of falling down there."

Doc got out of the technician's way so the hatchets could be collected.

As Doc climbed out of the rift, Lowry said, "I can understand one hatchet in the field, but not two."

Doc said, "Agreed. If these were ordinary camping hatchets. You'll see when they bring them up. They look forged out of one piece. The haft is almost long enough to qualify as an axe. They had nylon handles, which appear partially melted in the heat, for a good grip that would absorb some of the strike shock. But the overall design is for throwing. Or for fighting."

Wilde asked, "Like a tomahawk? Is he Native American?"

"Caucasian," Doc answered. "These things look like a modern take on an old, or even ancient martial use. Like Vikings, or Goths."

Van Sickel said, "Tell them what else you saw."

Doc obliged with, "The sternum tat. PNC. This guy's Pure Nation Comitatus."

Wilde said, "So he came from that MAIm group."

"That's over a mile from here," said Haberman.

"Who puts a sentry that far away? Your perimeter would be a sieve," said Wilde.

Van Sickel added, "Maybe he got lost. And PNC has guns. Up north at their compound, their sentries tote firearms. They hate trespassers. They don't screw around."

Doc said, "There could be a gun jammed in there behind him, but I didn't see one. What he dropped is what was in his hands."

Wilde said, "He *wasn't* guarding. The weapon choice says to me he was hunting, but it was a ritualized hunt. For a man."

"It fits," said Haberman. "Malthys's Hulu account has multiple viewings of that Vikings TV series. We're talking eight views of every episode of every season. He eats that stuff up. Binge watches."

"You monitor his downloads?" asked Wilde.

"He's a shitbird running a gang of shitbirds," said Haberman with a grin. "We monitor everything about him."

Van Sickel said, "Molly, Pershing, I asked you to take a look at this because of your person of interest. I've got a body here. Molly, you think he was out hunting. Why? How did he know to go hunting in the first place? Who sent him? Who did he run into?"

Lowry remained silent, but he looked at Wilde.

"I would be speculating," said Molly.

Van Sickel said, "It wouldn't be the first time an educated hunch helped us focus our resources. I've got two pilots missing. That pisses me off. So spit it out."

Wilde reflected for a moment before speaking. "Rufus Colquette makes an ill-advised brag to someone whom we believe might be Ben Blackshaw. Colquette evades apprehension in Richmond. He wants sanctuary, or at least protection, so he 'fesses up, maybe to one or all of the other doers in that photo. They, in turn, pass the word of this breach in protocol up the chain of command."

"To Malthys out here," said Lowry.

"So Malthys details this guy here to patrol out looking for Blackshaw," said Haberman.

"Why?" asked Van Sickel.

"Colquette and Blackshaw met on a bus," said Wilde. "Maybe they chatted about their itineraries. We're reasonably sure Colquette was on his way to the PNC compound to be honored for his kill. Wherever Blackshaw was traveling before he ran into Colquette, we have him on surveillance in Chicago buying a one-way train ticket into this area."

Van Sickel asked, "How did this guy here draw the short straw to go looking for Blackshaw? Why would Malthys send him into the field?"

Haberman said, "Malthys is cautious. The long range patrol might have been proactive. It might have been an honor for this son of a bitch here. Or, it might have been punishment for some kind of infraction. A make-good."

"You wouldn't send Colquette? He incited the problem," said Wilde.

"Like you said, he started this," said Lowry. "I'm not sure he would be my first choice to clean up. And where is he? Would he actually come here? Why not hole up at the PNC compound up north?"

Van Sickel shook her head. "Now the line of speculation's too long. Too thin to support its own weight. My question is, does shooting this guy fit your understanding of Blackshaw's behavior?"

"The shooter lived—" said Lowry.

"And he left," said Wilde. "Blackshaw's a possible for this."

Haberman said, "I guess we'll need to drop in on MAIm to break the bad news."

CHAPTER 57

THE ACRID WILDFIRE smoke reminded Blackshaw of the troubled world into which he was reemerging. Del still led the way, but a glimmer of daylight, and the increase in haze inside the chamber told Blackshaw that an exit to the surface was close ahead.

With barely yards to go, Del stopped walking, and rested his right knee on the stone floor. He said, "Get up here, Ben. You need to see this."

Blackshaw climbed up next to Del, who was shining his light on a strange object on the ground. "It's one of those drone things."

"Eight arms, like a flying spider," said Del.

"There were a lot of them." Blackshaw tilted the drone up to look at its underside. "That rig there used to hold something. A package."

That was when Blackshaw and Del each noticed something different, yet remarkable about the octocopter.

Del spoke first. "See that?" He pointed to a snapped of shaft of wood embedded with a steel point in the heart of the drone. "An arrow. Somebody brought this thing down."

"And left it here for us to find," said Blackshaw. "Or to kill us."

Del looked at Blackshaw for an explanation. It was Blackshaw's turn to point. "That's a fragmentation grenade up in there. I think this drone was hauling contraband, and either the right person was supposed to retrieve it, or else the wrong person would buy the farm. That little keypad must take a code to deactivate this servo that pulls the grenade's pin."

"What's wrong with people—" said Del. "Hold on. Wait! What are you doing?"

With the fingers of one hand clamping the spoon to the grenade's body, Blackshaw was deftly detaching the pin from the small servo. He said, "You might want to climb farther up and get yourself around a corner or two. If I screw this up—" He let the sentence hang unfinished.

Del did not stir. Blackshaw concentrated, and two minutes later, the grenade rolled free from the drone into his hand, its pin still in place. Blackshaw tucked the small bomb into an outer pocket of his rucksack. Then, with much less finesse, and more brute strength, he dug and wrenched a small black box out of the drone's body. "Transceiver," was all he said. Then he asked, "Who do you think shot this down and put it here where we were going?"

Del looked Blackshaw in the eye, and said nothing.

"That's what I thought," said Blackshaw.

After a few more minutes of gritty climbing through tortuous caverns, one of the system's exits lay before them. Blackshaw squinted in the new, diffuse light, and squatted down for a moment to take stock.

He asked Del, "Still got your map?"

Del dug into his pack, and soon the map lay between them on the stone floor.

Del said, "We're here." He pointed to a place on a hillside. Then he went on, "The big revival meeting is over here. Just a couple hills in between here and there."

Blackshaw asked, "Back up. Where'd we go in to the cavern?"

Blackshaw couldn't tell if Del's gesture at the map was intentionally vague, but if what he indicated was true, not only had they passed beneath a significant stretch of burning desert, they were now on the opposite side of the anti-immigrant gathering from their starting point.

"About here," said Del. "You covered about four miles as the crow flies."

"So it must have been much farther underground, with ascents, descents, and turns," said Blackshaw. "We made okay time considering."

"We spent a stretch in the water trying not to drown. That stream took us a good way, and fast," said Del.

"Wouldn't have minded walking instead," said Blackshaw.

"I hear you," said Del, "all except for that burning-to-death part." He waited with patience for Blackshaw to say more.

Blackshaw followed the light, and moved ahead to the crack in the earth, the exit from the cavern system toward which Del had been leading them. When he slowly put his head into the daylight, he was swept back to his tour in Iraq in the first Gulf War. There was the desert sand, the choking dust and smoke. In Iraq, the pall came from oil wells Saddam Hussein had ordered destroyed. Here, it was from the wildfire. Blackshaw shuddered as his mind wrenched him halfway around the world, across many years.

"You don't look so good," said Del.

"I appreciate your getting me this far," said Blackshaw finally. "I got it from here."

"You still think there's some work for you out there?" asked Del.

"More than likely."

"And that bio-weapon—"

"Wants neutralizing." Blackshaw's words sounded clipped, even to him. "Del, your world's still on fire. Maybe mine is, too. Each to our own."

"My crew gave me up for dead hours ago."

"I've played dead at times. Coming back to life isn't a breeze," warned Blackshaw. "They're likely worried sick over you. Don't you want to set them straight?"

"Soon enough. Ben, I think you're going to need some help."

Blackshaw was quiet. Then he let out a long, slow breath, as if preparing to squeeze his rifle's trigger between heartbeats.

"A friend of mine gave me a come-to-Jesus speech once," said Blackshaw.

"Why do I think you're about to do the same with me? I didn't take you for a missionary."

"I needed to hear a certain kind of gospel at the time. You might, too," said Blackshaw.

Del was quiet again.

"Ellis and I were in a tough spot," said Blackshaw. "He had a very big stake in the outcome of some difficult business, but evil men were against us. The difference here being, it's not your circus. Not your monkeys."

"Let me stop you right there," said Del. "Don't speak for me. Don't you *dare* speak for me. The PNC, and Rot-Irons, they hate Apaches. All Indians, but Apaches in particular. The assaults, on women who leave the reservation for work, or shopping, or visiting—there are crimes which the law hasn't seen fit to do much about. That'd be bad enough. But those people are stuck in cowboy-and-Indian movies. There've been disappearances. Lots of men, but women mostly. Gone without a trace. Ben, these stupid fascist bigots, they test themselves against us, knowing full well we aren't living how we used to, like guerilla fighters running and gunning through the hills. Going up against us to prove who they are. But never one-on-one. Always in a pack, singling us out. They're cowards, Ben. So sick inside themselves."

Fury and sadness choked Del, and he stopped speaking.

Blackshaw waited a moment, then said, "I'm not easy saying this, Del, but a few hundred years ago, my people on Smith Island, they took what, and sometimes *who*, didn't belong to them. They did what they had to for survival. Today, they're different. They find peace with religion now. It was Ellis who told me I couldn't duck out of my heritage. The situation we were in would call for blood if we were to win. I explained I'd done my share of reaping during the war. But Ellis is a smart man. He saw how reluctant I was to do more of that stateside, and in a time of peace."

Del asked, "He didn't want you jumping in?"

"No," said Blackshaw. "He was sure I would. He just didn't want me to be surprised when it happened, when I killed again in cold blood or hot. Ellis is a good man. He knew what was coming, and didn't want me to think less of myself. We sure didn't have time for wallowing around in a funk."

"And did you?" asked Del.

"Kill, or wallow after I did it?"

"I got an idea," said Del.

Blackshaw listened.

Del held Blackshaw's gaze. "How about you don't come around where I live, and tell me I don't have a stake in what you do," said Del. "And while you're at it, you should let me decide what I can live with. Do you know my name?"

"It's Del." Blackshaw watched Del's eyes, and hoped the boundless anger welling there could be checked by the man's good character.

"It's Del to *you*. In my heart, and where I'm from, I'm Delshay Goyathlay. Ben, they named me for *two* generals, to make sure I got the message. Red Ant, and Geronimo. Are you hearing me okay, Ben?"

"I read you five by five, Delshay."

"You've got a rifle and a couple spare mags. Now you've got a grenade. I've got some coyote poison. What else do you have?"

After a moment, Blackshaw admitted, "I have a pistol in my pack."

Del took a pistol from his own coat pocket. "Not anymore, Ben. Not for a long while. I'm glad you told me the truth. Good choice. Now, the question is, do you want it back?"

Blackshaw grinned, looking at his own Bersa in Del's hand. "You hold onto it."

"Good choice," said Del for the second time.

CHAPTER 58

TIMON PARDUE WATCHED the blacked-out CBP Suburban roll down into the heart of the MAIm encampment through the wildfire smoke. He noted that the driver kept the speed low and respectful, so no one was surprised, or forced to scatter or sprint out of the way like rural chickens in the road. Whoever was coming wanted to talk, not confront. At least for now.

When the car doors began to open, Pardue recognized Mike Haberman from the Tucson FBI office, and Wanda Van Sickel from the CBP. After introductions, he knew the black agent's name was Pershing Lowry, and that the pretty white gal was Agent Molly Wilde.

Missing from the delegation was Kirby Rumball, the current Cochise County Sheriff, and Pardue's successor after the recall vote. Maybe Rumball wanted no part of this cluster, and was the wiser man. Perhaps he had not been invited by these alphabet agents, a signal that this was a Federal matter, and men of Rumball's local stature were small potatoes, and easily mashed.

It was hot, but Pardue felt a surge of sweat on his back and from deep in his armpits. At the sight of Lowry, the black FBI agent, Malthys and Gunter Foss began to troll in from their respective factions. Pardue prayed they wouldn't do something stupid. Pleasantries were brief. Nobody bothered to talk about the weather.

Van Sickel said, "We lost a chopper overnight."

Pardue felt Foss's eyes boring a hole in the side of his head. "Oh no," said Pardue. "That's awful. They okay?"

Van Sickel continued, "We don't know, Timon. The crew is missing."

Pardue asked, "Are they walking out? How come they didn't stay at the crash site?"

"Again, we don't know," said Van Sickel. "Fact is, we think they were removed from the wreck. We have reason to think they couldn't have gotten too far on their own."

"Good Samaritan, maybe?" asked Pardue.

Haberman asked, "Run into anyone on your patrols?"

"No," said Pardue. "Fire's keeping the illegals south of the border. Only a damn fool would make a run for it now."

"But you're still sending out patrols?" asked Van Sickel.

"Plenty fools in the world," Pardue said. "We got a job to do."

Van Sickel said, "It's CBP's job. You should keep that in mind, Timon."

"I appreciate your taking the time to come here and tell me that," said Pardue evenly.

Haberman said, "Malthys, come on over."

Malthys and Foss picked up the pace, but avoided Lowry, though they glared at him. They did not extend their hands to any of the visitors.

Haberman lowered his voice. "When we were looking for the crew, we found some remains a couple miles southeast of here."

"Wets?" asked Malthys.

"From the ink on his chest, he was PNC," said Haberman.

"Who? What happened to him?" Malthys was tense. His breath was coming faster. Veins throbbed in his temples. He shifted weight from one foot to the other in agitation as his eyes darted across Haberman's face.

"Lucas Ford," said Haberman. "That's what his ID said. Any idea what he was doing so far from here?"

Everybody from the Suburban was watching Malthys. Foss and Pardue were eyeing him, too.

Malthys said, "No idea. Taking a walk."

"Bullshit," said Lowry. "He was out there looking for something, but it found him."

Foss and Malthys both hackled into a state of seething truculence at being spoken to like this by a black man.

"The spics might be superstitious, but we don't believe in duendes," said Malthys.

Van Sickel said, "He didn't run into a goblin. It's common knowledge that PNC mounts armed pickets outside your home compound, Malthys. Lucas Ford wouldn't go on walkabout without direction from you."

"He took off. Maybe the smoke got to him," said Malthys. "Who knows? We don't do bed checks here."

Pardue stepped in. "You didn't say what happened to him."

Haberman said, "Looks like the poor bastard brought hatchets to a gun fight. He lost, of course. Sorry to bring you bad news."

"You catch who did it?" asked Malthys.

"No. The killer is still out there," warned Haberman. "I'd keep your people close to camp until police can make an arrest. Was Lucas Ford quarreling with anybody you know of?"

For an answer, Malthys quoted John 14:27. *"Peace I leave with you; my peace I give you. I do not give to you as the world gives. Do not let your hearts be troubled, and do not be afraid."*

Van Sickel gave Pardue, Malthys, and Foss a slow, steady appraisal each in their turn. She said, "Please keep an eye out for our pilots."

Under Foss's beard, his grin did not reach his eyes. "Sure, Feeb. We'll get right on that."

CHAPTER 59

BLACKSHAW WATCHED THE visitors drive out of the encampment through the sight of his rifle. Downdrafts from the ridge dispersed fire smoke at his position. From there, he saw Malthys and a biker peel off from the other leaders and duck into a tent marked with a crude, spray-painted Rot-Iron patch on the flap.

Del said, "That's a lot of heat. Think it's just about the vigilantes? I mean, when we heard about them massing here, the fire boss almost sent us home for our own safety. We took a vote to come ahead anyways."

"There are two FBI agents in that truck from back east. I know them. More to the point, they know me. Reckon I can say they're here about the murdered boy."

"So they got your message after all," said Del. "Maybe you want to stand down and let them do their thing."

Blackshaw took his eye from the sight, and examined the Threadcutter from barrel to stock. "I need to check the zero after all the knocking around in that stream. Make sure all the water's out of this built-in suppresser."

"I take that as a *no*," said Del.

"Take it however you want," suggested Blackshaw.

"There's a ravine over the ridge behind us," offered Del, with a fatalist's resignation. "About a hundred yards straight shot. That do you?"

"Those fonny boy's won't hear a thing," said Blackshaw. He had fired the gun only twice before, but it amazed him both times with its muffled report.

They edged up the hill, keeping low to the rocks. At the crest, Del guided them through a low cut. His instinct against skylining their passage to the other side was in perfect harmony with Blackshaw's, though the camp and any watchers there were a mile distant.

The two men took less care, and moved faster down the other side into the ravine. When a helicopter flew past, they pasted themselves under a ledge out of sight.

"That bio weapon still part of your thinking?" asked Del.

"I got another look at it," said Blackshaw. "It's still sitting there next to that older white guy's tent like regular supplies."

Del took care in phrasing what he said next. "What are the odds they know what it is?"

Blackshaw said, "I'm counting on it. When push comes to shove, I hope they rely on it."

With the helicopter disappearing over the next ridge, Blackshaw pushed out from beneath the rock overhang and resumed his descent. Del's ravine turned out to be a small box canyon.

Del looked as though he were watching his step around a lunatic as much as taking care of his footing on the hillside scree.

At the floor of the canyon, Blackshaw tore down the Threadcutter as best he could. Fortunately, the gun's tolerances were loose by dint of their Soviet design, and its recent bath in the subterranean stream was all fresh water. Del watched the reassembly process, which was swift. Blackshaw snapped in the magazine, but only after each round had been wiped and inspected.

Blackshaw let his gaze range down the canyon for a few minutes. "I need to fire at least one shot to see what's going on with the scope."

"I get it," said Del.

"See where that light layer of rock jumps up into the darker layer on that wall?"

Del wasn't long in spotting the place. "About a hundred four yards, past that ponderosa pine."

Blackshaw appraised Del, and his estimate of distance, with new respect. "That's it."

"No good," said Del.

"What?" asked Blackshaw, confounded. He had struggled with rules of engagement on the battlefield, but never in an empty box canyon.

"If after everything you saw on the cavern walls, a bullet mark is what you want to leave behind here, that's on you," Del explained. "But look in that tree. Ben, that's a Plumbeous Vireo nest hanging there right close to your flight path."

"You think they're setting eggs?"

"Or chicks, by now. You want to find out with a stray round?" asked Del.

Blackshaw suppressed his exasperation, and reassessed the distant rock wall. After a moment, he called it. "The dip in the dark stratum to the right of the first spot. Ten *yards* to the right. We good?"

Del found the place, glanced back and forth between the new target and the Vireo nest twice, and nodded.

Blackshaw raised the Threadcutter to his shoulder, and peered through the sight. He squeezed his trigger hand, and the gun jerked, emitting a sound between a puff and snap. A small cloud of dust drifted away from the target on the light breeze.

"Kinda low," said Del.

"Ya think?" asked Blackshaw.

"And to the right. About five o'clock."

Blackshaw adjusted the windage and elevation. At least the sight's mount seemed not to have shifted in the buffeting waters of the cavern. He deemed that a miracle. "I'm going to try one more. Any bugs or flowers I should look out for?"

"I'd let you know," Del said, with a straight face.

"I'm sure you would," said a wry Blackshaw.

This time the bullet struck the rock wall where it was intended.

They both heard the returning helicopter's rotors at the same time, and hustled beneath a tree growing next to the canyon wall before the aircraft crested the ridge.

"They're flying a search grid," said Del.

The helicopter buzzed on without changing course.

Blackshaw asked, "If you have a problem with me shooting at rocks today what happens tonight—"

Del fixed Blackshaw with a look devoid of any sentimentality. "Live by the sword, die by it."

"The bad ones," agreed Blackshaw.

"I meant *you*," said Del.

CHAPTER 60

THE CUSTOMS AND Border Protection office was humming. The team in the conference room, including Lowry, Wilde, Van Sickel, and Haberman were seated in a strategy and tactics meeting.

They were joined by Otto DeGore from the Nogales Immigration and Customs Enforcement suboffice for Enforcement and Removal Operations. DeGore was wearing a suit and tie, but it was obvious he still wore thick Level IV body armor underneath the office threads as a hold-over from his days patrolling the border.

Another fresh face, one that was plainly aware he had received one of the last invitations to the party, belonged to Kirby Rumball, the current Sheriff of Chochise County.

DeGore asked, "Can you all catch Kirby and me up on where things stand? What did you see at the MAIm camp?"

Van Sickel, as their office host, led off. "We still have no word on our pilots. PNC doesn't have any Tahoes registered to it, but there are two known Rot-Irons who own the make and model sold with the same make and model tires of the tread marks we found near crash site."

Mike Haberman, from the Tucson FBI office, said, "The camp reeked of weed. We've got probable cause to toss the whole place on that alone."

"That's pretty thin soup, Mike," said Sheriff Rumball. "You want the DEA jumping in on this, too?"

"I like the way you're thinking, Mike," said DeGore, who was clearly a man in favor of action. "Pershing, Molly, what about the suspects in that photo?"

Wilde said, "So far, all we have is a PNC connection from Rufus Colquette's ink. Now, where the trend for hate groups is to steer away from brick-and-mortar sites to go underground to recruit from and disseminate information via websites, Reddit, and subreddits being among the foremost virtual town halls for hate-group sympathizers, Malthys still runs a large physical plant, his compound, and he has brought significant membership with him from there to this MAIm camp."

Rumball asked, "What about your unsub who initially passed the Sha'Quan Stewart photo to authorities back east."

Lowry said, "Technically, he's not an unsub. We believe his name is Blackshaw, Benjamin F. We're viewing him as a CI at this time."

DeGore pressed, "A Confidential informant? So where is he? Why isn't he informing?"

Wilde said, "Based on past experience, his value as an asset is at times—troubling. He doesn't spoon-feed on request. He can't, likely because he's not embedded with any known gang, or terrorist or hate group. But we believe he is also in this area."

"What's your leverage over Blackshaw. A reduction of sentencing? Do you pay him?" asked DeGore.

Lowry admitted, "He has never been in custody. He has never been charged with any crime. Evidence of wrongdoing against him is thin. Circumstantial, at best. Strong-arming him could cost us an asset who is more valuable in the field."

"Blackshaw's a birddog. He tends to get a ball rolling in a given direction," said Wilde. "And if his brief history with us is any indication, he might also be present when the ball—*stops* rolling."

DeGore said, "So, he's just like those people at Camp MAIm. He's a vigilante."

"For good or ill, Otto," said Lowry, "he's *our* vigilante."

"When he feels like it," said Rumball, with disgust. "What can we expect from him?"

Wilde said, "That's hard to say. He's a volunteer. A Good Samaritan with some interesting skills. But, as Pershing indicated, we don't have any real leverage over him."

An impatient Van Sickel spoke up. "Great about Blackshaw, but I want to get back to my pilots. Nobody but MAIm was running patrols two nights ago. It seems ridiculous to take them at their word that nobody saw the helo crash, or made contact with my people afterward."

DeGore asked, "Maybe your CI found the crew."

Wilde said, "My sense is that if Blackshaw is actually in the area as we suspect, and he did find the pilots, Wanda would have them back already."

"That's your sense, is it? *Jesus*," sneered Rumball.

"We do have one PNC fatality already," said Haberman. "No suspects at this time. Might have been an internal dispute."

Van Sickel added, "Or Blackshaw's good deed for the day. We don't have slugs to compare yet, or even type, since both shots were through-and-through, with whole lot of desert to comb to recover them. And no brass. Why the hell don't we go in and toss the place? It's Federal land. Do we really even need a warrant?"

Sheriff Rumball was quick to point out, "It's Federal land within the boundary of Cochise County."

Wilde said, "The Rot-Irons and the PNC are heavily armed. They make up a significant portion of the MAIm group. And the ranchers are no push-overs."

Haberman saw where Wilde was going. "She's right. There's a strong *sovereign citizen* ethos informing all of them and their actions. Even with every *i* dotted, and every *t* crossed, odds are good they won't give a crap about properly executed warrants and jurisdiction. They think laws don't apply to them. They'll say screw off, and if we don't, it's a stand-off at best, a shoot-out at worst."

"But on Federal land?" said DeGore. "I'd like to see them try."

Van Sickel said, "No, you wouldn't. Now I'm thinking the media would be on us before a single shot was fired. They haven't invested full camera crews yet, only because there's no story, no bang, and no blood. The wildfires are getting the airtime for now. It would be nice to keep it that way, eager as I am to go in."

Rumball said, "So you want to de-escalate again, like Bureau of Land Management did with those ranchers who owed back grazing fees? It's no wonder they're going after illegals themselves. They think you Feds got no teeth. No sand to go head to head."

"They're your flight crew, Wanda," said DeGore. "First, we look after our own. And it might put a pin in the MAIm balloon if CBP and ICE showed a little more leg in that area. That's their beef, right? Not enough man-power on the border there?"

"If Blackshaw is here, it's about Colquette," said Lowry.

"That's a damn big *if*," said DeGore.

Lowry continued, "It's likely Colquette unwittingly divulged intel to Blackshaw on where he was going. My point is this, Otto. Think of half the Western movies you ever saw. A lone stranger comes into town, and takes over law enforcement, overruling, and eventually outgunning a hamstrung sheriff who won't, or is too afraid to act against the threat, which might be an evil rancher, a dangerous gunslinger, whatever. You understand me. The stranger is a dictator pro-tem, welcomed by some, reviled by others. He comes, and does what others won't do in a vacuum of the rule of law. As the dust settles, he's typically offered a badge by grateful citizens. But he always declines it, and disappears."

"Rule of law hasn't failed," said Haberman. "This is an ongoing investigation."

Wilde pointed out. "To Blackshaw, maybe it failed in Richmond when police there missed Colquette after Blackshaw handed him over on a platter. I don't think he tends to offer second chances. To us, I mean. In Blackshaw's thinking, we're the weak sister. And he's not a man to shrug off the screw-up in Richmond and say, *oh well, too bad.* Blackshaw finishes what he starts."

"Sounds like a real head-case," said DeGore.

"Not to knock your CI, but it's the same mentality as those MAIm characters," said Sheriff Rumball. "Jumping in to plug a porous border. Volunteering in the face of failed authority."

Van Sickel cautioned, "That perception won't be changed by a show-down, especially a bloody one. We need to reallocate resources, and detain border crossers legally."

Mike Haberman said, "If I could make a suggestion, the Stewart murder is a hate crime. That, plus your CI's presence in the area, might be enough to get us a search warrant, and even an arrest warrant, for Colquette and the others in the photo. But not for the MAIm camp south of Bisbee."

"Then where?" asked DeGore.

"At the PNC compound," said Haberman. "We go there first, rule out that Colquette's there. Then a case could be made for serving a warrant at the MAIm camp. Most of Malthys's honchos are down here. Might be less trouble starting up north."

DeGore sounded angry when he asked, "With all due respect, Mike, are we letting fear of bad press wag our dog?"

Though not as bloodthirsty as DeGore, Van Sickel sounded skeptical for her own reasons. "Strategically, if Colquette isn't there at the compound, and he is at this damn camp down here, then Malthys gets word of the first search, and he can stash Colquette anywhere."

DeGore said, "Easy. We hit both places at once."

Van Sickel reminded everyone, "The Tahoes are not PNC. They're registered to Rot-Irons. If Rot-Irons have my crew, they might shelter Colquette, too."

Lowry asked, "Would Malthys turn a PNC asset like Colquette over to bikers?"

"Do you think Malthys sees Colquette as an asset or a liability at this point?" asked Van Sickel.

Wilde said softly, "We're talking about coordinating three high-profile, simultaneous operations with a very high potential for violence."

No one spoke. Ever the Hotspur, DeGore said, "I'm game." He leveled a challenging glare at the other four, waiting for their answers.

CHAPTER 61

RUFUS COLQUETTE SUFFOCATED in Malthys's tent. The sun heated the fragile shelter's fabric, which turned the interior into a sauna. Opening the flap exposed the interior to more smoke from the wildfire. Sealing the tent built up carbon dioxide, and made Rufus feel sick to his stomach, as though he would pass out. Anger kept him awake.

The car ride from Virginia to Arizona had been a different kind of hell. He had killed the little jig, but Nyqvist, Oren, and The Major had treated him like a damn criminal instead of a hero, just for sending Blackshaw the picture. Compared to the serial beatings dealt him by his three travel companions along the way, Blackshaw's interest and his praise for a deed well done were that of a proper sovereign gentleman. But maybe it was really Blackshaw who accidentally showed that photo to the wrong person. Blackshaw was the dumb-ass. Why couldn't Oren, Nyqvist, and The Major understand that? And now Colquette was under house arrest. They wouldn't even let him hunt for wets on their patrols. He wondered if maybe this was just more PNC initiation stuff, as if his kill wasn't enough.

The tent flap was unzipped from outside, and Malthys entered. *Thank God* thought Colquette. Finally, somebody who would get what he was about.

Malthys handed him a cold beer, which tasted so good going down that half the bottle was gone before the first swig was done.

"I appreciate you keeping a low profile here," Malthys said.

"Not like I got a choice," whined Colquette.

"And your kill. I'll be putting the picture up on the Monkeyland site, once the heat dies down. And once we tile out your faces."

"Tile out—" Colquette was stricken.

"You're a valued soldier, Rufus. But keeping your face in the shot, and the other guys', with the cops, the Feds—your courage is only as good as your anonymity. You understand, that, right?"

Colquette wasn't sure if he understood, but he wasn't happy about how it sounded. "I guess."

"The main thing is that everybody at PNC will know of your bravery," said Malthys. "When we're done here, we're going to have a triumph for you back up at the compound. Great food. More beer if you want it. I bet you'll have your choice of pussy, too. You're coming up in the world. I envy you, brother Rufus. I really do."

Colquette brightened. "So let's go back now."

"We still have work to do here, first. And I keep my best men close to me," said Malthys.

"But I'm not doing anything! I can't breathe!"

"With the fires, the air's not much better outside, I promise," said Malthys, cracking a smile. "Stay put for today, like you said you would. Tonight's another story."

Colquette asked, "What's happening tonight?"

"Patrol."

"I'm going out?" asked Colquette. He was eager to get to work on the wetbacks.

"You're not just going out," said Malthys. "You're going with Foss and me."

Colquette's emotions surged. He'd get away from this damn tent. He would be patrolling with the leader of the Pure Nation Comitatus. He'd get to meet Gunter Foss, a big player in the Rot-Irons. Not for the first time, he wished PNC were more into motorcycles. Peeking from the tent, he thought those Rot-Irons looked so badass riding by all together, their engines banging loud as gunfire. Regardless, soon he'd have another chance to prove himself in front of the right people, and he was ready.

"Thank you, Malthys, sir!" Colquette was embarrassed at how desperate he sounded.

Malthys did not seem to notice. "Finish your beer, and get some rest. It's going to be a long night."

Colquette reined in his tone when he said, "Will do."

Malthys left, completely zipping the tent closed again behind him. Colquette did not care. Nor did Colquette see Malthys nod to Foss outside that everything was ready to tie off at least one troubling loose end this evening.

CHAPTER 62

AGENT WILDE STOPPED Van Sickel after the meeting. Lowry waited down the hall. For now, Sheriff Rumball and ICE Agent DeGore were off to war-game the simultaneous three-pronged raid concept, though it had been voted down for now.

"Wanda, tell me more about your air crew. The uniform, I mean," said Wilde.

Not for the first time, Van Sickel scanned Wilde's high-end tailoring. "Why do you want to know about that?"

"At the MAIm camp," said Wilde, "there was a guy. A Rot-Iron."

"More than one. What did you see?" asked Van Sickel, growing intrigued.

"Bikers wear those sleeveless jackets, like vests. With their gang colors on them," said Wilde.

"Their *cuts*," Van Sickel clarified.

"Cuts. Right. But they wear them *over* their leather coats," said Molly, confirming. "Do your crews wear flight jackets?"

"In warmer weather, not often. Even at altitude, the aircraft all have heat. Some wear jackets for the extra pockets," said Van Sickel. "What did you see?"

"There was this biker wearing his cuts over a jacket. But the jacket looked nylon. A little shiny."

"We only issue in Nomex. It's fire retardant. A little shiny, I guess," said Van Sickel, catching Wilde's drift, and growing impatient. "What color was the jacket under this guy's cuts?"

"Your crew, Greenway and Eckhart. They're tall women. They would wear a larger jacket. Even if it were lightweight. Large enough for a medium build biker to take as a trophy."

Van Sickel stepped into Wilde's personal space. "Molly, what color?"

"It was khaki," said Wilde.

Taking a slow, deep breath of restraint, Van Sickel asked, "Did you see any patches on the coat sleeve? Emblems?" She grabbed a passing pilot by the arm and dragged the bewildered man over to Wilde. "Like *these*?"

"It's possible. I don't remember. Maybe," said Wilde, her usual confidence as an keen observer shaken.

Van Sickel called the team back to the conference room, yelling for everyone by name. To Molly, she growled with through gritted teeth, "You could have mentioned this sooner."

CHAPTER 63

BLACKSHAW AND DEL were back at the ridgeline of a hill observing the MAIm encampment. Blackshaw scanned the tents through the Threadcutter's zeroed scope.

Del said, "You want to pick off Colquette from here."

"Just want to see him again," said Blackshaw, without committing.

"And you'd be okay *seeing* Malthys too, I take it," said Del sounding wry.

Blackshaw said nothing. After several minutes, Del spoke again. "A sniper can really take camp morale down a notch."

"Reckon so," said Blackshaw. "Seems the guys running the show down there hang out around that table, about two o'clock."

"If you cut the head off the Hydra, two more heads grow back," said Delshay.

"Damn if you don't talk in riddles, Del. I don't know where you stand," Blackshaw muttered. "I wonder if you do."

A half hour passed. The smoke from the wildfire ebbed and thickened with the breezes, sometimes reducing visibility to a blur, and the camp vanishing like a desert Brigadoon.

Once, when the smoke became particularly dense, Blackshaw asked, "What's your take on the fire? What's happening with it around here?"

Del watched the smoke wafting through the hills around the camp, then turned his attention to the sky. Ten minutes passed. He sounded unhappy when he said, "The fire itself is building to the east. To the southwest, that's a thunderhead climbing up. In general, I'd say odds are against rain, but another round of lightning strikes could mean fresh starts, and restarts, with more wind. Dusk will get interesting. Overnight'll be fascinating."

"So, if we get more fire between us and that camp, the whole walk through those caves under the fire would've been for nothing," said Blackshaw.

"Do you mean a cool Zen kind of nothing, or a futile kind of nothing?"

Blackshaw took his eye away from the scope long enough to confirm Delshay was grinning.

Returning his eye at the scope, Blackshaw noticed a commotion near one of the tents. The smoke made immediate comprehension of what he was seeing difficult.

"See in front of that Rot-Irons tent?" asked Blackshaw.

"I got it," said Del.

A Rot-Iron had pushed out of one of the tents by the camp's edge, and had dropped to his knees, as if he were vomiting.

"Too much party," said Del.

"That's not puke," said Blackshaw. "It's blood."

Clutching at his throat, the fallen biker rallied comrades to his side. Then, at the tent's entrance, Blackshaw could only watch as a black woman in a stained khaki flight suit staggered into the open, looking confused by her surroundings. Noticing the scrub at the camp's edge, she pushed herself through obvious pain toward the desert. Three more bikers surrounded her, bashed her off her feet, and dragged her back into the tent, her mouth smothered by a Rot-Iron throttle hand.

"They got a hostage," said Del. "What do you think?"

Blackshaw was disgusted by what he had witnessed, and yet, not surprised. "A hydra's not real," he said. "Those bastards won't grow new heads."

CHAPTER 64

GUNTER FOSS WAS insensed. Cootie, the sentry he had posted to guard the pilot, was bleeding out in front of him despite the best efforts of Jimmy-Jim, a former army medic-turned-Rot-Iron, to staunch throat and abdominal wounds. Five feet away, the pilot lay on her cot barely conscious, balled in the fetal position, and rocking from the beating the three guys who caught her had dished out before Foss could intervene.

"What the hell happened?" demanded Foss.

Only Stork, a Rot-Iron so-dubbed because of his tall, scrawny look and an uncanny penchant for siring children with multiple women and then quickly abandoning them, dared to answer. "Cootie thought he heard something. He went in, and came back out a minute later all fucked up."

Jimmy-Jim, his hands slippery with blood, pulled a monofilament stitch tight in Cootie's neck with a big fish hook he used as a needle, said, "He needs a hospital."

Everyone in the tent knew there was no chance of Foss agreeing to that. Jimmy-Jim might as well have pronounced that Cootie was already dead.

Malthys flew in through the front of the tent and took in the scene. "Gunter?"

"She tried to get away," said Foss.

Stork was holding pressure on Cootie's abdomen with an oily rag, but even so, it was saturated with blood.

"Thanks, I picked up on that," said Malthys.

"What's happening outside?" asked Foss.

"The tent opens toward the desert," reasoned Malthys. "It was quick. Only Rot-Irons saw anything, and they aren't talking. Is she going to live?"

"Who gives a damn," said Foss.

"You should," said Malthys. "We need her alive if anything goes wrong."

"I'm about to lose a brother here, Malthys. I think something's wrong."

"Really," said Malthys. "This half-dead jig takes down one of your boys—if you ask me, she culled a weak one from your herd."

Foss lunged at Malthys, knocking him down and firing jabs at his ribs before Jimmy-Jim and Stork could pull their boss off.

"You shut the fuck up!" shouted Foss. "I'll fucking rip you apart!"

"A little louder," said Malthys, rolling to his knees. "I don't think Pardue heard you. He's going to bail on us as it is."

"Not a chance," said Foss, mastering his rage, and shaking off his men. "He's known about this bitch for hours. If we go down, he goes with us."

Malthys digested this.

Jimmy-Jim rose and said, "I'm out of fishing line. I got more on my bike."

Stork held compression on Cootie's gut and throat as Jimmy-Jim stepped outside. Every able-bodied man inside turned when they heard Jimmy-Jim grunt, then collapse to the ground, his left foot still inside, and a dark splatter blocking light high on the tent flap.

Malthys put his head outside the tent, but retreated inside right away. He grabbed Jimmy-Jim's boot, and started pulling. "Help me, goddammit! Get him in here!"

Foss and Stork got grips on the leg of their inert brother's jeans and yanked. Both men swore when Jimmy-Jim left a crimson smear on the ground on his way back inside. His head was missing from the eyebrows north; his brain was an addled scoop of oatmeal slopped into a bloody bone bowl.

CHAPTER 65

ON THE RIDGE, Blackshaw kept his eye to the scope, but with a sixth sense, his right hand snaked out to collect the ejected cartridge of the round he had just fired. The body of the biker he had plugged had been hauled into the tent within seconds of dropping him. *Taking in the trash* struck Blackshaw as fresh.

The quick glance from someone inside the tent could have made a second target, but Blackshaw wanted two things from the first shot; a thought-provoking commotion among the MAIm leadership, and no panicked stampede among the rank and file.

Del was quiet, his eyes wide. Blackshaw reckoned his friend had never seen a man killed with intent. He was wrong.

Del said, "Damn. You blew his hair off. Welcome to the club."

Blackshaw waited for him to say more.

Five, then ten heartbeats passed. Del said, "My sister, Gouyen. She can handle herself. She was with the Apache 8. All women wildfire fighters. But the day she turned twenty-one, she went out. She celebrated. It wasn't even a biker bar. A couple bastards, they were Rot-Irons. They came on smooth. A few more drinks, and Gouyen's girlfriends said it was time to get her into the car they'd come in. She said no to them, but she accepted those guys' invitation to go for a spin on their bikes. When they were done, they left her for dead in the desert. We looked and looked for her. She got home two days later. She walked. Too ashamed to hitch a ride."

"What club, Del?"

"I found one of the guys who did it," said Del. "I took him out to the desert." Del gently thumbed the edge of his axe. "He's still there, in different places. Scattered around. He didn't walk home. So, Ben, I guess it's the Killed-A-Rot-Iron Club. You're late to the party, but hey man, welcome aboard."

CHAPTER 66

MALTHYS AND FOSS stared at Jimmy-Jim's corpse, which lay next to Cootie, who had coughed up blood, convulsed, and pegged out just after Jimmy-Jim lost his head. Within the space of a few minutes, Foss had lost two Rot-Iron brothers-in-arms, and he was inches away from the kind of apoplexy that would get even more men killed if Malthys couldn't keep him focused. Foss didn't seem the contemplative type. He already had a pistol in his hand, with nowhere constructive to point it.

Foss demanded, "What'd you see when you looked out."

"Jimmy-Jim, and a whole lot of open desert."

Then the second most important question occurred to Foss. "Did anyone else see?"

"Besides the shooter? No," quipped Malthys, to his peril. "The tent opens away from camp. Your boys played it cool. You should, too."

That brought Foss's quivering gun muzzle within inches of Malthys's eye. "Don't tell me what to do!"

"Wouldn't dream," said Malthys. "But we've got bigger fish to fry. Last night was a test. It worked. Tonight, we take the big shipment, right?"

Foss eyed Stork as he lowered the gun. "You think a Fed just up and shot Jimmy-Jim?"

Malthys was thinking about the guy Rufus Colquette had blabbed to on the bus. *Blackshaw.* Maybe they were dealing with a vigilante who was praying on vigilantes.

"I have no idea," said Malthys. "Feds usually show up at company strength, try to intimidate, then negotiate, *then* they blow you to Kingdom Come. We've given them no cause. If it wasn't one of your own guys with a grudge against Jimmy-Jim, who knows? We didn't see. Maybe somebody's trying to cut in on our action, but I can tell you, my people have no idea why we're here."

"I haven't said shit about it to my boys," said Foss, glancing at Stork again.

Stork put up defensive hands, palm out, and said, "I don't know fuck-all what you're talking about, okay?"

Foss said, "See?"

Malthys said, "So, maybe it's some cockweed who's got a problem with bikers. Or maybe it was a coyote. If we really do stop the wets storming the border, that'd hurt their business, right? Anyway, he's probably long gone."

Malthys did not believe that line for a moment, but it seemed to calm Foss down. "Let's stay cool. We do tonight like we planned. Tomorrow, we do whatever we want. Stay for more. Leave, and do it again someplace else with a new cover."

Greenway moaned on the cot.

Before Foss could target the chopper pilot with his bottled rage, Malthys said, "And we keep her like we planned. Flip her back to the Feds if we need to, and we're the good guys. If we don't need to, she's all yours."

Foss shook his head. "I think she knows what happened to the other one."

"Okay," said Malthys. "Her family would still like to have a body to bury."

Foss drew his knife. "I'm not sitting in here while this tent gets ventilated by some wingnut."

He slashed a vertical slit in the back wall of the tent, and departed through the new exit facing away from the desert in a swirl of wildfire smoke.

CHAPTER 67

"THERE'S A HOSTAGE," said Del.

"I've got eyes," said Blackshaw.

They had retreated down the back side of the hill from which Blackshaw had shot the Rot-Iron. Blackshaw wanted to change his observation post right away, in case anyone in the camp had by some miracle spotted the shooting position.

"How do you think she's doing, now that you killed one of their men?" asked Del.

"Depends on whether the leadership has a good handle on themselves, and on whoever else is in that tent."

"You rolled the dice for her," said Del.

"She's valuable to them only if she stays alive."

"Their values are different from yours," said Del. "At least a little bit," he added, after a moment's thought.

"A few minutes ago, they just were wondering how to get through another dull day in the desert. Now, I reckon they're worried about getting killed any second," said Blackshaw. "We've put them off balance. They won't broadcast losing that man."

"What now? You can't whittle them down from out here. You don't have enough bullets."

"True. So we meet them out here," said Blackshaw. "They have those patrols, looking for the immigrants coming across the border. The patrols come out, the bosses among them. That little drone we found has

something to do with all this—the real reason they're here acting all concerned about the border. And if they change that patrol routine, or dial it
down, it signals to their men that they're cowards, or lazy. When they do
come, we need to be ready."

CHAPTER 68

ADELLE CONGREVE'S INTUITION was telling her things she would rather ignore. As she walked through the MAIm encampment, flashing her beautiful smile around like sunlight, and encouraging the patrols as they went into the desert, she sensed things were unraveling around her. It was a terrible mistake to bring Malthys here. Malthys had brought those disgusting bikers without anyone else's approval; not Dressler's, nor Cutlip's, and certainly without Pardue's okay. The usually straight-arrow PNC followers got into camp and acted like Amish kids on rumspringa, or spoiled college brats wilding in Fort Lauderdale during Spring Break. Malthys showed no interest at all in reining them in.

The outlaw bikers behaved exactly as one would expect; rowdy thugs perpetuating an adolescent rebellion long into adulthood, when mid-life crises blew even bigger holes in their existing moral deficits. Now Congreve felt it would have been better if the MAIm camp had been composed only of true-blue ranchers. When otherwise law-abiding citizens take the law into their own hands, it meant something. Congreve sensed that when religious freaks and miscreants took up her cause, the struggle became tainted.

Even Congreve's own behavior troubled her. Underneath she knew she should not have thrown herself at Timon Pardue. He was a little drunk at the time, and of course, Congreve's affections had once again proven irresistible. She felt bad about it. Though her husband Ricky-Ray was many years dead, every encounter with a man since then felt like a betrayal of her one true love. Pardue in particular highlighted her disloyalty.

That was because Congreve was discovering that her feelings for the beleaguered former sheriff ran deeper than a mere fling. This man had character, grit, and a quiet strength about him. Yes, she had chatted with him at county council meetings often enough, but when she flew out into the desert to visit him just a few days ago, she felt like she was seeing Pardue for the first time there in his natural element. He had served Cochise County with all his heart. Seeing him out here in exile, far from the petty concerns of politics, transformed him into a romantic figure. Adelle Congreve was nothing if not romantic. What a picture Pardue had made walking into camp with his pretty horse.

Could she start over with Pardue? She wondered if the damage she'd caused in that sweaty tussle could ever be undone. Did he think ill of her, view her as forward, or see her as some sort of camp tramp? There was no time like the present to explore these feelings with her chosen man. She changed course, and strode toward Pardue's tent.

CHAPTER 69

"THERE'RE *TWO* DEAD?" Timon Pardue could not believe what Gunter Foss was telling him. "Is one of them the pilot?"

Foss had burst into Pardue's tent as if he were terrified. The biker accepted the Solo cup from Pardue, and held it for a stiff pour from the former sheriff's whiskey bottle. He drank off half the measure, and savored the burn in his throat, waiting for its calming wave to wash through his system.

"That bitch is still alive," said Foss. "It's two of my men. Fly-girl had a damn knife, and took down Cootie. Jimmy-Jim was sewing Cootie up, went out for some more line, and *boom*! His head came off."

"I don't understand," said Pardue.

"Somebody shot Jimmy-Jim right outside my tent!"

Pardue waited while Foss slugged back the rest of his drink. Then he asked, "Was this Jimmy-Jim getting it on with somebody's old lady?"

"No, dammit!" wailed Foss. "Nobody *heard* a shot. Nobody *saw* anybody take a shot. It was somebody out in the desert."

Pardue was skeptical. "Somebody with a rifle that nobody saw or heard."

"That's what I mean."

"So your beat-up hostage—"

"*Our* hostage," corrected Foss.

"—killed one of your men, and somebody else killed another one. And you don't see that as an occupational hazard of being a Rot-Iron?" asked

Pardue, chuckling at the absurdity of Foss's complaint. Then Pardue got serious. "Why are you really here, Gunter? You and Malthys."

"We're patriots," protested Foss, taking umbrage. "We want to protect our borders from—"

"That's horseshit," said Pardue. "Patriots believe in something. They believe in law. In the Constitution."

"We believe in *freedom*," declaimed Foss, with pompous certainty his jingoistic statement would answer all questions, end all arguments,

Pardue shook his head. "Freedom to be jackholes, intimidating real Americans, and running dope wherever you want because everybody's scared of you. It's anarchy for you, and laws and rules for everyone else. Isn't that it?"

Pardue slapped the cup out of Foss's hand. "Get out of my tent and go to hell. You made a mess out of honest civil disobedience bringing that poor pilot here. My reputation's done. Go on. I said *git!*"

His fingers rendered clumsy from booze, Foss was slow to get a grip on his pistol. Pardue's gun was out in plenty of time. He gestured with it toward the front of the tent. Pardue may have had a drink or three under his belt, but there was no mistaking his unwavering willingness to shoot Foss dead then and there. Despite his justified concern about Pardue, Foss gave a glance through the tent's door looking for gunmen before stepping back out into the open. Nobody fired, but Adelle Congreve was marching straight at him, and she glared at him like he was a turd floating in a punch bowl.

CHAPTER 70

TEDDYBEAR CHOYA MOUNTED the lead truck. Paolo Estrella y Castro climbed into the passenger seat next to his boss. Choya was excited. He was driving the lead truck in a convoy of five vehicles filled with Estrella y Castro's little flying spiders, each one loaded with a kilo of cocaine. Too bad the Guinness Book of World Records didn't track the exploits of super-criminals like himself. Tomorrow morning, he would have some new entries, including most dope transported by autonomously navigated drone swarms, highest dollar value contraband ever shipped across the border without human mules or supervision. Maybe Choya would write the Crook's Book of Badass Records himself. He was confident his name would appear quite often.

They drove out of Choya's compound in Sonora past the fresh little grave belonging to the boy Manuel who had screwed up building the drone that did not return home. It was fitting that Manuel would not be going home either. There was a little cross made of wood to mark the patch of fresh-churned earth. Teddybear Choya wasn't a monster, after all.

They needed several hours to drive north to the spot where the drones would be launched. Gunter Foss still had to transmit the landing location. Choya hoped the place Foss picked would be large enough, and that he would have enough of his gang on hand to take the cocaine packets off the drones before they flew home. It was going to be glorious to watch the spiders take to the air. It would be amazing to watch all that dope, and all that money, drop out of the sky. Pennies from Heaven.

Now that the drones had been proven, Choya's deal with Foss made it clear that once the drones crossed the border, Foss owed payment for the drugs in full. Choya would not be held responsible for losses resulting from screw-ups on the other side. With that insurance in place, Choya felt in his bones that this was going to be an exciting evening.

CHAPTER 71

IT WAS DECIDED. Otto DeGore, of ICE/ERO, was prepping a
tactical team to serve a warrant at the main Rot-Iron camp in Wickenburg.
Mike Haberman of the Tucson FBI office would lead the detachment going
in at Malthys's main PNC compound in northern Cochise County.

Molly Wilde and Pershing Lowry, of the D.C. FBI office would join
with Wanda Van Sickel and other agents of the CBP, as well as Cochise
County Sheriff Kirby Rumball, leading a larger team hitting the MAIm encampment south of Bisbee.

A judge who was pals with the Chief Justice of the Arizona Supreme
Court coughed up the necessary warrants as soon as his superior learned
that one of the MAIm honchos was none other than Timon Pardue, who
had jailed his new appointee months ago.

Van Sickel's agents and Rumball's tactical officers were staging in the
CBP garage. The contingent heading into MAIm was fifty strong. Van
Sickel requisitioned and was granted clearance for three UAVs, one to get
intel from above each raid site in real time.

Van Sickel stopped by the pair from Washington. "I have preliminary
on the cause of our chopper's crash. I don't know what to make of it."

"Of what?" asked Lowry.

"NTSB guys were examining the boom that separated from the fuselage. You remember," explained Van Sickel. "Looking around those holes,
the ones that look like double-ought buckshot. One of the techs tilted the

boom, and slugs rolled out. Looked like a bunch of .22 bullets, but when we got them in the lab—"

"Bullets!" said Wilde.

"No," said Van Sickel. "That's the point. They're steel. Deformed steel balls, about an eighth of an inch in diameter. On a hunch, the lab tested them. They got residue consistent with C4 explosive, and some with epoxy resin."

"That's a bomb," said Lowry. "But the bearings came from *outside* the fuselage. That was obvious."

Molly said, "It's a specific kind of bomb, Pershing. Steel bearings, epoxy, and C4 sounds like an anti-personnel mine."

"Bingo. My guys think it was a Claymore," said Van Sickel.

"But how did a land mine get above the helicopter?" Lowry asked. "You confirmed your bird was the only aircraft up there."

Van Sickel said, "At the time of the crash, we got a Doppler return on a flock of birds close by. Now we're not so sure what it was. We're checking the data more closely."

"So all we know for now," said Wilde, "is what we knew before. This wasn't an accidental forced landing. It was a shoot-down."

"We know more than that," said Lowry. "Something cloaked, or something very small, took some kind of IED aloft and brought down a helicopter."

"I'll keep you posted," said Van Sickel. She moved off to confer with Sheriff Rumball about the evening's festivities.

Wilde said to Lowry, "This is going to be interesting."

Lowry said, "By *interesting*, do you mean a second Antietam?"

Wilde pursed her lips, not wanting to say more about her misgivings.

Lowry lowered his voice. "Van Sickel's looking for her pilots. Rumball's only too happy to stick it to this Timon Pardue character, the former sheriff. Neither of them is keen on Malthys, or the Rot-Irons, or anyone acting in a vigilante capacity. At the moment, it seems you and I are the only ones keeping Rufus Colquette and his friends in mind."

Wilde watched as the tactical team checked weapons and donned body armor and helmets. Lowry's feelings for Molly put him in two minds. He was concerned for her safety during what was to come; but he loved her enough never to ask that she compromise her career in the face of danger.

"You don't have to do this," blurted Lowry, instantly regretting it.

"Why not?" asked Wilde in a steady voice. "Just because I'm pregnant?"

Lowry stared. "You're—"

Wilde smiled at Lowry, assessing his reaction, and pecked him on the cheek. "Bad timing?"

Lowry continued to stare as Wilde took off her khaki Dior scarf, spread it on the hood of a nearby Suburban, drew her pistol, and began carefully stripping it.

PART IV
DEEP BLOOD KETTLE

CHAPTER 72

DEL PULLED THE red plastic bag from his pack. Blackshaw remembered it contained the large pellet of extremely concentrated coyote poison.

Del said, "The Plains Indians had buffalo jumps. Back when there were buffalo. They'd pick their ground, turn it into a drive lane, improve it with natural baffles, rock cairns, and when the herd came through, they'd kick off a stampede. Run them for miles until they went over the cliff at the end. Blackfoot called them *pishkun*. Deep blood kettle."

Blackshaw asked, "You going to run those bastards off a cliff?"

"In the smoke, it's hard to see. People lose their way," mused Del. "And a cliff can mean a lot of things. The place you fall. The place you die."

"I don't know, Del. What if they don't lose their way?"

"It worked for ten thousand years." Del held up the red bag containing the ten-eighty. "And in the end, it's all about the journey."

"I believe I've misjudged you," admitted Blackshaw.

"You mean, *underestimated*."

Blackshaw left that alone. He said, "The stampede. Those buffalo went in the right direction toward the cliff, because they were driven from behind, right? And from the sides. But weren't they also following a very brave, very fast guy wearing a buffalo skin?"

"Yes," said Del. "The bison felt confident they were going in the right direction because of him."

"Reckon we know a thing or two about decoys on Smith Island," said Blackshaw. "Who'd you have in mind?"

Del just looked at Blackshaw. His gaze was steady, but his meaning was not clear, as if he were thinking of other things, in another time.

CHAPTER 73

MALTHYS AND STORK remained in Foss's tent with the injured pilot. It was hard for him to think clearly in the stifling heat and with Stork's fidgeting. The presence of two bodies, Cootie, and Jimmy-Jim, was not helping the atmosphere. Either the pilot had slashed into Cootie's bowel, or Stork's nerves were making him flatulent. Either way, there was a fecal stench wafting in there with them like a bilious wraith.

Despite the Andersonville atmosphere, Malthys needed to get his plan in order. Tonight, he would address the matter of Rufus Colquette while on patrol. The kid was a bone-headed idiot, totally unreliable. Perhaps Malthys would include Nyqvist, Oren, and The Major in the purge for their poor judgement in letting Colquette loose with that photograph.

Foss was another matter. Malthys suspected the Rot-Iron would stay the course to reel in the larger drone delivery tonight, but he could not be sure. There was no way Malthys would ask to postpone the patrol. It was too long in the planning. The percentage that the Rot-Irons owed PNC for the two deliveries would keep Malthys's operation afloat for two years; longer if he culled out all the followers whose bank accounts he had already fleeced and who were now dead weight.

The shooter in the desert could keep things interesting. Though the mysterious gunman had proven to be a threat once, odds were good he had left the area. Unless it was this Blackshaw guy. Only a lunatic would stir the Rot-Iron hornet nest, and then linger to suffer the stings.

Malthys wondered if, once the drug money was wired to the PNC's off-shore accounts, Adelle Congreve might be persuaded to give him a lift back to his compound in her chopper. The wildfire was getting close, after all. Leaving the camp tomorrow was looking more like an evacuation.

Not for the first time, Malthys considered that army surplus container Pardue had outside his tent. Foss had no idea what it was, or the unholy plague it contained. Whether it was a gift from God, or from the Devil, Malthys would figure out a way to use it to his advantage.

CHAPTER 74

BLACKSHAW WATCHED DEL apply a tiny green glob of Ten-Eighty poison to the spines of a jumping cactus. He was using a stick and his leather gloves, which proved cumbersome when the first few cactus lobes he attempted to smear broke away from the main plant and dropped to the earth. After those failures, Del used a much gentler touch. Now, a trail of daubed cactuses stretched out over forty yards through a ravine behind them.

Together, they had decided that the buffalo jump concept needed an update. They could not rely on the camp patrols to follow a specific path close to the MAIm boundaries. Yes, there was a beaten path, but Blackshaw and Del figured it would be safer to create this toxic drive lane farther from the camp, and decoy the patrol they chose into it, as if it were a chemical ambush.

Blackshaw wanted Colquette, if he presented himself, but would accept Malthys. He would take the lead Rot-Iron, too, if he emerged beyond the confines of the camp. Del knew the topography in the area, and a number of natural bottlenecks and gauntlets had presented themselves. The patrols would likely take high ground and the ridgelines, since they had no fear of skylining themselves. The immigrants they sought were unarmed, unless their coyote traffickers stayed with their charges farther north across the border than expected, before abandoning them in the desert to find the American Dream on their own, or die of thirst, whichever came first.

While Del extended the tainted drive line, Blackshaw mused aloud. "I saw a lot of those drone things."

"I believe you now," said Del touching the outermost spines of another jumping cactus with the Ten-Eighty.

"They were built to carry more than just the grenade," reflected Blackshaw.

"My bet's on dope," said Del, moving with gentle caution to the next cactus.

"I think you're right," Blackshaw admitted. "You think they're remote controlled?"

"Isn't that how those things work?"

"The military ones can be autonomous. They work far beyond line of sight. The ones over the Gulf were flown from Florida, and they could fly themselves for a time. But I never saw a flock swarming together like that. That's right sophisticated."

Del kept working, and said, "That's enough for this one. I still have plenty of this stuff for one, maybe two more drive lanes."

"Let's do it," said Blackshaw. "Gives us more options."

"We're going to have to clean this stuff up," said Del. "We can't leave it lying around once we're done."

"Fair enough. I guess at least one of us has to survive to do that," muttered Blackshaw.

Del stood up looking thoughtful. "That was *my* plan. What the heck is yours?"

Blackshaw didn't answer that. Instead, he continued with his earlier line of thought. "They can't fly forever. They have to land someplace so the dope can be recovered. A big, flat landing zone. Preferably with access to a nearby road for hauling the stuff out."

"Makes a kind of sense," said Del. "A lot of hills out here. And some trees. Won't be too many places like you're talking about. That's if there're more of those things coming."

"Let's look around again," suggested Blackshaw. "I think dope and those fonny boys in that camp are connected. Hold off on putting out more of that goop until we find a likely spot. Close to camp. Close to a road. Open and flat. Not too many trees, like you said."

Del considered Blackshaw's words for a moment, and offered, "There's a place I know of."

"Night's coming," said Blackshaw. "Let's go give it a look-see now, maybe kill us a couple birds with one stone."

CHAPTER 75

LOWRY WAITED POLITELY, and perhaps prudently, until Wilde had reassembled her pistol and holstered it. As she retied her scarf, he asked, "When were you going to tell me, Molly?"

"Not before I was sure," said Wilde.

"You took a test."

"No. But a girl knows," said Wilde. "Those tests are just for confirmation, I think. I mean, nobody buys one for the heck of it, right?"

Lowry still could not believe what he was hearing. The moment was made all the more surreal by the martial preparations going on around them in the CBP garage, with men and women arming themselves to the teeth to descend on the MAIm encampment.

"In light of this—development, are you sure participating tonight is the best course?" asked Lowry.

"Are you worried about me?" asked Wilde, completely charmed by Lowry's concern.

Lowry treaded lightly. "Yes, but I'm worried about both of you now."

"In that case," said Wilde, "if it gets ugly, you can just think of me as shooting for two."

"I'm not sure a potential firefight with heavily armed vigilantes would be considered the best prenatal care."

"This is all very noble of you, Persh," said Wilde. "Now shut up and get ready."

"I am ready. If you are," said Lowry.

"Why Pershing Lowry," said Wilde, facing him. "That sounded dangerously close to a proposal. Are you proposing to me?"

Lowry cleared his throat and said, "Molly, would you make me the happiest man on this planet and be my wife? And please stand down from this damn raid?"

Wilde grew serious. "I'll do the one, but not the other. Tonight, we make the planet a little better for the three of us. Tomorrow, I'd be honored to marry you."

CHAPTER 76

BLACKSHAW NOTICED DEL was paying more attention to the sky. The sun was sinking westward as it often does, but wildfire smoke and now dark bruised roll clouds tinged with the yellows of disease were obscuring its brilliance, dulling it to a white orb, more moon than star. Then a breeze freshened, like the first breath of newborn trouble. It grew into a brief gust, turning leaves backwards and in other strange angles as if to say it could do anything it wanted, and soon would, *just you wait and see.*

"If I was home, I'd be looking to my mooring lines before this flaw," said Blackshaw.

"The lightning. That's what's coming. And the wind." Del looked to the line of fire marauding through the hills. "I should be there, but I guess it'll get here. Not enough crews to attack it. I should be helping."

"No rain in your personal forecast?" asked Blackshaw.

Del's laugh was mordant.

Blackshaw opened his pack. He removed the waterproof bag, broke the seal, and extracted a satellite phone. It took a few moments to power up. Then he punched in a number and listened.

Mike Craig, the reclusive hacker and weather guru, answered on the other end with a grudging "What."

"You know who this is?" asked Blackshaw, whose faith in his phone's encryption was so lacking he refused to say even his name if he didn't have to.

"Generalissimo," said Craig, "I'm glad your daughter's *quinceañera* went well, and that there was no rain, and that she is happy and grateful, but I haven't changed my mind. I still live in the mountains, and a boat, even the hundred foot Cheoy Lee long-range cruiser you described, would be of little use to me here. Your fee was enough. I beg you, sir, please do not send the boat up to my mountain like in that movie."

"Try again, *Fitzcarraldo*." said Blackshaw.

Mike Craig's proprietary climate modeling software, his hacks into every weather satellite and recording buoy around the world, and his uncanny interpretation of the data, kept him on the speed-dial of every warlord, dictator, and general planning military actions or personal events of state, and for a hefty price.

"Oh," said Craig. In tones devoid of pleasure, he went on. "It's you. You're not dead."

"Don't get so excited," said Blackshaw. "You got my location?"

"Yes," answered Craig. "I had a call from a mutual friend that you were out and about again. What do you want? I see by your signal you're in a very warm place in the world. Trying out Hades before you buy?"

"No, Mike. Now listen up." Blackshaw had fished the detached drone receiver from his pack. He read the serial number from the unit to Craig.

"Wow," said Craig, after checking the number. "Where'd you get that?"

"From a small eight-rotor drone with a grenade on it. For moving drugs, I think. This transceiver has its own battery. If I turn it on, do you have any assets close by that could spoof its guts?"

"Your phone," said Michael Craig, as if Blackshaw should have known. "Fire up that transceiver. I'll take a look."

A few minutes passed. Del and Blackshaw waited in silence. Then Craig spoke up. "This unit has full telemetry. It's networked into a swarm of other transceiver units, for proximity awareness, and autonomous navigation. I'm impressed."

"If these things flew again, could you—"

"Take command? It's not a business I want to be in, but I could do it," said Craig.

"I don't want the dope," said an angry Blackshaw. "I'm thinking more about a Return to Sender function."

Michael Craig actually chuckled. "I get it. Yes. I can reprogram the swarm's destination with a few earlier lines of go-home code, not to mention a few other things. It'll need to hack into some border ground sensing assets. The U.S. sending units seem to be close to the same frequency range as your drone. I can preload the commands."

"Okay. Now Michael, we're going to need water. A lot of it," said Blackshaw. "In just a few hours."

Mike Craig was a few moments checking his data streams before he replied. "Can't help you. There's convective activity in that area, but rain's going to come down fifty-three point seven miles east of your position."

Blackshaw thought the situation through. "Can you get me something standing by? Maybe from Mars, if you get me."

"Wow. That's big. Do I want to know why?"

"Just make a few calls, Mike. Please."

"Oh God."

"Now what's the problem?" Blackshaw wanted this call over and done.

"You said *please*. You never say please. This is going to be bad."

In addition to weather predictions with accuracy that could endure for days, or even weeks if the price were right, Mike Craig had provided Blackshaw with crucial tactical surveillance on past operations; missions that unfortunately had achieved undesirable prominence in worldwide media.

"I'm working on my manners," said Blackshaw.

"More like you're working on the End of Days. I'll see what I can do," said Craig.

"That's all I'm asking. I'll text you a position later. Please stand by."

"Stop saying *please*. Wait!" wailed Craig. "It's date night for me and Nicole!"

"She'll understand." Blackshaw terminated the call.

Del was staring at Blackshaw. "Did you just make a phone call for water?"

"You sure as hell don't want to see me dance for it." Blackshaw re-sealed the phone and the transceiver in the waterproof pouch, and watched lightning rip through the clouds like flashes of divine artillery.

CHAPTER 77

IT WAS A different Adelle Congreve who sat with Pardue in his over-heated tent. She was having trouble broaching what was on her mind. She hadn't come back for another tumble, which was just as well, since Pardue had only one Viagra. After their first go-round earlier, he'd made a respect-able showing without the blue diamond pill because of months of sheer pent-up desire. Had she wanted more, he'd need a pharmaceutical boost. She had declined his offer of whiskey, and that so disturbed Pardue that he passed on having any himself. He waited quietly for Congreve to begin, knowing that her obvious psychic pressures combined with a natural hu-man abhorrence of silence would get her going faster than any amount of cajoling.

Pardue politely extended a piece of beef jerky, which Congreve ac-cepted. She nibbled at it with an air of distraction.

"Timon," began Congreve. Then she stopped.

Pardue remained silent.

"Timon, I'm so embarrassed."

Pardue said nothing, but a part of him felt crestfallen. After just one brief moment of passion with him, she was already breaking things off.

"This morning—" she began again. "I don't want you to get the wrong idea about me."

"I got lots of ideas about you, Adelle, and none of them bad," said Pardue. "Nothing you need to feel ashamed of."

"How do I put this?" She was struggling.

Pardue put her out of her misery. He said, "It was the heat of the moment. All the excitement about what we're doing here, some of it spilled over. And it was a mistake. Is that it?"

"No!" Congreve said. "Is that how you feel? We did wrong?"

"Adelle, don't worry. I won't kiss and tell. I may be a lot of things, but I'm not like that."

"Hold it." Congreve hit her stride. "I didn't think it was wrong at all! The truth is I care for you very much, Timon. It's just that since Rickey-Ray passed, I've rushed into things a few too many times, and it never went anywhere. I so admire you. I don't want you to think I'm some kind of wag-tail tottie."

Pardue scratched his head. "You can have anybody you want. You know that, and so do I. It was nice you thought of me that way for a mi-nute. I won't forget. But, like I said, I won't embarrass you, either."

Congreve grabbed Pardue's hands in hers. "Are you completely dense?"

"You wouldn't be the first to think so," said Pardue. "Highly doubt you'll be the last."

"Timon, I am trying to say I don't want us to be a fling! I sure don't want you to see *me* that way, though God knows I'd understand if you did. Do you think we have anything that can survive what we've done here?"

The imploring look in Congreve's eyes stirred Pardue deep down. His time in the wilderness had left him feeling lonely. His brief sojourn in this camp was nothing more than a thorny vexation turned disaster. He had fooled himself into thinking his presence here would legitimize citizens protecting the southern border. That was a delusion, what with Malthys and those biker clowns taking part. Maybe Congreve could help work out what to do next. The way things were headed, they could be an item, sure, but she'd be visiting him in prison for a conjugal honeymoon.

Pardue chose his words with care. "It's complicated, Adelle."

Congreve's eyes welled with tears. This was not the answer she hoped for. "You've got a woman waiting for you."

"Not strictly speaking, no," said Pardue. "Not in any romantic sense. Here it is. You remember the feds this morning, looking for the pilots of that CBP chopper?"

"Yes. It's worried me. Them showing up made me think we all overstepped."

"You said a mouthful there," Pardue agreed. "Gunter Foss came back from his patrol covered in blood. Said he shot a javelina, wounded it, then rubbed up against some brush the pig bled on when it ran off. I didn't believe him then, but I let it go."

Congreve had her ranch owner's hat on now, all business. "Blood? What's going on? You're scaring me, Timon."

Pardue averred, "You have every right to be scared. You might want to rethink having anything to do with me after what I tell you. Some hours ago, Foss invited me into his tent. One of the missing pilots was right there. A woman. She's hurt pretty bad. That's where the blood came from."

"Oh my God." Congreve's hand went to her heart. "He shot her?"

"Not to my knowledge."

"Where's the other pilot?" asked Congreve.

"Foss said she didn't survive the crash," answered Pardue. "He left her in the desert."

"Animal. Was this before the feds came?"

Pardue hesitated. Then nodded. "I'm ashamed. Foss said now that I knew about the pilot he took, he'd make me an accessory to everything. The kidnapping. And the other pilot's disappearance. Maybe I'm drinking too much, but I believed him. With my reputation as it is, it made sense I was done for."

Congreve took Pardue's hands again. "That bastard! You poor man. He's out of his mind! Nobody'd believe you had anything to do with that!"

"But Malthys must have been party to it. They were out on that patrol together. I was afraid for my life, as much as for that pilot's if I made a move. I've been a coward today. You see, whatever the law says later on, right now, between the PNC and the Rot-Irons, there're over a hundred men against me, most of them armed."

Congreve did the math. "You mean *against us*. Dressler, Cutlip, and I have maybe forty, fifty men, all hands tallied. But they didn't all bring weapons. It wasn't supposed to be like Waco, for God's sake!"

"Foss was just in here telling me the pilot shanked one of his men trying to get away. He's dead."

"Good for her!" said Congreve, clapping and smiling like she just got her first pony. She had the utmost respect for a female chopper pilot who could take care of herself. Their sorority was small.

Pardue went on. "But here's the kicker. Foss said somebody shot another one of his boys. Put him down right in front of Foss's tent. Took his head clean off. He said it was somebody with a rifle out in the desert."

"Two less sonsabitches if you ask me." Congreve's cool was remarkable under the circumstances.

"So you see, Adelle, we've got bigger problems than me falling in love with you."

Congreve could not contain her joy. She beamed when she said, "You love me—"

"Of course I do. You're everything, Adelle. The full package. How could I *not* love you. But I'm nothing. And I've got less than nothing. Not even my good name, though we both know I lost that before I even left town."

"Timon, you *love* me? Not just *want* me for a roll in the hay?"

Pardue drew himself up. "I swear it, Adelle. You're the bettermost woman in all the world. It might not be much, coming from me, but I'll be the happiest con' in Folsom if you still care after everything I've told you."

"*Care?* I told you, stupid, stupid man, I love you."

Congreve kissed Pardue hard. Before he knew it, his right hand was kneading her left breast. She moaned, growled, leaned back, and then drew his hand away.

"No time for that now, cowboy," she scolded. "We got to buckle to."

CHAPTER 78

LOWRY AND WILDE were ready. Wilde thought Lowry looked handsome in his ballistic vest and FBI windbreaker. Food and coffee had been ordered into the staging area below ground in the CBP garage. Wilde was tucking into a turkey sandwich with gusto. Lowry was torturing a bag of corn chips, eating them so slowly that Wilde wondered if he were still feeling anxious about the raid.

Van Sickel approached them, her face a mask of calm, and only her eyes betraying sadness. No amount of time on the job would make her immune to the news she bore.

"Cell signals come down here to die," said Van Sickel.

"It's been a pleasant respite," said Lowry, who usually maintained very close contact with his office in Washington.

Wilde took Van Sickel's meaning, and said, "You've heard something."

"Mike Haberman got me on the landline. He relayed from your office when they couldn't get you. They found human remains. In the woods."

"Sha'Quan Stewart?" asked Lowry.

Van Sickel took a deep breath, then said, "Young adolescent African American male. They're working on the ID still."

"What's the hold-up?" asked Wilde.

Van Sickel's voice was flat, as if she were trying to quash any emotion as she spoke. There was still an underlying quaver to her words. "The remains were found in a hollow north of Roanoke, south of I-64, well inside the perimeter of the George Washington and Jefferson National Forest. There was no scalp. But there wasn't much else, either."

"What's with that?" asked Wilde.

"This is preliminary, but as it was told to me, it appears the remains were field dressed, like a game animal. Like a deer. Gutted, and skinned."

"Skinned. *Jesus*," said Lowry, who was never given to profanity of any kind.

"It appeared to be a camp site. Very secluded, but recently used," said Van Sickel.

"But there's no doubt it's Sha'Quan Stewart?"

"One of them could be," said Van Sickel.

Lowry said, "I don't follow you."

Van Sickel explained, "It's a dump site, Pershing. There are at least eight sets of remains. Likely more. A lot more. I'm told the cadaver dog earned his kibble."

"So, they've been at this a while," said Lowry, who had thought until now that nothing could faze him.

But Van Sickel went on. "And there were teeth marks on bones at the scene."

Wilde said, "That's consistent with animal activity at outdoor scenes."

Van Sickel said, "Again, this is preliminary, but the teeth marks are human."

"Okay, now I'm going to be sick," whispered Molly.

"They're cannibals," said Lowry, lost in the horrific images forming in his mind.

Van Sickel said, "Bind, torture, kill, *eat*. But you need to know, the way the most recent victim was found, with animal hide tourniquets at the wrists and ankles, he might have been alive when the hands and feet were amputated. Guys, it may be that the victim was forced to watch them cook and eat his limbs before he was killed."

Lowry and Wilde were both struck dumb.

"Don't let them take you alive," said Van Sickel, as she turned to complete preparations for the raid.

CHAPTER 79

DEL WATCHED BLACKSHAW eat a protein bar under the rock ledge. They were trying to stay out of sight of the occasional helicopter patrols passing overhead in the dusk.

Del reviewed a list he had been making in his head. "So there's this Colquette kid, Malthys, the pilot, and that WMD. Not to mention the Rot-Iron. He's Gunter Foss, by the way. No creampuff."

"And Colquette's pals. It's going to be a busy night," said Blackshaw.

"Ben, you have that phone. Why don't you do like folks do sometimes, and call 911? Call in the cavalry." Del heard himself. "Never thought I'd ever say *those* words."

"There's a credibility issue," said Blackshaw.

"It's all kinda far-fetched, true," said Del. "You don't think they'll believe you."

"The other way, Del. I don't believe they can, or will do a damn thing," said Blackshaw.

"You have serious trust issues."

"I rely on myself. You can leave anytime," said Blackshaw.

"And miss this? I was just wondering how you saw all this playing out. With an eye toward still being alive tomorrow," said Del. "I've got part of the picture. The rest of it would be useful."

"You mean, like a plan?" asked Blackshaw.

"If you don't mind," said Del.

"I'm still working that out," Blackshaw admitted.

"Oh." Del leaned back against the rock face, and draped a neckerchief over his eyes. "Wake me when the lightbulb goes off."

A few moments later, Del snored softly. Blackshaw watched the lightning ripple deep in the clouds and plotted his own mayhem at ground level.

CHAPTER 80

CONGREVE WAS SMOOTH. She stood at the camp table, which bore a small Stonehenge of rocks to hold down the charts in the rising wind. She even gestured from the maps to the terrain around the camp, but she was talking with Cutlip and Dressler on an entirely different matter. Malthys and Gunter Foss were not yet present. Congreve had called the patrol planning meeting to order by first making Pardue's excuses.

Congreve said, "You boys just listen to me while I've got time, and don't interrupt. Those two sidewinders, the biker, and Malthys, they've got the pilot of that CBP chopper in Foss's tent. Foss showed her to Timon, and is threatening to kill her and implicate him if he talks. Even so, the pilot's hurt and tried to get loose. She cut a biker, and he died. The other pilot's already dead and they buried her someplace. And Foss also told Timon there's somebody in the desert plinking bikers. One got shot dead. All clear so far?"

Dressler and Merton nodded, their faces revealing no more concern than if Congreve had mentioned she had a touch of poison ivy.

She went on. "Our whole MAIm movement has been undermined by their actions. It's over, boys, before it ever began. Any patrols we mount now are window dressing so those assholes think everything's fine, and Timon's playing ball. But he's laying low until we all decide what to do. I say first order of business is free that pilot, for her safety, and to clear all our names, but she's under guard in Foss's tent. Second order of business, neutralize Malthys and Foss. We can't do that here in camp. There's too many witnesses, and too much chance of an outright firefight. That said, if they go out looking for illegals tonight, maybe it happens that they don't come back. Inform your men. Clear?"

Cutlip said, "Sounds about right to me."

"What sounds about right, Farrell?" It was Malthys strolling up to the planning session with Foss. Congreve wondered what they had heard. They were quiet as cats, especially Foss when he wasn't riding his noisy hog. As it was, Foss was looking very nervous, always looking out toward the desert.

Congreve said, "The plan for tonight. For those who bothered to show up, that is."

"I'm here," said Malthys, the picture of Biblical innocence.

"Where's Pardue? Looks like he's a no-show," said Foss, fractious as always.

"Said he wasn't feeling well. Taking a siesta," Congreve explained.

Foss said, "When he finishes acting like a wetback, he should come out with us on patrol. Tonight."

"He asked not to be disturbed," said Congreve, thinking on her feet.

"I'm not asking," said Foss. "He's supposed to be leading us out here. He can't do that from a tent. It looks bad. He's coming with us. Got a problem with that, Miss Adelle?"

Congreve's heart sank. After a moment, she said, "I'm sure he'd like a chance to stretch his legs."

"That settles it," said Malthys. "How 'bout that, Gunter? The big cheese is coming with us."

Cutlip and Dressler swapped a quick glance. Though neither of the steely ranchers spoke, an understanding had been reached. Action would be taken. Men would surely die.

CHAPTER 81

DEL JOINED BLACKSHAW up on the ridge overlooking the distant camp, and said, "That's enough beauty sleep."

Blackshaw studied Del, and said, "No. Still ugly."

Del ignored the jibe. He asked, "What's happening down there?"

The wind was a steady twenty knots, gusting to thirty-five. It wasn't clearing the smoke. It seemed to be wafting more into the area.

"Losing the light, but it looks like there's patrols going out," said Blackshaw. "The ranchers are leaving their horses in camp. They're prepping ATVs."

"They're fools, whatever they take," said Del. "Fire's quicker than those buggies. We're going to have to move off this ridge soon. The ravine behind us is working like a flue."

"You can go. I need to see where Malthys is headed tonight," said Blackshaw. "I need to meet that guy."

"Been meaning to ask you about the biker you shot before," said Del.

"What's on your mind?"

"You know I've got my reasons for not bitching that you took him out. If he's a Rot-Iron, he's no saint. But that one hadn't done anything to you," said Del. "You did it in cold blood. Just the way they're killing the folks *they* don't like."

"Cold blood's good. If I get too excited, it makes the gun all jumpy," said Blackshaw.

Del said nothing.

"You can't believe I'm like them—" Blackshaw was in no mood to explain himself, but he made the attempt. "That biker—whatever his name was—he and I met at the apex of two very long chains of decisions made and actions taken. He's been headed toward me, and I was stalking in on him, for all our lives. Before he even put on his gang colors, he was doing the things that meant one day he'd put those colors on. He was on the path. At any moment he could have turned off it, and been someplace else, been somebody else. He didn't veer. Neither did I. Bound to be trouble."

Del said, "You seem to know lots about him."

Blackshaw wondered about that. Then he said. "I knew him well enough because he and I are the same. Del, I never killed another man lest he was exactly like me in the way of temperament, and coming hard for me and mine. I suppose the idea of who's mine to look after has broadened some, perhaps too much for your liking. But there's only certain people who find their way onto that path I mentioned. I'm going in one direction. Woe betide anybody running toward me."

"I think you might be crazy," said Del.

"Reckon I'm going through a rough patch."

Del laughed low. "A *rough patch*. Is that what the kids are calling it these days?"

"Complaining doesn't do me any good, Del. Taking steps seems to make the difference."

"Let's take some steps off this ridge before we cook," urged Del.

"Not until I see Malthys."

Blackshaw looked down the hill behind him, rubbing his hand over his jaw, feeling the whisker stubble rasp his fingers. The arroyo seemed like a fissure leading into the Underworld. He would have gone there gladly, and not looked back, if it could have saved LuAnna.

CHAPTER 82

TEDDYBEAR CHOYA DROVE his truck like a lunatic toward the launch site, lurching hard across dry gullies in the savage terrain. The four other trucks followed as best they could despite the vehicles' age and the drivers' prudent sense of self-preservation. Paolo Estrella y Castro debated asking Choya to slow down. As it was, he was having a bad time trying to log in the coordinates of the new, bigger landing zone that Foss had texted in moments ago. His fingers kept dancing off the keyboard. That, or the text screen on his phone would wink out because of some annoying battery saving setting. Estrella y Castro had to be sure he programmed the drones to perfection, or they'd end their flight in somebody's back yard swimming pool.

Each truck contained fifty drones. As on the shipment the night before, each of the forty-nine drones carried a fragmentation grenade to protect its kilo cargo of cocaine from unauthorized tampering on the receiving end. If Foss couldn't retrieve it, nobody would. Not without high velocity shrapnel mixed in.

And as before, one drone per truck was built purely to protect the swarm, with its M-18 Claymore antipersonnel mine that could be deployed with devastating results, as the shoot-down of the CBP helicopter had proven. Forget how fragile the drones themselves were, thought Estrella y Castro, that was a hell of a lot of explosive to jostle across the Sonora like this. If any single grenade or mine went off, the cascade of sympathetic explosions would obliterate truck, cargo, and crew in an instant.

A grinning Choya socked Estrella y Castro in the shoulder, and said, "Relax. This is going to be good, right?"

As the truck bottomed-out in a rut, Estrella y Castro's kidneys rattled, and he gasped. The grenades and the Claymore were remarkably stable unless they took a bad shock from another explosive, but Estrella y Castro did not want to tempt fate.

The nervous engineer said, "You want me to take a turn driving?"

Choya said, "No. I'm good. You ready to make history two nights in a row?"

"I'd rather *make* history than *be* history, or make a crater," said Estrella y Castro. "Maybe we could slow down."

"I know we could slow down," replied the boss, "but we won't. We're almost there."

Estrella y Castro decided he could hang on a little longer, as if he had any real choice in the matter. After all, he reasoned, if something went terribly wrong, it's not as though he would have the slightest notion what happened to him.

CHAPTER 83

GUNTER FOSS BARGED into Timon Pardue's tent, with Malthys close on his heels. Foss's pistol was already in hand, negating Pardue's advantage of a quicker draw.

Tucking the gun he frisked off the sheriff under his own belt, Foss barked, "On your feet, old man."

Pardue looked up from the newspaper he was reading, which Congreve had been kind enough to lend during his self-imposed house arrest. "Come on in, assholes."

Foss aimed the gun at Pardue's head. "Let's go!"

"Where'd you have in mind?" inquired the former sheriff.

Malthys answered, "You're coming on patrol with us. Now!"

"I'm drunk, and my feet hurt. You all go ahead."

Foss and Malthys seethed. They were unused to defiance of any kind, especially in the form of indifference when they held a weapon in play.

Malthys said, "You're coming with us."

"So you mentioned," slurred Pardue. "You're repeating yourself, son. Hey Gunter, how's our pilot doing?"

Foss's hand went white on the pistol. "She'd be a lot better if you were moving."

Pardue sucked his teeth once, and then a second time, eyeing Foss. "How am I supposed to believe you? Last I saw, she was in pretty bad shape."

Foss said, "Like *you're* going to be. Get up! I won't tell you again."

Pardue said, "Oh go ahead and shoot. You ruined my name already. I got nothing else."

Foss felt as though his synapses were melting from rage. "Okay. *Okay!* You want to hang out? That's cool. How 'bout I turn my boys loose on Adelle Congreve for a few hours before I cut her throat? You can sit on your fat ass and watch *that!*"

Suddenly, Pardue didn't look so drunk. Without another word, he rose, and with a deliberate step led Malthys and Foss out of the tent. Outside, they found four others waiting; Malthys's rejects. That skinny kid with the peevish glint in his eye was there with three rough-looking skells. Foss gave Pardue a casual shove—might have looked playful, might have looked mean—to reassert who was boss. Something in the hard set of the sheriff's shoulders told the biker this old man would not die easy.

CHAPTER 84

BLACKSHAW SAW MALTHYS. He hadn't expected the PNC messiah to patrol in the wilderness alone, but when he climbed behind the wheel of a 6-seat Yamaha ATV, the other five places were quickly taken. Next to Malthys, there was Rufus Colquette wedged into the middle seat. To Colquette's right was one of the other killers in the photograph, Oren, if Blackshaw remembered right. In the back row Nyqvist sat behind Malthys, with the old sheriff in the middle. The man Colquette called The Major sat on the far right. Gunter Foss got in train behind the big ATV. He was riding solo on a smaller 2-seater.

Del said, "That's a lot of heat for one patrol."

"Maybe they're going to split up once they get farther out."

Then, through the rifle scope, Blackshaw saw something that changed his entire sense of the party moving out southwest into the smoke-palled desert hills. The sheriff in the back seat. He glanced over his shoulder at someone back in camp. It was subtle. All he did was shake his head *no*. Just one movement.

Blackshaw traversed the rifle to the right to see who the sheriff was looking at. Near the edge of the encampment, he saw a buxom older woman in a big white Stetson watching the patrol roll out. Looking heartsick with worry, she took an involuntary step forward as if to follow the patrol. Then she checked herself, and stood still wringing her hands. Yes, thought Blackshaw, she looked miserable.

Blackshaw kept his scope on the woman as a tall, thin rancher moved to her side and put his arm around her shoulders in an offer of comfort. A squat-looking bull of a man standing close by turned and nodded to a group of five other men, ranch hands who had been watching the farewell. Then the two older men, along with the hands all walked with purpose, but at a pace calculated not to excite attention, to a small motor pool of ATVs, and fired up the machines. Every one of them wore a sidearm.

Del said, "Foss is following up to keep an eye on Malthys, or somebody else in that big ATV."

"Foss isn't watching his own six. And Del, that's no patrol," said Blackshaw. "It's an execution party."

"But who's the turkey in that shoot?" Del asked.

"Maybe Colquette's too hot, too much trouble now, even for PNC," said Blackshaw. "The other men in the big ATV? They were in that picture with Colquette, just so you know. The fourth one in back likely took that picture. They're party to that child's death. Except for that guy you said used to be sheriff around here."

Del spat on a whetstone and ran his axe blade over it twice. "You think Foss and Malthys are going to do them all?"

"If they don't, I will," Blackshaw said.

"Because you're the helpful sort," said Del. "I'm surprised Pardue's in on it."

"By the concerned looks of those ranchers, his number's up, too," Blackshaw speculated. "And there they go."

The ranch hand posse on the ATVs revved, dropped into low gear, and slowly followed the first patrol into the wilderness.

"It'll be way more complicated now," said Del.

"Killing's like that in the best of times," observed Blackshaw. "Let's get off this ridge like you said, and see where they're headed."

CHAPTER 85

SOMETHING HAD CHANGED. Colquette might not be book smart, but he could feel the shift, like the beating to come if his pappy stank of booze. Malthys was barely speaking to him. When he did, it was with grunts, or a word or two. Now that they were going out in the ATV, there wasn't any of the big pep talk Malthys had given Colquette back in the tent before. Maybe Malthys was tense about the patrol. Something felt off. Having that old man in back, the one who used to be a sheriff, made Colquette squirm. Made him bust a sweat the way he did when he saw the two cops crawling all over that bus he'd just gotten off in Richmond. That was close. This felt like that.

One thing Malthys was right about was the smoke. They were riding through hollows and gullies, topping out over ridges, and sometimes they drove through smoke so thick, he couldn't see three feet ahead of the ATV, and that was with the lights on. One time he glanced over his shoulder to check what that old man was up to, and he could barely see the light of Gunter Foss's ATV behind them. Colquette's throat and nose burned. His eyes felt hot and gritty, and seemed to scratch every time he looked around. Sometimes, he coughed and had to wipe tears and snot on his sleeve. *Great.* Doing *the work* back east was lots easier. *And the chow was better.* Colquette made himself smile with that one.

Nyqvist had said it. Colquette always knew it. A true hunter eats what he kills. Of course, nobody ate *raw* meat. They weren't *animals*. Oren had a special sauce he liked to use for basting. It gave the jungle jerky a right tasty tang.

Colquette looked back again. The ex-lawman said, "Turn around, boy."

"I ain't no—"

Pardue slapped Colquette hard across the face. The kid's head snapped sideways, his ears rang, and he swore he saw stars like in the cartoons. Nyqvist, Oren, and The Major just giggled! When Coquette looked at Malthys to see if he had anything to say about one of his soldiers getting used hard like this, the look he got was pure poison.

Holding a hand to his burning cheek, Colquette wanted to go back to camp. The tears were really coming now from smoke and from shame. He wanted to go home to Virginia, and to his mother. She was a total bitch, but he could handle her if she acted up. That's when Malthys slowed the ATV down, and then stopped.

CHAPTER 86

BLACKSHAW AND DEL waited at the edge of what they believed
to be the right spot. The area was wide, level, and windblown clean of
brush. The sun was down, but lightning flashed glimpses of the kill zone
often enough. When the time came, the night scope on the Threadcutter
would fill in the darker gaps.

Del said, "They should be here by now. We came on foot. They're on
ATVs. Did we jump to too many conclusions?"

"My gut says you were right. This is the place."

"So? Where are they?"

Blackshaw thought about this. "They've stopped. That's it. I doubt
they're lost. Let me work back down the trail toward them."

"You want me to sit around here and miss the fun?" asked Del, coming close to griping.

"You'll think of something. I know you won't be bored."

Blackshaw moved around the plateau, and inched down into the ravines and arroyos. After twenty minutes of careful stalking, he thought he
could see the hazy loom of the two ATVs to his left, around the bend in an
arroyo. Blackshaw crept to higher ground and moved in.

He didn't mind the wind wrapping smoke around him. The dark palls
that hid him were just echoes of what lurked within his heart. Or that's
what LuAnna would have told him, if she were awake and by his side. Why
had he thought of her now?

The wind covered the sound of his footsteps. Facing danger, battle, or even death, Blackshaw was always tranquil during a solitary stalk. In this peaceful interlude, his mind ranged back to his last conversation with Knocker Ellis. His friend had said LuAnna's coma might still allow for a kind of deeper listening. Could that mean she might also be capable of an unfathomable means of talking to Blackshaw here and now? This land, Del's country, with its earthen waves, and dry, bright storms, was a mystery to Blackshaw. And when mystery hung close like so much smoke, Blackshaw was less vulnerable to surprises of any kind, and more open to the strange actions of spirit.

So he crept forward, let his mind broaden, and listened for anything otherworldly on the wind. He listened for his bride's voice, which had fallen into a deathlike silence on this side of the veil. And then he knew. When he and LuAnna had hunted the marshes together, they did so in a perfect duet of soundlessness so as not to flush the game ahead, speaking only in glances, easy nods, and feather-soft gestures of hand and gun. Blackshaw smiled in the hellish dark. LuAnna was right there with him after all. She was present, but was letting him move in for the kill without distraction.

Blackshaw honored the nerving power of his huntress bride by turning from mystical and melancholic thoughts to the deadly business before him. The ATVs were just over the ridge now. To avoid skylining himself in a lightning silhouette, he crept to a dip in the hill that was backed by a higher thrust of ground. He lifted his eye behind the gnarled trunk of a tree. Through the lower leaves, he saw seven men below him.

Malthys and Foss stood apart from the loose cluster of Colquette, Nyqvist, Oren, and The Major. The former sheriff was quietly trying to remain aloof from both groups, but Foss kept checking Pardue, always turning so the old man stayed in view. The quickened stances of the men in the ravine shouted that everyone knew this was a stand-off, but they all were affecting easy, even casual voices. The wind whipped their words down the ravine. The tones Blackshaw could discern were not triumphal, but gentle, in the way of men confident of a quick kill just moments away, if only they could pretend that death was lurking in another country, not seething closer in their hearts.

CHAPTER 87

THE KID STARED at Pardue until the slap. That took the little bastard down a peg. The old man wondered if he'd overdone it when Malthys pulled the ATV over and stopped. Looking down the backtrail, he saw that Foss had stopped and dismounted his ride. The drivers had left the engines idling.

Malthys and Foss kept sheep-dogging Coquette and his three dimwit pals into a loose cluster. Pardue was momentarily relieved not to be the focal point of the PNC boss and the Rot-Iron. It seemed the four newcomers were in bad odor.

There was no question in Pardue's mind it was going to get ugly. Foss and Malthys had pistols. And Foss still had Pardue's go-to automatic. Colquette was likely not armed. But Pardue thought the three others, Oren, Nyqvist, and The Major, might have been packing heat, the way their hands hovered around their waistbands which were hidden by untucked shirts.

Malthys said, "Rufus, I want you with me."

Colquette bloated like a tick with pride. "You got it."

Pardue figured Colquette was a dead man.

Foss said, "The rest of you come with me."

Pardue said, "This isn't anywhere near where we decided to patrol."

Foss was quick. "It's close enough. We walk from here. We don't want the ATVs to give us away to the wets, right, old man?"

Everyone watched Pardue to measure how he'd take the slur. He said evenly, "If we're stopping here, why not shut down the engines?" Before anyone could say a word in reply, the situation deteriorated.

CHAPTER 88

BLACKSHAW SIGHTED ON Colquette's chest, for a CBM, or Center Body Mass shot. He took a slow, controlled breath, then relaxed, and adjusted his aim, close as the target was, for the gusting wind. He gently took up the little bit of the Threadcutter's trigger slack. He was on the verge of squeezing the trigger when he heard a distant *crack*. A nanosecond later, Foss clutched his left shoulder, staggered, and swore. In the same instant, Oren settled to his knees, grabbing his neck with both hands, gawping and bleeding like a gaffed fish. Blackshaw traced the trajectory in his mind's eye. The round that nicked Foss had struck Oren.

Blackshaw had not accounted for another shooter in his planning. Of course, he realized that at least one of the ranchers from the posse had crept in from their own parked ATVs, and sensing the same tension Blackshaw had, he tried to take Foss down, protecting Pardue. The result angered Blackshaw, sending an unsettling surge of adrenalin through his body. A moment ago, he had a tight group of relatively stationary targets. At the back of his mind, he had prepped a firing sequence for moving from Colquette to the other targets, and might have made hash of at least four of them before anyone gave a thought to taking cover. Then he could've put down two more slowpokes before the storm and gloom swallowed the rest. Blackshaw could've mopped up the wounded at leisure.

Now the plan was blown. That single bullet hit the men downhill with all the shock and speed of a pool shark's cue ball in an open break. Foss bolted out of the beam of his ATV's headlight and was lost in the shadows, though his spew of cussing would have been good enough for Blackshaw to echolocate a snapshot with decent odds of finding meat. Yes, Blackshaw knew he could have taken the biker with the rifle's night scope, but he'd wanted Colquette first.

Malthys swore only once, then gazelled out of the light with only a few long strides. Colquette followed right on Malthys's heels.

The Major dived across the front row seats of the big ATV, squirmed out the other side, spooning low and tight behind the vehicle like it was a new girlfriend.

Pardue was surprised, and mortally slow, though he was clever. He had a good idea who was firing, and took cover putting a sizeable rock between him and the shooter on the backtrail. Once there, he drew his small backup pistol from an ankle holster. Blackshaw could still see Pardue with the naked eye from his high vantage and the ATV headlight beams, but he had no argument with the former sheriff, and so held his fire.

Oren flopped from his knees onto his back in the glare, with his life-blood jetting into the sand from his throat. Now he only had strength to press the wound with one ineffectual hand. That hand quickly fell limp and slick at his side. His heart pumped three more times before giving out; Oren was done for the day, and forever.

Nyqvist showed bold and crafty instincts for survival. He too went for the front seat of the big ATV, staying low, and in a blinding sequence of moves, he switched off the headlights, threw the gear shifter, and punched the accelerator with his fist. The Yamaha, with its fat horned tires spinning and throwing plumes of dust into the smoky air, lurched forward behind a small butte. Nyqvist must have put an eye over the dashboard to steer, because the whining engine receded into the night.

That left The Major lying on the ground with no cover, writhing and gripping one arm with the other hand. A Yamaha tire must have spun on The Major's arm as Nyqvist sped off. Blackshaw aimed, squeezed the Threadcutter's trigger, and took The Major with one shot just below his nose. The bullet carried through the teeth, bone and tissue, and snipped the man's cervical spine. Lights out.

Pardue's eyes bugged when he realized there was a shooter somewhere on his six. Rather than cower in the open, he made a run for Foss's idling

ATV, and hopped aboard. He gunned the machine in a tight, drifting circle, thumped over The Major's corpse, and charged like a demon back down the trail toward camp, hollering, "Don't shoot, you cockeyed sonsabitches! It's *me*!"

Foss's head emerged from behind scrub-covered rocks, and with it, his pistol. He fired a volley of shots at the receding Pardue. A second after the last report cracked, Pardue slumped over his ATV's handlebars. The ATV drove on.

Blackshaw scanned the kill zone, and finding no more targets there, he faded back down the hill into the dark to go hunting.

CHAPTER 89

NANCY GREENWAY LOST all track of time, and was not even certain she was still among the living. She was devout in her belief in God, and the afterlife, and wondered if she was in some kind of metaphysical transition from her former existence to whatever came next. A rare moment of lucid thought set her straight. She would not still be in such grotesque pain in the Heaven of her understanding. And Heaven would not stink like a hog sty. This was earth. She was alive. Or maybe it was hell.

The man who watched her was agitated, caged. She knew his name was Stork. Perhaps she had heard him called that by someone during one of her feeble climbs up to twilight consciousness. He would part the front flap of the tent to peer out, then he'd shuffle back to a slit in the tent's side, and look out there. Back and forth went Stork between his two loopholes, never giving Greenway a glance.

Greenway used her time wisely to reconnoiter as best she could from her cot. The lantern light in the tent was turned down low, but she could see the forms of two bodies beneath the careless toss of an old wool blanket. She could account for one corpse, from her surprise attack with her rescue knife. Had she cut and killed two of these bastards? No matter. In the end, her slashing blade had failed her. She was still a prisoner. She wondered why these monsters continued to let her live.

Greenway sensed her injuries were about to submerge her again into unconsciousness when the hallucination began. Stork had just moved from the front flap of the tent that looked out into the desert side. He was wearing his usual groove in the ground toward the slitted canvas at the back of the tent. But now, there was a new presence in the enclosed space. She saw the silhouette of a big man, with long ungathered hair waving below his shoulders.

The man barked, "Hey asshole!"

Stork jerked, yelped, and whipped around to see who had accosted him.

The stranger said, "My sister sends regards."

Then Stork staggered back a step, and looked down. Greenway was almost as surprised as Stork to see an axe handle extending from the left side of his chest, the blade buried deep in his heart. She knew she was dreaming. It was too good to be true.

The big man with the long hair let Stork drop to the ground. Then he planted a boot on Stork's body and wrenched the axe, which came free with a wet sucking noise. Then he wiped the blade on the dead man's clothes. Greenway giggled, wondering if using Stork's filthy clothes to clean anything would ever work. As she slipped into unconsciousness again, she felt herself lifted off the cot in strong arms.

CHAPTER 90

ALL THE TRUCKS were unloaded. Estrella y Castro had the drones set out with enough space between them for a clean launch. He had given each little craft extra room because of the vagaries of the gusting winds. Whether Foss had allowed for that in his choice of the landing zone was another matter. Estrella y Castro had already warned Teddybear Choya that some of the drones might make a rough landing on the other end because of the weather, and so might not be in good enough shape to relaunch for the trip home. Choya seemed to have registered what Estrella y Castro was saying, but it was clear the boss didn't care. In Choya's eyes, the drones themselves were expendable, and replaced much more easily than missing kilos of cocaine.

Choya danced around the drones, filled with excitement about the launch. Estrella y Castro was making final checks on the two hundred fifty flying spiders. The robust telemetry program he had coded allowed him to make most of the systems' inspections from his laptop. After a lengthy visual check, the cargo drones were ready. The hunter/killer Tarantulas carrying the claymores were next. All processors and circuitry were miraculously intact after the hard ride to the launch area.

Estrella y Castro stood back from his arachnids and their deadly payloads, and gazed up into the turbulent sky. He caught Teddybear Choya's eye, and said, "They're ready."

Choya grew quiet, which for him passed as solemn. He soon broke the spell, commanding, "Fucking *do it*, man!"

All the systems icons on Estrella y Castro's laptop were green. With his finger poised over the launch key, he had a change of heart, and said, "No, Boss. This one's yours."

Choya stepped over to the hallowed computer. Estrella y Castro pointed to the correct key on the board. Without another word, Teddybear Choya pressed the key so hard, the laptop almost tumbled out of Estrella y Castro's hands. As Estrella y Castro got a grip on the controls, two thousand motors whirred to life, and the little creatures raced into the sky and away to the north with the buzz of raging hornets.

CHAPTER 91

LOWRY AND WILDE rode through the night from Bisbee with
Sheriff Rumball and Van Sickel in the lead CBP Suburban to stage one mile
away from the MAIm camp before the raid. There were seven other vehicles, including two ambulances, and a six-wheeled, armored Lenco BearCat
personnel carrier, with a ten-man tactical team.

The timing was arranged to allow Otto DeGore of ICE/ERO to be a
similar distance outside the Wickenburg base of the Rot-Irons, with smaller
detachments covering known Rot-Iron safe houses in the area. Mike
Haberman had already checked in that he and his FBI-Tucson contingent
were in place outside the Pure Nation Comitatus compound.

Van Sickel slowed, and pulled off the highway into the desert. There
were no MAIm sentries at this turnoff. CBP scouts had already determined
that the MAIm lookouts were busy watching their own well-traveled access
lane to halt media crew incursions, and had not thought to post sentries at
other points where more determined federal forces might make their way in
close.

Van Sickel conferenced Haberman and DeGore in on her cellular
phone in case anyone was scanning federal or local law enforcement radio
frequencies. She said, "Van Sickel here. We're go."

Haberman's voice came through strong over the Suburban's bluetooth
speaker. "Haberman. We're go."

DeGore followed up. "DeGore. We're five minutes out. My safe
house teams are go."

Van Sickel said, "Don't take all night, Otto." She ended the call. "Not like him to be late."

Lowry said, "Any sign of media at this point?"

"Still nothing," said Van Sickel. "The wildfire's the big story. It's getting close to Hereford. We've kept our concerns about the pilots off their screen saying that it is likely that unknown Good Samaritans have intervened. We held the last presser four hours ago, and told the newshounds to call it a night. Very low key."

"Let's hope it stays that way," said Wilde.

The Suburban's dash speaker burred, and Van Sickel opened the line. "Van Sickel here."

Otto DeGore said, "DeGore. We're go."

Haberman reaffirmed, "Haberman. Still good to go."

Van Sickel took a breath, then said, "Van Sickel here. Godspeed everybody. Let's roll."

She eased the Suburban forward into the smoke-shrouded desert toward the MAIm camp.

CHAPTER 92

NYQVIST DROVE BLIND for a few seconds, then risked putting his head up to glance over the ATV'S dash. He spun the steering wheel just in time to miss diving over a cliff into a small box canyon. At this point, he'd put a few yards between him and that shit-show in the clearing.

He sat up into a hunched driving position, nose to the steering wheel, but he still had that prickly sensation of cross-hairs or iron sights resting between his shoulder blades. He slowed the ATV, and tried to use the flickers of lightning to pick his way through the desert. His only thought was to get farther away.

Nyqvist always had a feeling that Malthys would plan to do Colquette, ever since the photo got loose and screwed them all. What Nyqvist had not bargained on was that the Dean of the PNC would want to take out everybody having to do with the hunt and barbecue back east. You can't found a new cell someplace distant if you keep knocking off the membership. It made no sense. At least that idiot Colquette hadn't yacked about the hunt supper. But that hadn't mattered. Flashing the picture around, and the scalp trophy had done enough damage.

When the intervals between flashes of heat lighting grew too long, Nyqvist winked the headlights on and off to illuminate his next few yards of travel. He was getting into thicker brush and cactus, and wondered if he would be faster on foot. No, something about having mechanized transport, open as it was, made him feel safer.

He had just flipped the headlights off after a brief glimpse when there was a loud clang in the engine. The whole vehicle jerked, like he'd smashed into a rock. Oily smoke roiled up into his face, and the machine slowed and stalled. He dismounted with the flashlight from the dash, and looked up front. There he saw a bullet hole in the cowling. His breath quickened with panic. He calmed himself with the thought that the round had struck the ATV way back at the clearing where the trouble began, but had only now crippled the vehicle, putting loose metal into the gearbox, or holing the oil pan, and letting the lubricant or maybe the coolant run dry. He had no idea what was wrong with this damn thing, or how to fix it, and wasn't going to figure it out now. It was time to start that walk after all.

He grabbed two canteens and walked fifteen minutes, wandered really, wondering where the hell he was going, how he was going to get there, and what he would eat and drink on the way. The canteens wouldn't last long. He had no idea in what direction the nearest road lay. The stars were a mystery to him. He only hunted by day, and spent nights in the field back east drunk off his ass by the fire like a real man.

Cautious and scared in this alien world, he flashed the beam of his light all around him from time to time as he made his way forward. Once, he caught movement behind him about fifty feet back, and stared. Nothing stirred. Coyotes? Wild pigs? Malthys had made sure Nyqvist was unarmed, and now he couldn't take an animal down. If he found any wets out here, they'd do in a pinch. A man's got to eat. A real man will do whatever it takes to survive.

Nyqvist heard movement behind him again. A rustling noise. Closer now. He was too slow with the flashlight to catch sight of anything. He redirected the light to the ground, searching around him, and picked up a small rock. He hefted it, and got his grip right so its pointed edge was ready to deal a blow. Christ, he felt like a damn cave man.

Nyqvist heard a man's soft voice in the wind. "I know what you did to that boy. I'm coming for you. I'm going to lift your hair."

Nyqvist's heart pounded in his chest. The flashlight revealed nothing. Just scrub blowing in the smoke and wind. Holy hell, somebody or some *thing* out here knew what he'd done, and had a problem with it.

He turned started moving away from the voice, just trotting at first.

"Don't bother running!" cried that voice. "I'll still take you."

Nyqvist's last tatters of dignity fluttered away, and he began to sprint, tripping every few steps, and keenly aware that the front of his pants were soaked with piss.

Nyqvist shouted, "He was just a little nigger runt!" as if that excused everything, and would earn him the mercy he had failed to show all through his life.

He stumbled hard on his next step, and went down, picking up stings in his legs, arms, and face to go with his skinned knees, like he'd dropped on a bed of nettles. The flashlight revealed a goddamn cactus! He got back to his feet, and tried to pluck out the spines as he struggled on, but he only managed to drive them deeper into his flesh, and bed a few new ones into his hands and arms.

He heard the voice again. "You're going to pay for what you did!"

Nyqvist ran on through the wilderness, ignoring more cactus spines that seemed to be jabbing into him at every step. He dashed blindly, his lungs pumping the smoky air without benefit of replenishment.

There were pop-up wildfires along his path, but he dodged them, weaving his way like it was an infernal obstacle course. He finally faltered at the great wall of flames in front of him. There was nowhere to turn. When he looked, there was unbroken fire on both sides of him now, and a vengeful fiend in pursuit.

He leaned over to catch his breath, lost his balance, and fell to the ground, suddenly weak. Nyqvist's leg muscles twitched, then spasms racked his whole frame. His shaking hands could not pick up the flashlight or the rock where he'd dropped them. He vomited his guts out. His heart felt as though it was galloping in a spastic tattoo, skipping beats, then racing to catch up. His stomach twisted into agonizing knots. He dry-heaved, ejecting only a sticky thread of bile.

Nyqvist tried to focus his eyes, which jumped and jittered uncontrollably in their sockets. Amidst the jumble of confused signals caroming through his optic nerves, he thought he could make out the presence of a man bending low to study him. Nyqvist whispered, "Help—help me."

The stranger gave a glance at the flames that were blowing closer to where Nyqvist lay helpless. The stricken man appealed again, but his voice was a rasping croak. "Bastard! Help!"

Finally, the stranger spoke. Nyqvist recognized the voice from moments before. It was *him*!

The demon said, "No. I won't help you. My name is Blackshaw, and you're dying."

CHAPTER 93

COLQUETTE DASHED INTO the darkness. It was chilly. He had no coat. He thought the desert was supposed to be hot. He scrambled on hands and knees up a steep field of scree toward a ridgeline, and was about to cross it and descend the other side, but the entire descending face was engulfed in flame racing up the hill to his position. He stayed on the clear side, and stumbled and slipped west along the ridge, flames to his left, and a glowing desert swathed in smoke to the right.

The heat on the left side of Colquette's body was searing, drying his flop sweat to salty scum. His hands were cut and scraped, but he kept going, trying hard to put as much distance as possible between him and Malthys. He kept on like this for half an hour. Through his terror and confusion, the only satisfaction he could find was in the thought that any wets trying to come into America from Mexico tonight were frying like bacon.

Colquette ran until the ridgeline teed into a high escarpment of rock. He tried climbing it, but fell back for want of cracks and ledges wide enough for him to grip for more than a second or two. When he fell back the fourth time, he realized he was not alone. Not twenty feet away, there was a man seated on a rock with a rifle resting across his lap. Colquette looked closer.

It was Blackshaw. From the bus. And all he said to Colquette by way of greeting was, "I want that scalp."

Colquette's fear bloomed into righteous anger. "No! You didn't earn it!"

"It's not for me, Rufus. I'm going to give it back to that boy's mother to be buried with him."

"No way in hell." To Colquette, the very idea was crazy.

Blackshaw leveled the rifle for a hipshot. "Up to you. Hand it over, or I put a skylight in you where you stand."

"You're a goddamn thief!" wailed Colquette.

"You don't know the half of it." Blackshaw raised the rifle and acquired Colquette in the scope. "Now's not the time to think I'm joking."

Colquette erupted in a spew of foul language. All the while, he was fiercely digging around in his front pants pocket. Finally, he removed the scalp, and threw it on the ground.

"There!" said Colquette, his voice cored with plaintive injury.

"Now you can go," said Blackshaw.

Colquette angled down the hill as if to work his way around Blackshaw.

"No," said Blackshaw.

Colquette stopped as the rifle canted toward him again. "You said I can go."

"No that way," explained Blackshaw. "If you go that way, I shoot you."

"Then which way, you asshole!"

Blackshaw nodded toward the brow of the hill.

Colquette shouted, "That's Mexico!"

"Nice country. Nice people," said Blackshaw.

"But that whole damn hill's on fire!" shouted Colquette. This guy was out of his mind.

"You start walking, or I start shooting," said Blackshaw. "Your call, big hunter man."

"That's no choice at all!" Even Colquette could see that.

"It's more than you gave that child," said Blackshaw. "It's more than you deserve. Make up your mind. In two seconds I'm shooting your legs. Try walking to Mexico like that."

Colquette glared at Blackshaw, then made a dash down the hill. Blackshaw fired the rifle, and a stinging burst of rock and sand danced up in front of Colquette's feet.

"Okay! All right!" Colquette stopped, and quickly worked his way back up the hill to the ridgeline. "Take it easy!"

At the ridge, Colquette stopped, the glare of wildfire waving over his face. He took a step down the other side of the hill.

Blackshaw jerked the rifle to his shoulder again, and fired. Colquette felt a punch in his side, his body twisting. His legs went limp, and he tumbled into the flames below.

CHAPTER 94

BLACKSHAW SNATCHED UP the fallen tuft of hair before it could blow away.

Del's voice reached him from the lightning riven hollow down the hill. "You suckered him."

"I let him get away once," said Blackshaw. "Never twice. Where you been?"

"I looked in at that camp," said Del. "Who was the woman?"

"I don't know what you mean," said Blackshaw.

"It's dark and smoky, but I swear there was a gal standing right there." Del had climbed to Blackshaw's elevation, and now pointed to a spot three paces from where the waterman stood. "Nice looking woman, but I guess silhouettes can lie. Could have been an illegal lost out here. I was a good ways off."

"Del, it was just me and Colquette," said Blackshaw.

"I know what I saw, Ben, but if that's your story—" said Del.

"Then where's she now?" demanded Blackshaw. "Look around. You see her?"

"No. I must've been mistaken," said Del, not wishing to press the point with the likes of an armed and moody Blackshaw.

"Guess so," said Blackshaw, but he was disturbed by Del's weird sighting. Blackshaw trusted his new friend's vision more than he cared to let on.

CHAPTER 95

ADELLE CONGREVE COULDN'T believe what she was seeing. From the direction of the highway, a convoy of SUVs, ambulances, and what looked like a tank came screaming into the encampment. It was the Feds again, sure, but this wasn't a polite howdy like before. This was all business.

But the raid was a gadfly distraction compared to the doings on the other side of the camp. The boys who had followed after Pardue, Foss, Malthys, and that quartet of nimrods were streaming back in. She couldn't see Pardue, until she realized he was riding double with one of the skinnier ranch hands. Pardue looked ill. Then she saw the blood high and on the right shoulder. Somebody'd plugged him.

Congreve ran to meet Pardue. Cutlip, Dressler, and the ranch hands were helping her ashen swain off the ATV. She wailed, "Timon! Oh my God, Timon!"

"It's a scratch," lied her brave old lawman.

Congreve bulled a helpful cowboy away and put her shoulder under Pardue's to support him. Her hand felt warm and wet. She looked at Pardue's back. "You're shot in-and-out! Dammit you fool!"

A lady FBI agent had her gun and her ID out as she ran to them. "Special Agent Molly Wilde, FBI! Can you talk? Who shot you?"

Congreve saw agents and S.W.A.T. guys in tactical gear and machine guns fanning out through the camp while their honchos flashed paperwork.

Warrants, she figured. She was seeing the entire MAIm movement collapse before her very eyes, and none of that mattered because Timon was hurt.

Pardue's voice was feeble as he gasped out, "It's Malthys and that biker, Foss. One of them did it. And Foss's got one of those lost helo pilots. In there." Pardue grunted as he tried to point to Foss's tent.

Wilde spoke into a walkie-talkie and then said to Congreve and the hands helping Pardue, "Take him to that first ambulance. The medics will meet you on the way."

Congreve and the men dragged the stumbling Pardue toward the distant ambulance. Wilde and another woman, this one in CBP gear, went for the tent with two tactical operators watching their backs.

The burly EMTs didn't seem to mind that they had a civilian patient so early in the operation. They opened the double back doors of the ambulance to extract the stretcher, and held still in surprise. Adelle craned over their shoulders to see what was riveting their attention. There was already somebody on the stretcher. Congreve recognized the top of the flight suit, and the CBP insignia of the unconscious woman.

"Be damned! That's her! That's the pilot!" croaked Pardue.

The medic placed Pardue on the side bench with pillows and a blanket to make him comfortable. One of them assessed the pilot, and soon both the pilot on the stretcher and the former sheriff had IV lines flowing saline into their arms. Pardue also sported a pair of trauma dressings, front and back.

Congreve said, "You boys stay back here and get busy. I'll drive."

The taller medic said, "You can't do that, ma'am!"

Congreve shouted. "Son, I own this ambulance and most of the hospital we're going to. And if you *ma'am* me again, I'll snatch your job for good. Now shut up, and hang on!"

CHAPTER 96

MALTHYS NEEDED LEVERAGE. His presence at the drug pick-up would have to wait. Foss could handle it. It was his deal. It was his problem. Foss knew the landing site coordinates for the Mexican drug lord to program into the flying spiders. Foss would tell his pick-up crew the code to keep the onboard grenades from blasting the neighborhood sky high as the cocaine cargo was detached. Malthys had only been riding shotgun on these phony patrols as a manager interested in his stake. If Foss failed to pay Malthys his share for providing cover at the MAIm hate revival, there would be trouble. Wrath-of-God kind of trouble for the Rot-Irons.

It had been a long, dark hike back to the camp following all the ATV tracks. As he trudged, he wondered who had been shooting at the patrol. A coyote who didn't want his trafficking interrupted? A traitor Rot-Iron, maybe. Perhaps even one of his own PNC believers bucking for better rank.

Malthys veered off the trail for the last two hundred yards. He could see the lights, from generators, and from campfires, too. Lighting fires struck Malthys as idiotic with the smoke already choking the air, but everybody had that Kumbaya spirit of childish unity and purpose. Some of his people had even brought marshmallows for s'mores, for God's sake! Malthys stopped short when he noticed flashing strobes from cop cars. Feds most likely, unless somebody was having a heart attack. He crept closer.

The camp was crawling with agents. Rows of Rot-Irons were face down on the ground, their hands zip-tied at their backs. Some of his PNC groupies were eating dirt, too. A damn *raid*. Okay, so what? It didn't matter. The whole camp was a distraction; scream and bluster about Mexicans crossing the border, so nobody would notice the Mexican dope Malthys and Foss welcomed with open arms.

Malthys reconsidered his plan. If Pardue had made it back to camp alive, he might be talking, cutting a deal with authorities in exchange for light treatment. As a former lawman, and half-senile in the bargain, it would be an easy sell that Pardue had been intimidated into silence about the pilot. If things got really hairy, Foss could take some of the heat for the kidnapping off Malthys, but by no means all. Malthys needed to get ghost for the time being. He needed to bring leverage along with him wherever he decided to go. A gun by itself wouldn't cut it. He needed that weapon of Pardue's. The M-388V. If he handled things right, maybe he could abandon the faltering PNC and all the dipshits he had to tolerate, and instead hold an entire country for ransom. Fewer moving parts. Bigger return on investment.

That old fool Pardue thought the thing was junk. Malthys understood its power was truly Biblical. He could visit an Old Testament plague upon the world. He could be God.

CHAPTER 97

GUNTER FOSS RAN until his lungs felt like they would blow through his chest wall, with his heart close behind. His wounded shoulder hurt like hell. He knew the site he'd selected for the mass drone landing was somewhere nearby, but the storm, the smoke, the thunder, lightning, and the damn wind, not to mention the unfamiliar element of panic, these had him all turned around. Millions of dollars were about to rain down out of the sky, and he had to be there to see it, and recover the goods.

Foss slowed to a shambling gait at the bottom of a ravine. He'd need a minute to catch his breath before he could make the climb out to continue his search for the landing plateau. He also wanted to clear his head. How had getting rid of that punk Colquette and his three stooges gone so wrong? Who was shooting at them? Ranchers, most likely. Foss saw at least two of Malthys's people go down; Oren, and The Major. And he thought that he'd tagged Pardue. Any day he could fire some lead into a cop, even an ex-cop, was a good day.

The real problem was if he was being trailed by somebody who knew about the coke, and wanted to find out where it was coming down. Foss stumbled. His pistol flew out of his hand. He heard it land in the dirt. The next flare of lightning revealed the dense bed of cactus in which the gun had landed. *To hell with it.*

Foss looked up at the ridge of the arroyo. He saw the silhouette of a man with a rifle. Foss scrambled toward the opposite slope, and was a third of the way up before he saw another man, and an axe blade swinging and glinting in the lighting up top there.

Foss yelled, "Get away from me! I got friends. You do not fuck with Rot-Irons!"

Foss glared at the men above him. They didn't move. They didn't speak. Foss slid back down into the arroyo. Maybe they were coyotes, and didn't speak English, didn't understand the shit-storm he could bring down on them. Out here, his brother Rot-Irons meant nothing to these weird bastards. Foss was the only man from his club present. He should have tried harder to find his gun. He picked up a rock and heaved it at the rifleman. The stone flew close. The man didn't move.

Foss tried to appear calm as he strode along the arroyo floor. The men on the ridges above moved in the dark along with him. Only the lightning revealed that they had changed position, following him. If the storm would die back, then the lightning would stop showing where he was. Maybe he could change directions, or climb out without being seen. But the storm was relentless, getting worse if anything. Where was the rain? That would have given him cover.

He came to the end of the arroyo. The wrong end. The ground did not rise gradually, nor did the walls widen into open desert. The long depression terminated in a steep V formed by two rock walls, as if he had been deep in the bilge of a ship of stone, and had walked forward to the bow. The two men were closer, staring down at him. The one with the rifle looked like he was talking on a phone, likely whistling up reinforcements. That's why these guys weren't coming down the hills at him. They were too scared to take him on.

Foss backtracked down the deep swale, and started to climb up the side of the ravine with the axe dude at the top. Over the wind, Foss thought he heard the lumberjack chuckle. Three jets of dirt erupted in the hill in front of his face; bullets from the rifle guy. He hadn't heard a single shot. Foss swiped at his eyes, which felt like they'd taken a bucketful of grit. His footing gave way, and he tumbled back down the arroyo floor, crushing cactuses and acquiring a pelt full of fiery spines somewhere on the way. He rolled to a halt cursing his tormentors. He should have looked harder for his gun.

CHAPTER 98

BLACKSHAW HAD TOLD Michael Craig to direct the drop on his current position. Danger close. Craig had relayed the coordinates of Blackshaw's satellite phone directly to the crew of the massive four engine Martin Mars waterbomber. The WWII era Navy transport with its two hundred foot wingspan had been Blackshaw's idea to support Del and his crew to fight the wildfire. Now, there was an additional purpose the plane might fulfill.

The Mars pilots had likely been using the aircraft's storm scope to navigate the big plane between the worst embedded cells to remain on station. It was doubtless difficult horsing the aircraft's controls in the best of weather, but in this sky-churning system, it was dangerous, even foolish. Blackshaw had authorized Craig to offer an enormous bonus to the crew if they hung in for the whole turbulent ride. In an hour's time, the four men in the flying leviathan would be rich enough to retire, or dead.

Crackling fire fringed the ravine. Trees downhill from Blackshaw exploded as heat boiled sap and moisture deep inside the bark. If the water-bomber didn't show, Blackshaw and Del would burn. A roar, deeper than thunder, felt first as a throb through his boots, grew in the distance.

Blackshaw turned to the west, and with the next ripple of lightning, he saw the great wings of the avenging bird. It loomed out of the dark like a Jurassic behemoth, blackening all light except a hazy orange glow from the ground. The four Wright Cyclone engines of nearly three thousand horsepower each banged in Blackshaw's head. Foss was staggering, and hopping on one foot, then the other, plucking at cactus spines, wiping at his eyes. When he heard the duplex radials growl down in the acoustic center of the ravine, he twisted, looked to the sky, and cowered.

The aircraft's water bay vents opened, the crew perfectly timing the drop. At its usual altitude of one hundred fifty feet above the ground for a water bombing run, the Martin Mars could inundate four burning acres in a few seconds. On this special run, it came in low, very low, concentrating its payload on a much smaller area. The converging lay of the land did the rest to channel thirty tons of water cascading from the belly of the plane. It sluiced down the narrow ravine walls taking debris with it, and turning dirt and scree into a speeding wall of mud in an instant. Blackshaw and Del stood back from the arroyo's edge and watched as the water washed Gunter Foss away like a dead leaf in a flash flood.

Above, the aircraft soared on into the troubled night to find big water to land on until the storm passed. Below, steam rose from the superheated earth.

Blackshaw's ear drew his eye to the air once again. A broad formation of multi-legged shapes was moving north overhead from Mexico. Blackshaw extracted and dialed his sat-phone again. When the line opened on the other end, "Return to Sender," was all Blackshaw said before hanging up.

Del hollered to Blackshaw, "You coulda shot him!"

"Coulda stayed home. Coulda done plenty else," said Blackshaw, speaking more truth in his quip than he cared to admit.

CHAPTER 99

MOLLY WILDE PARTED the tent flap with her pistol drawn and raised. Shining her flashlight inside, she could not comprehend what she saw. Three men lay on the dirt floor. Lividity, stillness, and stench let her know these were corpses.

Wilde said, "Clear. Get in here."

Wanda Van Sickel, who had been covering Wilde followed the FBI agent inside, and said, "What is this!"

Wilde checked the first two bodies. "This one's cut, torso and throat, but partially stitched. And this one's missing a lot of his head. Cooler. Dead for some time."

Van Sickel examined the last body. "Deep chest wound here. Through sternum and ribs into the heart. A lot of force. Still warm. Recent. I feel like Goldilocks from Hell checking her porridge."

"All Rot-Irons," said Wilde. "Bad day to be them."

"Think it was Blackshaw?" Van Sickel asked.

"Different times of death at one scene," Wilde observed. "Hard to say. He could make this head shot. See that cot in back?"

"Somebody bled on it for a while," said Van Sickel.

Wilde pointed to a knife hilt tucked into the belt of Chest Wound. "Look. See that?"

"Damn!" spat Van Sickel. "Standard issue CBP rescue knife. At least one of my pilots was here. My God, Pardue wasn't lying."

Van Sickel's radio came to life. "Van Sickel, EMS 1." The man sounded excited, his voice overwhelmed at times by a Diesel engine whining and roaring in low gear at high RPMs.

She answered, "EMS 1, Van Sickel."

"Van Sickel, Nancy Greenway is in our ambulance. Transporting her with Sheriff Pardue now. And Adele Congreve is also aboard. She's driving."

"Greenway! Where's Eckhart? Where'd you find Greenway?"

The EMT answered, "She was already on the stretcher when we brought the sheriff aboard. No sign of Eckhart."

Van Sickel said, "How is she?"

"I'd bet on internal injuries. Bad left arm. Pretty banged up. Alert and oriented times two." came the radioed reply.

"Take care of her. Move!" shouted Van Sickel.

"Congreve's going like hell, ma'am," answered the EMT. "Might kill us all."

CHAPTER 100

THE AMBULANCE BOUNCED hard out of a deep rut. Congreve would have driven faster, but between her own worries about shattering an axel, and the EMTs cries of protest for a smoother ride for Pardue and Greenway, she fought her urge to floor it.

Two other reasons for Congreve to slow it down were the dark and the wildfire smoke. She was navigating out of the desert along the tire tracks of the incoming federal vehicles. Sometimes smoke cut the visibility down to a few feet, like dense fog. She didn't want to back-track the ambulance over a cliff.

She rounded a blind curve to the left, and slowed down even more. From the corner of her eye, she caught the right passenger door wrenching open. Malthys launched himself into the seat next to her. He hauled a heavy olive drab bin in behind him by worn canvas straps, and wedged it on the floor between his feet.

"Turn this thing around now," ordered Malthys. "We're going to your helicopter."

"The hell I will!" began Congreve, but she stopped when she saw the pistol's glint in Malthys's hand.

Congreve braked to a stop. "You're out of your mind. Timon's shot— as if you don't know. And there's a pilot hurt bad."

Malthys said, "The track's on fire up ahead. Nobody's leaving that way. Turn around. Do it! *Now!*"

Congreve shifted into reverse.

CHAPTER 101

BLACKSHAW AND DEL skull-dragged in close to the MAIm camp on their bellies. A federal raid was in full swing there. A glance into the back of a prisoner transporter revealed it was being filled with arrested Rot-Irons and PNC followers. There was no shooting. A few bikers railed about rights as they were hauled by agents toward the transporters. It was an orderly take-down. Blackshaw respected that.

Del nudged Blackshaw and pointed. "Seem like a bad direction for that ambulance?"

Blackshaw put his rifle sight on the ambulance as it pushed through the camp. A number of agents also thought something was off, as they watched it drive past, lights flashing, sirens blatting to get agents and MAImers out of its path.

Blackshaw said, "Maybe somebody's hurt over there."

The ambulance left the beaten path, and pushed into the brush for several hundred yards. Blackshaw noted the only thing lying ahead in its lights was that helicopter.

The ambulance braked hard. Malthys covered Congreve at gunpoint as she stepped out of the cab. Malthys descended next, toting a heavy bin.

"That's not good," said Blackshaw.

"What's not?" asked Del. "The hostage situation?"

"That, and Malthys has the WMD I mentioned."

"You got a clear shot?" asked Del.

"Nope. Trees. Smoke. Wind gusts. Might hit the lady. Or that bomb."

In the glare from the camp, Blackshaw saw the blood drain out of Del's face. And for now, all they could do was watch.

After Congreve trotted around stripping the gust restraints off the rotors, Malthys forced her aboard the Cayuse, then followed her into the other front seat. The rotors started turning, then buzzing. In a few moments, the helicopter lifted into the stormy sky.

"What about the engine? Go for the engine! Ben, what's one crazy rancher against the lives of millions?" Del sounded desperate and angry.

Blackshaw said, "That weapon's container might leak after a crash. Wouldn't be good for anybody around here, including us."

CHAPTER 102

CONGREVE WAS FURIOUS. Malthys had forced her to turn around and drive the ambulance back to the camp, then he had threatened an EMT in back with the pistol until the terrified man got on the radio, said that Pardue had gone critical and only a helicopter flight would get him to the hospital in time, and the track out to the road was blocked by burning brush. Then Malthys had opened fire back through the companionway between the cab and the box, shooting twice, killing both the EMTs. It was lucky Pardue and the pilot were passed out, or Malthys might have shot them, too. Congreve had no illusions about her fate at Malthys's hands. Right now, her only value to him alive was as a pilot.

She raced through the big items on the checklist with Malthys's gun denting her side. When the RPMs were in the green, she threw the Cayuse into the air. And right away, she noticed. Any noise out of the ordinary is a pilot's alert to trouble that might not show up on the instrument panel. And the whistling rush of wind from the opposite side of the cockpit told Congreve the far door was ajar. Malthys grabbed at the seat belts. He wasn't strapped in.

Without a moment's hesitation, Congreve nosed the helicopter over. Malthys went weightless in his seat, and started grabbing at the cyclic, the overhead, anything. The old green bin floated up with him. Congreve rolled the chopper to the left, and raised the collective. Malthys dropped fast in the cockpit, and his door flew open under his weight. Lightning flashed, and Congreve saw the stroboscopic moment, a rictus of horror in Malthys's face as he disappeared into the smoky black, the green bin following him out into the void.

CHAPTER 103

DEL POINTED UP at the chopper and shouted, "Now!"

Blackshaw already had the rifle raised to his shoulder, angled upward into the sky. In the night scope, he saw Malthys swinging below the helicopter with a death grip on the left skid. The PNC prophet's other hand clung to a carrying strap for the heavy weapon container. As Congreve contended with the turbulence, the human pendulum whirled beneath the Cayuse. Then Blackshaw saw the stenciled letters on the canister. All of them.

Knowing he risked Congreve and the chopper, and setting that thought aside, Blackshaw exploited a momentary lull in the wind and fired the Threadcutter. The bullet took Malthys in the hand clamped on the helicopter skid. Severed fingers spun away, and Malthys dropped, howling, a true falling angel bound for Hell. The green canister plummeted with him. The helicopter wheeled back down toward the ambulance.

Blackshaw and Del wended through arroyos and over ridges toward their best guess as to where Malthys pounded in.

"That canister!" shouted Del. "It might have broken open. Why go closer? There's no way Malthys survived that fall."

"I want to be sure," said Blackshaw.

Del paused, wondering if he really needed that degree of confirmation, then ran after Blackshaw. Several more turns through the ravines brought them to the bottom of a steep hill.

There was the green canister. Blackshaw went up to it, and examined its faded stenciling. Then he unlatched the few fasteners still intact on the lid. He opened the top, and slid a bulbous bomb with fins from the battered casing.

"What are you doing!" shouted Del.

"I reckon you could make a handsome lamp out of it if you wanted," said Blackshaw.

Del was angry with confusion. "Ben, you said it's a bio-weapon of mass destruction."

Blackshaw smiled for the first time in weeks. "I was wrong. See that T in its designation? T for training. It's a training round, Del. For practice. No bugs. No wonder it was lying around out here for somebody to find. It got lost on some exercise, but after a while, nobody cared."

Blackshaw heard a snuffling grunt from around the next bend, and followed the sound. He discovered a long rut was scored in the scree from the top of the hill to where Malthys lay. His limbs were twisted, and bone jutted through raw abraded skin, and splintered ends even burst through bloody clothing. And yet Malthys still breathed with a bubbling agonal snore.

"Lucky he landed on the top of the incline up there," said Blackshaw. "Skidded all the way down here. Steep as it is, he decelerated a lot slower than if he frapped on level ground."

Del swung the flat of his heavy axe blade down hard on Malthys's head with a wet, splitting thump. "Yes indeed, Ben. His lucky day."

CHAPTER 104

TEDDYBEAR CHOYA WAS surprised when Paolo Estrella y Castro jostled him awake.

"They're back!" yelled the excited engineer. "A little early, but they're back!"

Choya checked his phone, and found it odd that he had no text message from Foss that the shipment had been delivered. He eased down from the cab, and joined the other truck crews to wait for the drone swarm's arrival. Despite the storm, lulls in the wind gusts permitted the buzz of the little copters to reach their ears.

The swarm came in like wicked crows, silhouetted by flashes of lightning. Instead of landing, the units held off the ground fifteen feet. The noise penetrated their ears to the point of overwhelming. Seconds ticked away.

Choya said, "They supposed to do that? It's creepy."

"Maybe they're positioning for a clear landing," said Estrella y Castro.

"You programmed for that, right?" asked Choya.

"Not really—" said the puzzled engineer.

Suddenly, there were clinking, jingles, and ringing sounds as numerous small metal objects detached from the drones, fell on their heads, or struck the earth.

Choya bellowed, "What the hell, man! They're falling apart!"

Estrella y Castro knelt to pick up one of the objects. It was the spoon from a drone's fragmentation grenade, which could only be loose if the pin had been pulled. The ground was covered with them.

"Run!" screamed Estrella y Castro. "Grenades! The grenades!"

The engineer sprinted for the edge of the clearing, desperate to get out from under the veil of death snarling overhead. He glanced over his shoulder. He was going to make it to safety, but just barely. Then he saw the Tarantulas, the drones hefting the Claymore mines. Five of them were tracking him. They could see him! They could *see him*!

The first drone grenade exploded in the center of the swarm. The succession of blasts ripped out to the edge of the formation in less than a second. It was bright as lightning. It was deafening as a broadside from the *USS Missouri*. A blizzard of metal fragments screamed down at the engineer. Paolo Estrella y Castro began to fall as an intact human being. What thumped onto the ground an instant later was a smoking shredded mass of meat and bone.

* * *

Teddybear Choya's ears rang as he crawled from beneath the truck. He had no idea how long he had been unconscious, but it was still dark. All his men lay dead around him. His right calf and foot were punctured, bleeding. When he finally understood what Estrella y Castro was screaming, Choya had thrown himself under the nearest truck. His leg was not under cover when the heavens split wide to release hell's shrapnel.

Choya felt a hard kick in his ribs, and looked up. He focused on the two eight-pointed stars of Chief Inspector Obregón, Federal Police. A platoon of Obregón's officers were assessing the killing field, the pock-marked trucks' body work, the shattered windows.

"Why'd you kick me?" whined Choya.

Obregón smiled, "To make sure you're awake when I arrest you."

Choya's anger bloomed in his chest. "I pay you so you *don't* arrest me!" he roared.

Obregón shrugged, still smiling. "Somebody else paid me more to arrest you. A lot more."

"You know I can beat any offer," blustered Choya.

Obregón gazed at the destruction around him and said, "You look out of business to me, my friend."

Teddybear Choya considered his options. He needed medical attention. He had excellent attorneys. Even before his leg was treated, he would marshal his cash and his legal team, and make quick work of Obregón. So Choya played along. He held out his hands so Obregón could cuff his wrists.

"What are you doing?" asked Obregón.

"The handcuffs. Let's go," said Choya.

"But you're resisting arrest," said Obregón, looking at his fellow officers as he drew his pistol. His officers nodded agreeably.

"I'm not resisting! What are you doing?" screamed Choya, as Obregón aimed the pistol at his head. "You were paid to arrest me! What the *fuck*!"

"Did I say *arrest*? I think Señor Craig said to *detain* you. Dead or alive."

Two shots from Obregón's pistol rang out in night. Teddybear Choya lay still, two bullets cooling in his skull.

CHAPTER 105

BLACKSHAW WALKED FAST along the highway. He was so
tired he feared that if he stopped, he would sit, and not be able to rise again.
The wildfire smoke was still dense, wreathing across the road. His throat
burned. Traffic was rare, but Blackshaw wasn't hitch-hiking. With his fatigued stumbles every few steps, there wouldn't be too many offers of rides
to someone who looked like a filthy drunk. The federal transports clearing
the MAIm camp were moving in the opposite direction toward Bisbee.
That was one bunch Blackshaw had no wish to meet.

Blackshaw and Del had exfiltrated through the hills as the sun rose.
They had spoken very little about where they would go next. Del shouldered his axe and talked about getting centered again, but was vague on
how or where that would happen. Blackshaw did not want to mention that,
wherever he was going, he wanted to travel alone despite all the camaraderie he felt for Del after the last couple days. He need not have worried.

After scrambling down a brush-covered hillside, and skidding to a stop
at the bottom of a ravine, Blackshaw realized he was alone. He studied the
high face of the hill, but could see no cavern entrance. That didn't mean
that somewhere on those rocky heights, there wasn't a way in to the wonderful network of cavern galleries. Blackshaw called Del's name once, and
receiving no answer, he moved on toward the highway.

That was four hours ago. Blackshaw slowed his march up yet another
long hill when, through the smoke, he saw the car pulled over on the
shoulder ahead. He recognized it. A green convertible, top down, with

curving rear fenders bracketing an angled trunk; it had snarled past him thirty minutes before. As Blackshaw approached, he got a better look; a roadster, with its long hood couchant between the sweeping front fenders. The white racing roundel bore the number 28 in black. The right-side hood was raised and folded back on itself so that a figure dressed in black Nomex coveralls could reach inside to the engine.

Blackshaw miss-stepped again, scuffing pebbles and small rocks with the toe of his boot. The noise startled the person under the hood. Or *bonnet*, thought Blackshaw, upon recognizing the British Morgan. The driver was a lovely woman with laughing eyes, and bright, open features. Her red hair was snatched back, but wisping free in places from underneath a bright, elegant scarf. Blackshaw remembered the road race from his chat outside the hotel with Louis, the old Bisbee fire chief.

He said, "My name's Blackshaw. Are you with that Fireball rally?"

"It's the Gumball, and no, I'm not with any race at the moment, as you can see," answered the woman, who became even more beautiful when she smiled. "I'm Sharlie. Pleased to make your acquaintance, Mr. Blackshaw, provided, of course, you're not an axe murderer."

"Reckon not, miss. What's going on with your Plus 8?"

"You know your Morgans," observed Sharlie, her smile now a beacon in the smoky morning.

"I'm a fan. I brag I had me a quick ride in a 3-Wheeler this past winter up in Wakeham Bay, in Canada."

"I suppose they have roads there," muttered Sharlie.

Blackshaw said, "This isn't the best place for a pit stop."

"Agreed. My problem, Mr. Blackshaw, is that I pulled over to stretch my legs, and shouldn't have switched her off. And now she won't start again. I spat on all the cylinder heads. All hot. Battery, I think."

"Call me Ben. You're almost at the top of this hill," said Blackshaw. "Maybe a bump start would do it. That help you catch up?"

Sharlie beamed. "That would be wonderful. But I'm not catching up to anybody, Ben. At the moment, the rest of the pack is quickly catching up to *me*. If this works, may I give you a lift somewhere by way of thanks?"

"I got important business over to East Somewhere, so that'd suit me fine," said Blackshaw.

He tossed his rucksack into the Morgan. Together they pushed the green racer, which Blackshaw learned was called Sweet Pea, to the top of the hill. There, they continued shoving it along until the flat asphalt angled downward, and gravity took over. Sharlie hopped behind the wheel. Blackshaw kept pushing to help build speed. Sharlie shifted the transmission from neutral into first gear, and let the clutch out. The engine started right away.

Blackshaw vaulted the low door sill and took his seat, arranging his feet around his rucksack. He felt an intermittent vibration at his ankle that seemed out of synch with the powerful engine. Opening his pack, he dug out the sat-phone, removed it from its waterproof bag, and opened the line. After applying lipstick from the glove box, Sharlie lit a bright pink cigarette, and got down to the business of extending her lead.

On the phone, Mike Craig said, "You're still alive."

"Reckon so," said Blackshaw, a smoky wind making his eyes tear.

Mike said, "Seems noisy, Ben. Can you read me okay?"

"Five by five," shouted Blackshaw.

"Good, because I have somebody on the other line wants to hear your voice."

"Who's that?" asked the waterman.

"A *Mrs.* Blackshaw."

Blackshaw's heart hammered hard in his chest. "Put her on, Mike. I'd very much like to hear what she's got to say."

CHAPTER 106

WANDA VAN SICKEL had to wait five days until the wildfire was contained before she and Mike Haberman could put teams in the field around the MAIm camp. Infrared footage from the CBP drones helped trace the movements of the principal actors. There were two unknown persons who appeared, but who could not be accounted for. In the space of a few frames, they disappeared as if the earth swallowed them up. In later frames, and after many hours, the earth seemed to spit them out again. Now closer to the camp, they came into contact with key members of the MAIm leadership, as well as a few lower ranking persons of interest. Everyone with whom those two unnamed suspects crossed paths remained missing—until the fire was contained.

It turned out to be a crime scene that covered many acres. There were several sets of human remains that had burned, and another set that was burned but also had one gunshot wound. Congreve had been able to tell Van Sickel where Malthys had fallen from the helicopter. The intense fire had swollen the silent tongues of the dead making a moist barrier between the flames and the DNA inside the cadavers' molars. Even where dental records failed, the teeth would still have their say one final time to give names to the bodies.

The strangest discovery of all was finally locating Gunter Foss, who had somehow drowned in the middle of the desert.

Pardue was cooperating as much as he could, and would likely squeak through this mess with probation. No one wanted to turn him into a *cause célèbre* again. Shunning the media limelight, he showed an inclination to quietly lick his wounds at Congreve's Double-R ranch, and to hell with the rest of the world.

Greenway was traumatized, but strong, and doing her best to reconstruct her ride in the truck so they could find Eckhart's remains. Van Sickel hoped a Rot-Iron still might roll over on his buddies and shorten the search, and let Eckhart finally rest in peace in holy ground.

Otto DeGore's team had found a cache of cocaine at one of the Rot-Iron safe-houses. One of his agents had been wounded in an exchange of gunfire there. Three Rot-Irons had died.

Without Malthys, the PNC compound was changing in the following days and weeks. The more hardened zealots were finding themselves unwelcome among the majority of members who wanted a gentler existence without guns, or any other concerns outside more usual, less aggressive Christian observances. Like the religious zealots, Malthys's cadre of bigots dispersed and moved on to find like-minded company. The keyboard commandos of the PNC social media corps soon shifted their focus, and hired themselves out as a marketing team for churches and businesses. A smaller, happier community had survived Malthys, the false prophet.

CHAPTER 107

MOLLY WILDE OPENED the package with more than her usual care. It was small, and in her mind, *small* often went hand in hand with *delicate*. The parcel had arrived through regular mail at her home address, but in the confusion of moving Pershing Lowry's belongings in, she had not paid it proper attention until she had gotten into work at the FBI's Metropolitan Office in Calverton, Maryland. The return address was from someone, or something, called *Ribauldequin*, with a Portland, Oregon UPS store address.

There was white tissue paper beneath the box's cardboard flaps; more promise of something important, special, and fragile. The box was incredibly light. Wilde probed the paper carefully, not daring to tip the box over and shake. Had Lowry ordered something for her? Had there been confusion about a gift that was for *her*, but that should have been addressed to *him*? She pressed her fingers deeper into the box and felt thicker, coarse paper, like an old grocery bag. She drew out a paper packet. It wasn't even taped closed. She unfolded it, and was overcome by a nausea that had nothing to do with her pregnancy.

Her memory flew back to that photograph of Sha'Quan Stewart, and she remembered the anguish in his terrified eyes. She gently placed the small dark curls to one side, and read the message written on the packet.

I am sorry to be sending this sad bit of a thing to you.
Reckon you can find who it should go to for sanctified rites

and customs proper. I could not undertake it with my own hands so sullied. Expect no more troubles from the one who did it. BB

EPILOGUE

THE CAVE MOUTH was just deep enough to shelter Ascensión Huerta and her remaining children. As they ate, she reflected on this new country. Ascensión had sacrificed in untold ways to come this far, suffering the abduction of her beautiful daughter, savage violation, and the cruel necessity of committing murder. Even in the last day, she had seen duendes killing men, flying spiders, fires and floods in the desert, a devil dropping from the sky, and storms with no rain. She wondered if she should press on with her family into this upside down land.

Then she had found the ATV abandoned in the wilderness. It wouldn't start, but the back seat had a zippered bag with water, food, an old pistol, and even a new mobile phone, which was still in its package. She made the sign of the cross and stole all these things. Her babies were starving.

Ascensión thought of the almost-handsome Eduardo in Mexico City, and of her brother in Tucson. When next she looked at her children, they were quietly looking back at her, waiting. She packed up the remaining food, and stood up. Her beautiful kids stood with her. And then Ascensión walked north. She vowed that when these children were finally safe in their uncle's care, she would return to Mexico alone with the pistol and take back her lost lamb.

ABOUT ROBERT BLAKE WHITEHILL

Robert Blake Whitehill is a Maryland Eastern Shore native, and an award-winning screenwriter at the Hamptons International Film Festival, and the Hudson Valley Film Festival. In addition, he is an Alfred P. Sloan Foundation award winner for his feature script U.X.O. (Unexploded Ordnance). Whitehill is also a contributing writer to *Chesapeake Bay Magazine* and *The Audiophile Voice.*

Find out more about the author, his blog, upcoming releases, and the Chesapeake Bay at:

www.robertblakewhitehill.com

SLUDGE

A Ben Blackshaw Short Story

By

Robert Blake Whitehill

With

Taylor Griffith

For my friend, Bobby Villanova. You would have handled things differently.

RBW

To my family, friends, Westtown School faculty and staff, and my writing mentors, RBW and Julee W.

TG

CHAPTER 1

WHEN LUANNA WOKE from the coma, she had no precise concept of time or its passage. It felt as though she rose from a dream, a long cold swim under dark waters. The thrashing strokes had no beginning she could recall. She felt as though she were carrying something wonderful along with her, something that eased a sense of loneliness. Yet it was a swim that left her limbs sapped of strength. More than anything, she felt confused; that was the word for it. LuAnna felt confused and disoriented as unspoken questions knotted like dry hanks of yarn on her tongue. How did she end up here in a bed in their living room? Why couldn't she move? Why were so many familiar faces fussing over her? But of greatest importance, where the fuck was Ben?

Kimba Mosby, the reverend's wife, had gently explained the situation to LuAnna as her fighter's mien slowly reasserted itself. LuAnna had been shot. Shot *twice*, bless her heart, during a death match between her crew of Smith Islanders and a pack of ruthless human traffickers. Loss of blood brought on severe hypovolemic shock. A team of trauma surgeons and nurses, and later, the round-the-clock care from the women of the Smith Island Council, had served to keep her alive, but nothing they did could raise her back to consciousness. When LuAnna could mouth a few words, she asked after Ben. Her well-meaning nurses told her to rest, and to be patient, and that her husband was away, but would be home soon.

So, Ben was away now, much as LuAnna had been. Her only other recollection from her long sojourn in darkness, and it was a vivid, lucid memory, was a dream of hunting with Ben, stalking Evil with him through a burning nighttime desert. She could feel the heat of fire all around her. For now, it made no sense, just as Ben's absence now was inexplicable.

LuAnna's nurses mapped her path to full recovery. It lay over difficult terrain. Soon LuAnna could speak more clearly, and could swallow without aspirating liquids. When her gut could be trusted to digest properly, meaning that, to her utter embarrassment, she had broken wind to her nurses' satisfaction, her feeding tube was removed from her stomach, and she was given a solid diet of proteins and healthy fats to help restore her muscles. Her soul healed more slowly than her body, but the comfort of familiar flavors like goose pie, crab soup, and the occasional indulgence in nine-layer cake helped. A cup of joe now and then, instead of water helped maintain her sanity.

Even while eating became more tolerable, physical therapy was painful and slow. As her limbs were pushed and twisted, LuAnna wondered how muscle that was so weak could also be so damn inflexible. She was learning the hard way about muscle disuse atrophy. LuAnna would tough it all out if it meant getting back on her own two feet, and casting aside those crutches, then the cane, and most vexing of all, the helping hands poised to catch her if she stumbled.

Within a few days, she was allowed to go for short walks, but never by herself. LuAnna hated having a minder. She was also permitted to squeeze a tennis ball, or toss it back and forth with whomever was babysitting her. She felt like a circus dog, or an idiot, by turns. Bench presses were out of the question.

LuAnna barely tolerated the attention. Confusion was giving way to anger, which masked a fear that she would never be her old self. She had to argue and threaten bodily harm to use the bathroom alone. Her persistence soon won out on that magical day when she was able, and yes, permitted, to venture out through the front door of her house unattended. She could not walk far, but at least she was breathing fresh air, and taking steps of her own volition and direction.

After a few short afternoon walks, LuAnna realized she needed a friend along after all, not to watch out for her, but to catch her up on the weeks she had been away from Smith Island. That's how she thought of it, that she had been on a journey, and needed the gossip. Mary Joyce, LuAnna's neighbor and one of her closer friends on Smith Island, was kind enough to accompany her. Mary talked of births, engagements, illnesses, affairs (including Mary's own romance with Sonny Wright), deaths, (Mary was now a widow, with the gallant Sonny to thank for that, too) the run of crabs, new boats bought, and old boats sold as retirement took watermen down. Neither of them brought up the absent Ben Blackshaw, though the matter lay heavily on both their minds.

CHAPTER 2

ETHAN LAHARPE FELT truly accomplished for only the third time in his life. Looking at his run-down home next to Smith Island's failing wastewater treatment unit (*facility* was too grand a word) it was hard to believe how far he had come. Though the house was in poor condition, to LaHarpe, it represented a crucial part of his plan.

His first big achievement was getting out of the shit-hole he called home in Baltimore. LaHarpe's drunken father had never believed his only son would amount to anything. His mother was too high to give a damn about either of them. At twelve, LaHarpe had realized he could rely only on his wits, which led him to take drastic action.

He moved in with his surly grandfather, Micah LaHarpe, at age thirteen. His parents were officially ghosts of the past. A successful builder with a reputation for a firm, sometimes punishing hand, Micah had disowned his son for marrying a flaky poet. Perhaps the LaHarpe gene pool had a chance in Ethan. Micah paid for his only grandson's education, later supplying him with the connections to get into a business school which was barely a cut above community college in its rigor. Degree in hand, Ethan LaHarpe took over the reins of his destiny from there, and managed the second biggest accomplishment of his life; he landed a job at O'Bannon Filtration Company.

Despite his degree, O'Bannon started LaHarpe in a low paying gig under a hardhat so the new guy could learn the business from the ground up. After only a brief taste of this drudgery, he calculated what his lifetime earnings might be if he took the usual path up the O'Bannon executive ladder. He decided he deserved to reach even higher, and for much more, and certainly sooner.

By sucking up to every person who came his way, LaHarpe built a strong network within the company's upper echelon of executives. By pretending to idolize his superiors, LaHarpe lodged himself firmly in mid-level management. Soon he was overseeing larger commercial and municipal public works.

Landing the Smith Island wastewater project was the greatest catch of all for LaHarpe. Nobody else at O'Bannon wanted to trek from corporate in Falls Church, Virginia to Smith Island on a regular basis unless it was goose season. To LaHarpe, the distance was ideal for his plans; it meant he would not have to suffer close corporate oversight.

Then LaHarpe went one better. As a goodwill gesture, he had volunteered to live in the old house next to the failing water works for as long as the construction and renovation project required. The O'Bannon higher-ups admired LaHarpe's gung-ho spirit, parceled his other projects off to other managers, and cut him loose to concentrate on Smith Island. As LaHarpe saw it, he, the wily fox, and been ushered into the henhouse.

CHAPTER 3

LUANNA STILL COULD not recall exactly how she had almost died, no matter how often Mary Joyce explained it. She believed her friends when they told her the gunshot trauma could make hash of other important memories as well. When she failed to recognize the man outside her saltbox, it might have been that he was a stranger. It might have been that he was a dear friend she could not remember. This thought terrified her.

Mary Joyce had once again joined LuAnna for the stroll. To take her mind off the stiffness of her limbs, LuAnna used the windy, overcast day to pose more questions. Smith Island was still Smith Island, as Mary Joyce had put it, walking slowly so her friend could keep up. After years of grant applications and surveys, state and federal funding had been released to rebuild the decrepit, cranky, wastewater works. The old plant was losing capacity faster than Smith was losing residents. Now it was even overflowing after heavy storms. Close to two million dollars were to be invested in the new works. There was ample illicit cash stashed around the island these days to cover such a big project, but using it in such a visible way would have attracted the wrong kind of attention.

Talk of sewage became tiresome; LuAnna told Mary that she had finally spoken with Ben by phone. He had been somewhere out west, but was making his way back home. She dearly wished he were here already. LuAnna would recognize her husband from any distance. The gentleman now peeping inside her saltbox's windows was certainly not Blackshaw.

LuAnna felt Mary Joyce tense beside her as they approached the stranger. LuAnna did not need protection. She had snuck her little Beretta Jetfire .25 pistol in her waist band before they had left the house this afternoon. She didn't know if her reflexes could draw the weapon fast enough, so upon seeing the creeper, she shifted the gun from the waistband to the hand warmer pocket of her jacket.

When LuAnna called out to him, her commanding law enforcement voice sounded alien to her, but there it was. She never spoke like that to anyone, not since she had resigned from the Department of Natural Resources Police the year before.

"Can I help you, sir?"

The man turned around with a start. LuAnna sized him up immediately. Caucasian male, about 50 years of age. He had brown eyes, greying blond hair, and stood five-foot-ten in workman's Dickies. Soft pudding features under a receding hairline.

He might have been fit once, but he was running to fat. His over-polished, low-top work books were lazily tied on the big-toe side, as if he propped each ankle on the opposite knee to make the knot. That meant soft abdominals.

His canvas satchel did not appear to be weighed down by anything heavier than papers and a wallet, certainly not a pistol.

In a voice roughened by smoke and time, and roped in phlegm, he said, "Oh dear. I can see how this might look." His smile, with little teeth that reminded LuAnna of Silver Queen sweet corn kernals, didn't touch his eyes.

There were fewer than three hundred inhabitants on Smith Island. Despite her clouded memory, LuAnna soon realized this man wasn't one of them.

The stranger came forward to meet the women at the end of the walkway, no trace of being abashed.

"I just thought I'd come make myself known around these parts. I'm new to the island."

"Normally, people who want to nose around their neighbors' homes just ask to borrow a cup of sugar," LuAnna said with a salty-sweet smile of her own.

The man's face tensed for a second and a vein bulged in his neck. As if sensing its emergence, he looked away to clear his throat, and adjusted some stray wind-blown hair before looking back to the women.

He rebuilt a fresh smile, and said, "Why don't we start over? Ethan LaHarpe, general contractor for the new wastewater treatment facility in Tylerton. Perhaps you've heard of me."

LaHarpe extended a hand.

"LuAnna Blackshaw," she answered, giving his clammy, dead fish a firm grip. Soft for a contractor, she observed. No callouses whatsoever. "This here is Mary Joyce. And I haven't heard about you."

"I suppose that makes sense."

LaHarpe took out a handkerchief and knelt down to wipe a smudge of dirt from his gleaming boot. The spot was so small that LuAnna wouldn't have noticed it had he not be compelled to tidy up. He stood again and dusted non-existent flecks from his sleeve before pulling a small bottle of hand sanitizer out of his bag.

He went on, "Fresh, clean water is so important to me, I guess I can't expect everyone to care. No matter. Everybody's got a life."

Squirting the sanitizer into his palm, he made quick work of wiping down his hands, looking more at ease now than a few moments before.

LuAnna had heard enough from this fusspot. "LaHarpe, is it? You've yet to explain what all this has to do with you staring through my windows."

LaHarpe held onto his mask of composure. "I'm moving into the old house next door to the water works," he said. "Thought it could use some sprucing up. I figured some other houses here would give some inspiration."

Mary Joyce narrowed her eyes. "If that's the best excuse you've got for being a peeping-Tom, then I'd be more careful. People out here tend to shoot first."

"And ask questions later?" LaHarpe finished.

"No," said Mary. "Just shoot."

LaHarpe's eyes shifted back and forth between the women, clearly appraising them, their attractiveness, their smarts. The resulting chuckle did not sit well with LuAnna.

"Then I guess I better count my lucky stars it was only you two ladies I ran into. I apologize for the inconvenience; I meant no harm. I'll just be on my way."

LuAnna said, "Hold on a second, Mr. LaHarpe."

She could tell when someone was bullshitting her, and LaHarpe's neighborly façade could be smelled for miles. Mary Joyce's clipped tone indicated she felt the same way. Now LuAnna wanted to learn as much about LaHarpe as she could.

She said, "Where are our manners? Why don't you come inside for that cup of sugar, and let us show you some Smith Island hospitality. Tried our layered cake?"

LaHarpe glanced at his cheap digital watch while once again fixing his drifting hair. "I suppose I could spare some time for two such lovely faces."

CHAPTER 4

BLACKSHAW CAME HOME to a locked front door. There was a time when this was unheard of on Smith Island; it would have been an abrogation of neighborliness. And yet, he knew his wife had not done it out of spite, but as a precaution. Not one year ago, LuAnna had been kidnapped and brutalized. It cost the life of their unborn baby girl, and a piece of LuAnna's soul. Neither of them wanted the horror of another attack.

Retreating from the door for a moment, he fished the house key from the guts of one of his found-art kinetic heron sculptures in the yard. A chill shot through his chest as if he were breathing in ice water. The last time Blackshaw set foot into his saltbox was before his shammed death the previous December. He had volunteered to abandon his home to draw hostile operatives away from everyone and everything he loved. Instead, he had chosen a life of monkish solitude in a New York City basement where he could transform several tons of stolen gold bullion into precious works of art. He was surprised to find his homecoming left him so nervous.

Unlocking the door as quietly as he could, Blackshaw slipped into the house. His place looked the same as he had left it. Other than the lingering odor of antiseptics in the air, he would say no one had lived here for months. Then another aroma, that of freshly brewed coffee, welcomed him toward the kitchen where he found her standing by the counter.

LuAnna Bonnie Bryce Blackshaw. Though she stood with her back to him, Ben could see the commanding set of her shoulders, and the erect parade ground posture as she reached for the coffee pot. He could not see the cause of her tension. She was vigilant, as if she were protecting something. Her movements were still graceful, yet there was an underlying urgency. He felt the crisp chill of a winter's Chesapeake flaw piercing his core. Like the first time he went diving for oysters, his body ached with apprehension.

Her honey-blonde hair, cut shorter in her illness for utilitarian ease of care, brushed the nape of her neck. Something brittle about LuAnna made Blackshaw wonder if she would ever grow it long again.

She had not turned. She had undoubtedly heard the Atomic 4 engine of his deadrise, *Miss Dotsy*, come in at the pier. As a matter of fact, he couldn't understand why he was playing this game at all. The distance between him and the love of his life had left him in an all-encompassing sense of a loneliness, a void that only she could fix. But now that LuAnna stood just a few feet away, pouring a cup of joe into a mug, he stood rooted, immobile, as it must have been for her upon waking from the coma.

Blackshaw found that he couldn't speak. What would he say? What *could* he say? He found no words to express the joy he felt at seeing her, the relief that washed over him from knowing she was finally awake. Yet, guilt still stung him as he realized this remarkable woman found him, and his fevered missions, worth the risk of her own life. He could not begin to explain any of this, especially why he had not come to visit her. He had been compelled to spend his time anywhere except at the bedside of his fierce and fearless wife.

LuAnna saved him the trouble of figuring out how to begin again.

"Piping hot," she said, setting the mug down on the counter. "Just like you." She went on to pour herself a cup. "There's cake in the fridge, too. Mary Joyce helped me bake. Actually, she's helped with a lot of things around the house while I'm getting back on my feet."

As she stirred a bit of sugar and cream into her coffee, she turned to Blackshaw with a gentle smile that left crinkles in the corners of her eyes. "And before you ask, yes, the cake is chocolate."

There was a slight pause before Blackshaw managed to speak. "Nine layers?"

"Eight this time. But I'll make up for the last one with something special," she said suggestively. "Now stop staring at me like I'm one of those cheeky ghosts from Christmas past. I want to talk to you about the new water works. Just met the general contractor, and something's not right about that man."

Blackshaw wrapped her lean form in his arms. She put her mug down quickly, and held onto him, snuggling into the embrace she had long been awaiting. They stood there for a time, inhaling the scent of each other's skin, each reveling in the solace of the other's company.

"LuAnna—" Ben started before she cut him off.

"We can talk about it later." She added a kiss to his abraded knuckles for good measure. "I'm sure there's a damn good reason why you weren't here all those nights. If not, you can still make good by never leaving my side again."

"It's a deal."

LuAnna went on, "I'm telling you, Ben, that fonny boy sees this island as ripe for the picking. I just don't understand how."

"I thought you quit the NRP," said Blackshaw.

LuAnna's hands encircled her mug as she blew gently on the coffee. "I did. This is more for my peace of mind. I'm just trying to get back into the swing of things, hon."

Blackshaw understood what his wife meant. Though he wouldn't admit it aloud, LuAnna had come back to him a different person. Her native sweetness lay obscured beneath a brusque defensive verve that ran from her eyes, to the set of her chin, to the stance of her feet. Her traits as moral enforcer seemed to help ground her as she inched her way toward healing. Blackshaw thought he got it. They both needed to find their way back to Smith Island, and to each other.

"Mary Joyce says LaHarpe has the whole Island Council's haunches bristled. But I think we can handle him."

Blackshaw beamed with pride at his practical and resilient wife. "What's the plan, chief?"

LuAnna took Blackshaw's hands and said, "I think it's about time for you to go kiss and make up with Knocker Ellis."

CHAPTER 5

BLACKSHAW HAD TO hammer three times before Ellis opened the door to his saltbox. Had his old friend waited any longer, Blackshaw might have left Ellis's marshy hummock and returned the next day, or never. Upon opening up and seeing who it was calling, the black man blocked the doorway with a cross-armed stance. Not a word escaped his mouth.

Blackshaw said, "Well, are you going to just stand there?"

The old man didn't respond.

"Look, Ellis, I'm sorry. Rough times."

"No shit."

"And I shouldn't have treated a friend that way," Blackshaw went on. "Especially when you were just trying to help."

"Damn straight."

"Good," said Blackshaw. "Glad we settled that."

Ellis appraised his friend a few moments longer before flashing out a lighting quick jab to Blackshaw's solar plexus.

Blackshaw staggered back a step. "What the hell was that for?"

A smirk broke onto Knocker Ellis's face. "Not sure. I'm old. Sometimes I just do things. Get inside. You up for a second round with my gorgeous, sexy expresso machine?"

"Don't count on it," grumbled Blackshaw.

Ellis, the most wealthy man on Smith Island, had amused himself splurging on Kopi Luwak coffee beans which were intentionally processed through the digestive tract of a civet cat. The brew had tasted okay to Blackshaw until the moment Ellis explained how it was made. Then, one very expensive slug of coffee had been dumped out into Ellis's the sink, much to his delight.

Blackshaw said, "Let's talk on the way."

"Where're we going?" Ellis asked, as he followed Ben to *Miss Dotsy* where she lay tied at the pier.

"Tylerton. LuAnna's got a feeling about Ethan LaHarpe."

Miss Dotsy's Atomic 4 revved to life and took the men out into the gray bay.

Ellis eyed Blackshaw for the volatile man that he was. "Trouble ain't find you, and now you've got to go find trouble? Again?"

"LaHarpe sits okay by you."

"Didn't say that. Did you *hear* me say that? But if I went about knocking down every fella that didn't sit right with me, then there'd be a lot more space on the planet. I believe the same could be said for you."

"Ellis. This fellow might be nothing. I'll be damned if we went through Maynard Chalk just to get trod on by some slick contractor from Baltimore."

They stopped at the gas dock for LuAnna on the way.

Not long after, they reached the construction site. Three Smith Islanders pulled in to a nearby pier, tied up, and stepped ashore. On the other side of the pier lay a small barge on which they noted stacked bags of anthracite, sand, garnet, and other media that would make up the cleansing layers in the filter tank. There were several lengths of eight inch diameter PVC pipe on the ground. Long, grooved indentations in the mud told Blackshaw that much more pipe had lain in this stack, but it was now gone. Blackshaw could not see any pipe in the new works, there was a freshly filled trench running from the old facility down through the marsh to the water.

A small cement mixer at the site had been used to pour several large foundation pads for high and low lift pump wells, sedimentation tanks, the coagulation and flocculation units, as well as a chlorinator. At least that is what the plans posted in the weatherproof information kiosk indicated would be built. Yet, it was a Wednesday, and there were no workers at the site.

Next door, the old water treatment plant hummed, coughed, and gurgled.

Ellis said, "One more good storm'll take Old Faithful down."

Adjacent to the plant lay the ancient saltbox that Ethan LaHarpe had rented.

Blackshaw asked, "How much was granted for this thing?"

LuAnna said, "Two million dollars."

Ellis said, "Okay. That's a lot. How much you reckon has been spent so far?"

LuAnna answered again, "Not that much."

"I agree," said Blackshaw. "Not even close."

The screen door of the rented saltbox twanged open, and a man stepped out onto the small stoop.

LuAnna said, "There's the big man himself. What the heck is he wearing?"

"He's a dandy," said Blackshaw.

"He was in Dickies a couple days back," LuAnna reported.

Ellis kept his voice low. "Orvis shooting jacket. That hunter-orange shirt is prolly from Kevin's. Those are Beretta relaxed fit jeans. And that's a Rolex!"

Blackshaw and LuAnna eyed Ellis, who said, "Don't look at me like that. I like to keep abreast of trends so I can avoid them. Oh, and by damn if those aren't custom Gokie snake boots he's wearing."

"Do we have a snake problem?" asked Blackshaw.

"It seems we do," said LuAnna, glaring at LaHarpe.

"Gawd, what is that stink?" asked Ellis. "I know the old plant can get funky, but *wow*—"

"I smell it too," said Blackshaw. "But it's an onshore breeze. Like something died way out in the water."

Over the end of the Cuban cigar he was lighting, LaHarpe finally caught sight of his visitors. He called, "Is that you, Mrs. Blackshaw?"

LuAnna waved, and answered, "Just having us a look, Mr. LaHarpe."

"Come on, and welcome," said LaHarpe, descending the steps and strolling over. "And who are these gentlemen?"

LuAnna made introductions. LaHarpe shook hands all around. "Pleased to meet you, Mr. Blackshaw. You, too, Mr. Hogan. Mighty pleased."

"Where're your men today?" asked Ellis.

LaHarpe studied Ellis, gauging his answer before he said, "We're waiting on some parts to ship. New pumps, the chlorinator. Things like that. And somebody said there'd be some weather blowing through this afternoon. I didn't want the boys to get stranded out here, so I gave them the day off. But I can assure you, we're on schedule."

Blackshaw asked, "How many on the crew? We've got nice bed-and-breakfasts. Can't beat the food. There are plenty worse places to be marooned for a night."

LaHarpe said, "Thank you kindly. I'll be sure to look into that. At this phase, it's only two fellas on the job," said LaHarpe. "But we'll be ramping up in the next phase. I save you money if I run things a little lean at first."

"It's not our money," said LuAnna.

"You can say that again," quipped LaHarpe.

CHAPTER 6

BLACKSHAW FISHED A satellite phone from behind a loose panel at the back of the closet in his saltbox parlor, and pressed a speed-dial number.

The uber-hacker and weather tracker, Michael Craig, answered after several rings. "What."

"You know who this is—" Blackshaw asked.

It was apparent that Craig did not know, when he said, "Governor, really, I am so glad that squall helped cover your brother's extraction from the Shining Path camp, and I appreciate your generosity. The wired funds arrived in full and on time, and so that's all fine. I don't follow football, and I'm happily married, so a Super Bowl skybox full of energy drinks, boner pills, and *cheerleaders* as you call them—"

Blackshaw cut in, "Do I always sound like a client to you, Mike?"

"Oh. Of course not. To sound like a client, you'd have to actually pay me."

"You've made a tidy bundle helping out. You hurt me."

"Not enough to stop you calling."

Blackshaw paused for a moment and said, "I need you to check on some financial transactions. We have a contractor out here on the Smith Island working for a wastewater treatment company. Ethan LaHarpe, of O'Bannon. He's upgrading the works, and the budget's about two million."

Blackshaw heard a mini-gun firing over the line, then he realized the sound was Mike Craig's fingers rattling away in a fury on an old keyboard.

It was a full two minutes before Craig said, "Oh."

"Can you elaborate?" asked Blackshaw.

Craig obliged. "About five hundred thousand of the grant money has already been received by O'Bannon. Then it gets dodgy. LaHarpe is submitting spreadsheets to corporate for funds spent on parts and for labor. It's a big crew. Fifteen guys."

Blackshaw said, "Nobody's been on the site for a couple weeks. Before that, the headcount was only two."

Craig said, "That explains what I'm seeing here. Funds for payroll are wired from O'Bannon to the workers' accounts. But all the workers happen to be dead people, surprise-surprise. Oh, and when the money hits the accounts, it is wired out again—within thirty seconds—to a single account in the Caymans. Money for materials and some very pricey components is going pretty much the same, but LaHarpe seems to be replenishing that operating account to the right threshold just before the O'Bannon bean counters do their monthly audit. Payroll can disappear, but it would be easy for O'Bannon to check with suppliers about LaHarpe's orders."

"How much has been spent on the project out of that half-mil'?"

Craig said, "sixty-seven thousand, three hundred twenty-two dollars and—"

"I get the picture—"

"—eighty-seven cents. Should I give O'Bannon the heads-up? LaHarpe's going to ruin their reputation. They'll be on the hook for the money, and you won't get your plant."

"Would you please wait to tell them until I give you the word?" asked Blackshaw.

"Oh no," said Craig.

"What?" asked Blackshaw.

"You said *please*." Craig sounded weary. "That is never a good thing."

"But, I'm a gentleman," said Blackshaw.

Michael Craig might have contradicted, but he dared not.

CHAPTER 7

MISS DOTSY BORE Blackshaw, LuAnna, and Ellis on an approach toward the Chesapeake waters that lay offshore of the Smith Island wastewater treatment works. With gentle winds from the west where the sun was setting, *Miss Dotsy* rode smooth and true in an easy swell. LuAnna enjoyed the fresh air as she kept an eye on LaHarpe's house.

"Nobody working on the plant but, it's past quittin' time," she said.

Blackshaw was already encased in his ripped, patched old wetsuit. He was donning the front-mounted LAR V Draeger MK25 closed circuit rebreather which would allow him to dive to seventy feet without releasing any telltale bubbles. The fancy unit was a Welcome Home gift from LuAnna. Though stealth was not required now, using the MK 25 meant Knocker Ellis would not have to tend the noisy air compressor or the air hose of the old hookah rig they had needed back in the days when they were oystering in earnest.

"I don't smell it now," said Ellis as he cut *Miss Dotsy's* Atomic 4.

"But I don't hear the plant running either," said Blackshaw. Then he recalled, "The breeze had a little more north in her this afternoon. Maybe round out straight offshore, say a hundred yards."

"Got to start someplace," Ellis answered as he fired up the engine again.

Ten minutes later, with *Miss Dotsy* anchored in twenty feet, and her motor once again clicking and pinging as it cooled, Blackshaw eased over the side into the water. LuAnna bent over the side and kissed the top of his head.

Blackshaw glided toward the bottom. Using his compass and dead reckoning, he swam a rough grid as best he was able, searching through the mud, and over the oyster rocks for some clue as to what was happening on shore.

With his oxygen cylinders and CO_2 scrubbers close to timing out, he found it. A PVC pipe, the same diameter as he had seen at the water treatment job site, rose toward the marshy beach to his left, and stretched down into the murk to the right. Blackshaw followed the pipe into deeper water, and found its open terminus at a depth of sixty-five feet.

With no distracting bubbles to interfere with the submarine soundscape, Blackshaw heard a distant pump clatter to life. He touched the conduit before him, and felt it give a shudder, which settled into a regular vibration. When he realized what was about to happen it was too late to swim away.

The end of the pipe disgorged a jet of brown muck that enveloped him in a dark cloud. Moments later, Ellis caught sight of Blackshaw bobbing off *Miss Dotsy*'s stern, and reached a hand down over the gunwale to help him aboard.

"Oh my God!" shouted Ellis, as he pulled back his hand in disgust. "What happened to you?"

Blackshaw was covered in brown scum. "I found where the sewage is going. I think it's raw."

LuAnna joined Ellis at the stern. When the smell reached her, she clapped her hand over her nose, bolted to the leeward side like a savvy sailor, and vomited. "You are too nasty to come aboard."

"She's my boat," said Blackshaw. "Give me a hand."

"I'm not touching you," said Ellis.

"She's *our* boat, and you're not setting foot on her," corrected LuAnna. "You swim ashore, rinse off best you can on the way, and then we'll see how you smell. Pray to God we have enough bleach in the house for you and your gear, 'cause boy, you're headed for a Silkwood shower."

CHAPTER 8

WITH NO FURTHER deliveries of water treatment components scheduled to arrive on the *Captain Jason* or the *Island Belle II*, LuAnna, Ellis, and Blackshaw's threshed ways of dealing with LaHarpe's apparent fraud. The three of them were taking a moment on the brick patio on the waterside of the saltbox amidst Blackshaw's graceful sculptures.

They talked for half an hour. Still unsure how to proceed, the trio got a very sudden, and surprising glimpse of LaHarpe. The fussy little man was speeding along comfortably perched behind the wheel of a new golf cart customized to look like a miniature H1 Humvee. LuAnna could barely suppress a giggle at the sight. She was suddenly annoyed when LaHarpe veered off the road, and rutting her yard, drove straight onto the patio.

Blackshaw and Ellis noted LaHarpe neither dismounted, nor reached out to shake hands. Blackshaw wondered how any man could be so unaware of how he rubbed folks the wrong way.

"Well that's some kind of ride, Mr. LaHarpe," said Blackshaw.

LaHarpe smiled with an air of complacence. "Fifteen inch wheels, aluminum chassis, a chrome grille, and enough voltage to power a small town for a week, or Tylerton for a month."

Ellis was wry as he said, "Transport's a good idea. Guess you were wearing out those Keds hopping back and forth next door to the job site."

A vein bulged in LaHarpe's neck. "Keds, Mister—what was your name again, sir?"

"Call me Knocker Ellis."

"These aren't Keds. They're Brioni."

Ellis said, "Aw, I was just fooling. Them's the Brioni James Two-Tone leather sneaker. Anybody knows that."

"Indeed. The James." LaHarpe regarded Ellis with a fresh, discomfiting appreciation.

Blackshaw suddenly said, "Mr. LaHarpe, you're doing so much for us Smith Island folk, looking after us and our water, we want to show you some proper appreciation."

LaHarpe suspected a joke in the making, with himself as the butt of it. "Not necessary, I'm sure."

Blackshaw went on. "I'm serious. That house you're in needs some work. If it wouldn't put you out, maybe we could renovate some during the day while you're on site. Tighten up the windows for you. Caulk some seams. Maybe sand those floors. You'll be here nigh into winter. You'll be glad of the work. I can get some of our best boatwrights on it. We know our way around a project, doncha-know."

LuAnna had no idea where Blackshaw was going with this, but even so, she chimed in, "Maybe even some paint would help brighten the place."

"Some paint!" said Blackshaw. "There's a *great* idea."

LaHarpe made another token show of refusing. "I couldn't possibly put you all to the trouble."

"It's just Smith Island hospitality is all," cornponed Blackshaw with a simpleton's grin. "And for all your help to us, you deserve it."

The angry blood vessel in LaHarpe's neck slowly settled back into his flesh. Ellis stared at Blackshaw in consternation.

CHAPTER 9

SMITH ISLAND'S BEST boatwrights and other fine woodworkers shooed LaHarpe out the front door of his saltbox, and went to work. For the next several days, the displaced refugee contented himself with strolls, and more often, high speed drives around Smith Island, beaming with condescending good will at the neighbors who loved him so much they would fix up his home for free. Not a twinge of guilt disturbed his smug regard of the little people of his new home. He basked in their ingratiating serf-like obeisance, accepting one invitation after another for coffee and cake, lunches, and suppers. At night, he picked his way carefully through all the gutted disorder of his first floor. Within a few more days, the floors and drywall seemed to be going back together nicely. LaHarpe could see these Islanders worked like U.S. Navy Seabees. Thank goodness they weren't working on the wastewater plant, or it would already be finished!

CHAPTER 10

THE FIREHOSE WOULD just be long enough. Blackshaw, Ellis, and Sonny Wright had organized gathering several lengths of hose from the old fire truck, which still left the new truck ready for action should there be a need. They carried the borrowed hose to the old treatment plant under the cover of night. Blackshaw disconnected the land end of the effluent pipe that drained into the bay. He replaced the pipe with an adaptor valve he had fashioned. Its other end fit the firehose perfectly. It was a wonderful, simple piece of engineering.

The next day, the report finally came to Blackshaw that LaHarpe's house was ready. That night, LuAnna and Sonny Wright had stationed themselves in the old wastewater treatment plant, and shut down the pumps.

They ran the firehose from the old plant through a ground floor window in LaHarpe's saltbox. Since the contractor had been a dinner guest of Mary Joyce, and since she had laced his coffee with her Ambien, they were assured that LaHarpe was sound asleep.

It was time. LuAnna restarted the old plant for its most important flush.

CHAPTER 11

ETHAN LAHARPE DREAMED. He dreamed of receiving a promotion party at O'Bannon for his good work on Smith Island. At the party, he climbed on top of the table, unzipped his trousers, bent, and mooned his bosses and coworkers.

The dream quickly shifted to a beautiful beach. Pink sand girding a far-away island. LaHarpe worked at the cork of an insanely expensive bottle of wine. The islanders, some from Smith, others from this tropical paradise, had decorated one of their beach cabanas as a grand party venue. The dream was so vivid. LaHarpe's euphoria bubbled over. The music blared. The islanders danced. He could not wait to pour himself a celebratory glass. He opened the bottle. It was a cabernet, but vomit churned in his gut, and rose in his gullet. The dark liquid smelled like a pig farm.

Disoriented and confused, LaHarpe woke from the party dream, but the horrid stench still seared his nostrils, and coated even his tongue. For a moment, he felt as though he could even feel the odor on his flesh. Driving his feet into his slippers, the contractor rushed out of bedroom and down the stairs. In a moment, LaHarpe was standing in the darkened first floor waist deep in a brew of untreated sewage. The entire lower story was a foul, putrid grotto of shit.

CHAPTER 12

ETHAN LAHARP'S DEPARTURE was big news the next day. He was spotted boarding the seven o'clock boat to Crisfield, with a hastily packed bag, and still reeking like a tipped-over county fair porta-potty. Now the Island Council had to figure out what to do with a house full of sludge, but disposing of that would be much less disgusting than keeping LaHarpe around.

Ben made breakfast for LuAnna.

Over coffee afterward, she asked, "Does Mike Craig have a line on the money LaHarpe swindled?"

Blackshaw said, "Mike already grave-robbed that account in the Caymans, and sent it all back to O'Bannon."

"And no thought of keeping it?" LuAnna asked.

"My first thoughts get me into trouble," he answered. "I try to sit tight until the second thought tolls in."

"Any second thoughts about me?"

Blackshaw pulled LuAnna to her feet and took her in his arms. "Nope. And that's why I'm still in such an ever-lovin' predicament over you."

"Sweet boy," she said. "You remember before the shooting, before I got hurt, we doubled out on that old wreck?"

"It wasn't the most romantic spot in the world, but I'll never forget it."

"Okay," she said. "I need to tell you something, Ben. I'm not the only one survived."